THE DEVIL OF PINESVILLE

CRITTER CATCHERS
BOOK 4

HANK EDWARDS

MITTEN GINGER MEDIA

CONTENTS

SUMMARY

An old friendship shifting to a new romance. An ex-boyfriend extending an invitation. An urban legend in the flesh.

Critter Catchers and amateur monster hunters Cody and Demetrius are building their friendship into something hotter and deeper. Both are way out of their comfort zones, but willing to work at things. It will just take a little time until Cody feels comfortable "coming out" to their friends, family, and the rest of Parson's Hollow. Demetrius is trying to be patient and understanding about Cody's position, and focuses on their business. Or, rather, the lack thereof.

When Demetrius's ex, Oliver Berridge, invites him to come to Pinesville, New Jersey for a case that might be right up their alley, Demetrius is intrigued. Sensing not just physical but romantic danger as well, Cody makes certain to accompany Demmy on the trip.

Things in Pinesville are soon complicated by a competing animal control company and a group of monster trackers from a low-budget TV show. As the case intensifies, tempers flare and loyalties are tested, finally forcing Demmy and Cody to decide if they're willing to save their business, their friendship, or their romance.

The Devil of Pinesville ©2017 Hank Edwards
Cover design by Adrian Nichols
Book design and production by Hank Edwards
Editing by Jerry Wheeler

First Publication, 2017

CHAPTER ONE

The day was hot for mid-September, and Demetrius used the sleeve of his Critter Catchers coverall to wipe sweat off his forehead. He peered around the dark, cluttered garage interior that smelled of paper mold, musty clothes, gasoline, motor oil, and something disturbingly close to egg farts.

"This is a nightmare," Cody said from a few feet away. "I mean, this is worse than being stuck out in that swamp in Florida."

"Worse than the swamp where a flesh-eating monster made of moss, logs, and evil stalked us during a tropical storm? That swamp?"

"Okay, fine. It's not worse than that. But you have to admit this is pretty bad."

They jumped at the sound of scrabbling claws from behind a cluster of boxes.

"I know they're not dangerous," Cody said in a low voice. "But they're freaking me out."

"They're not werewolves," Demetrius said.

"Wolf *men*."

"Or chupacabras."

"Drug enhanced dogs."

Demetrius sighed. "Do you always have to correct me?"

"Say things correctly and I won't need to." Cody grinned. The sight sent a flutter through Demetrius despite the stuffy single car garage, their stifling coveralls, and the horrible smells.

"You're impossible," Demetrius said, and he turned away to hide his own grin.

"Impossible not to like, you mean."

Before Demetrius could respond, two small furry shapes darted out from behind a stack of boxes. He jumped back and watched as they raced across the oil-stained concrete. Before Cody could dodge out of the way, the small fur balls launched themselves at his legs and proceeded to climb him.

"Claws!" Cody shouted as he bounced from foot to foot and waved his hands. "Ow. Ouch! Dammit! They're like little needles jabbing right through the coveralls. Ow, goddammit!"

Demetrius could not help laughing. He held a gloved hand to his mouth to try and disguise his laughter, but Cody looked up and scowled when he caught him.

"A little help, please?" Cody attempted to pull one of the kittens off, but its claws were snagged in the material of his coveralls. Or in the skin of his leg.

Demetrius got his laughter under control and stepped forward. "Sorry. I'm here, I'm here."

He got hold of the other one and removed it with careful side-to-side movements. He held up the squirming ball of multi-colored fur and peered at the bright blue eyes and pink nose. A tiny mouth opened, revealing small, sharp teeth before it let out a high-pitched mew of agitation.

"Oh my God, they're so cute," Demetrius said.

"Ow, son of a bitch." Cody finally managed to pry the second kitten off his leg and held it at arm's length as it squirmed in his grip. "Cute? You didn't have their little needle-claws stuck in your legs. They probably gave me hepatitis or something."

Several hard knocks from behind them drew their attention. The pull up garage door had two plexiglass windows, both smeared with dust and dirt. Through one of the windows, Demetrius could just discern the blurry image of a face peering in at them.

"Stop fawning over the cats and catch them!" the figure outside the window shouted.

Lucia Durant was a tough as nails sheriff's deputy, and one of Cody's many ex-girlfriends they continually ran into around Parson's Hollow.

"We're not fawning!" Demetrius shouted back.

"You are most definitely fawning, Singleton," Lucia said. "You're not getting paid by the hour, so knock it off and get back to critter catching."

"She's even worse than usual," Demetrius grumbled as he joined Cody at the large animal carrier they'd positioned near the side entrance to the garage. He deposited the crying kitten inside to join Cody's.

"Can't blame me for that," Cody said. "It's been years since she and I dated."

"Maybe just looking at you riles her up."

Cody glared. "If you weren't so cute, I'd be tempted to stuff one of these flea- and tick-ridden kittens down your coveralls."

"Good thing I'm cute. Come on, I hear more of them in the back corner."

Thirty minutes later, they had chased down and crated all ten kittens. Sweat ran down their faces, and Demetrius's T-shirt was plastered to his back beneath the coveralls. He and Cody made one more lap around the garage to make sure all of the kittens had been caught.

"Let's get out of here," Demetrius said.

Cody picked up the carrier full of noisy kittens and Demetrius reached for the door knob, but Cody grabbed his arm and pulled him around.

"You know," Cody said, "it's a little strange. Even standing here surrounded by pussy, I'm turned on by you."

Demetrius laughed and blushed. When Cody leaned down for a quick kiss, Demetrius had to remind himself to keep it short and sweet. He sometimes got a little lost when he was with Cody. The physical aspect of their relationship was all so new; he didn't really know how to react and what to say when Cody started being romantic.

And he wasn't sure he completely trusted it, yet.

"Such a smooth talker," Demetrius said once Cody pulled away.

"Which is why you like me."

Demetrius shook his head and turned away, the word "like" echoing in his mind as he opened the door and stepped out of the detached garage. The cool, fresh air was water in a desert, and they both paused to take deep, grateful breaths. As he unzipped his coveralls, Demetrius wondered about Cody's use of the word 'like'. They'd only been back from Florida for four weeks. During that time, they'd managed to spend nearly every night together, at one or the other's apartment. It was fun and exciting and definitely more than satisfying sexually, yet Demetrius couldn't help but wonder where it was headed.

And he knew better than to try and think too far ahead. Especially with Cody, the master of wait-and-see. Still, Demetrius was a planner, and he needed to have some kind of map in place for something this important.

"Oh please," Lucia said from where she leaned against the front quarter panel of a tan mid-70s Cadillac Sedan de Ville with a white vinyl roof. "You're gasping like fish out of water. It could not have been that bad in there."

"Would you like to step into one of these coveralls and go inside for an hour?" Cody asked.

"I'll pass. Thanks for the offer to stew in your juices though." Lucia pulled out her phone and turned her attention to the tiny screen.

"Where are we taking these little bundles of flea-ridden cuteness?"

Lucia shrugged. "Don't ask me. The Widow just called the station and asked for someone to come get the cats out of her garage. Since the good mayor and city council decided to slash the budget and wipe out the city's animal control center, you're the third party vendor we call for all city animal control detail." She flashed a grim smile. "Aren't you the lucky ones?"

"So the entire animal control center is closed?" Demetrius asked. "Like, the building and cages and office and everything?"

"Yep. Like the building and cages and office and everything that has to do with animal control is gone. If there's no money for staff, there's definitely no money for overhead. That space has been turned into storage, so right now the City Hall Santa Claus is riding out the season in some fenced in kennel area."

"What should we do with these cats?" Demetrius said as an annoyed and nervous tremble started in his belly. When they'd received the call this morning from Lucia, he'd been excited about the opportunity to work with the city. It would possibly mean more of a steady income. But now he was pretty sure the money wouldn't match the amount of work.

"Where would you take a raccoon or a possum?" Lucia asked.

"The woods," Cody replied. "But we're not turning these kittens loose in the woods. They wouldn't stand a chance."

"Not my problem." She pushed up from the Cadillac and adjusted her gun belt.

Before Demetrius or Cody could respond, the Widow Monroe stepped out of the side door of the house. She stood less than five feet tall—five and a half if you added in her silver beehive hairdo. Her face was a tanned mask of wrinkles, severely weathered from decades spent working in her yard and attending every outdoor town and church function. Demetrius thought she looked like an old chamois his father had once used to wipe down the car after washing it by hand.

"Who's this now?" the Widow asked, squinting up at Demetrius. Her watery blue eyes flicked over to Cody and widened. "Hoo boy, you're a big 'un. How tall are you?"

Cody smiled down at her. "Six foot five, ma'am."

"Six five?" The Widow waved dismissively. "Hell, my husband, God rest his soul, was taller than you." She turned to Lucia. "Who are you?"

"Sheriff's Deputy Lucia Durant, Mrs. Monroe. You called about cats in your garage?"

"Sheriff's Deputy? When the hell did they start hiring women?"

Demetrius pressed his lips together to keep his composure, but heard Cody snort a quiet laugh behind him. Lucia's smile stretched wider, but Demetrius could tell she was working to keep her patience intact.

"For a long time now, ma'am." Lucia gestured toward Demetrius and Cody. "I wanted to let you know I contacted animal control on your behalf, and these men have caught all the cats that were in your garage."

"Cats?" The Widow turned and glared. "I don't want any damn cats. I've got enough trouble with the wanton slut of a cat that uses my yard for a whore house." She threw her hands up in the air and stomped around the front of the Cadillac. Shaking her head, she grumbled, "I don't need any more damn cats around my house. Take them away, I'm not interested. And get rid of that harlot feline while you're at it, too."

"But you called us," Lucia said.

The Widow waved off Lucia's statement before she hauled open the Cadillac's driver door. She tossed her shiny black handbag inside and climbed in after it. Once she settled into the driver's seat, her eyes were barely visible above the dashboard. When she started the car, the yellow revolving light on the white vinyl roof spun into life. The light had been installed by the sheriff's department many years ago, when the Widow had simply refused to quit driving. It served as a beacon to all motorists and allowed other Parson's Hollow residents to keep track of where she was.

As they watched her back out of the driveway, Cody said, "She's going to kill someone someday."

"She did kill someone. Farmer Wilkes, remember?"

"That's not the official story," Lucia said in a snappish tone. She winced as she watched the Widow swerve off down the street, then shook her head. Her talk with the Widow must have worn her down a bit, because she sighed and said, "Call Homeless Pets, they're a no-kill shelter just outside of town. They might be able to take the kittens."

"Thanks for the info," Cody said. "Finally."

Lucia took a couple of steps toward him, and Demetrius swallowed hard. Why did it always have to turn ugly between these two? Was it simply left over resentment from when they had dated back in high school? Lucia had broken up with Cody before he could end things and had been the only girl who had beaten him to the punch. Maybe some attraction still simmered beneath the surface for the two of them, and Demetrius wondered if he should feel more jealous and threatened about Lucia than he actually did.

"You know what, Bower?" Lucia said with a sneer as she jabbed a finger at him. "You're a third party vendor contracted to perform animal control duties for the city. And per that contract, you are to transport any animals you have contained to facilities licensed to handle them. I'm not supposed to give you names and numbers and a nice little list of places waiting with open arms to take animals off your hands. I'm supposed to uphold the law and keep the citizens of this town, including your sorry ass, safe. Is that clear?"

Cody's jaw was set and his eyes cold as he stared at Lucia. Demetrius had seen the same expression hundreds, if not thousands, of times over the years. Cody did not like to be told what to do.

He did not snap back at Lucia, however. Demetrius was surprised and impressed as Cody stood and returned Lucia's stare. Instead of saying a word, Cody simply adjusted his grip on the handle of the carrier and gave a single nod.

Lucia returned his nod and lowered her arm as she stepped back. "Good. Once you've dropped off the cats, come by the station and fill out an application for a purchase order agreement so you can get paid."

She walked down the drive to where her patrol car was parked by the curb. Her blonde hair was pulled back into a pony tail, and the gun belt rattled with each step. She walked and looked like a complete badass, and Demetrius wondered how Cody and Lucia had avoided killing each other in high school. And in the years since they'd all graduated.

"Well, that was stressful," Demetrius said after Lucia had driven off.

"Such a bitch," Cody grumbled and stomped past him.

Demetrius followed, walking fast to keep up with Cody's

longer strides. "Yeah, she's tough and doesn't take any shit. But she did get us this job with the city."

Cody grunted, and the kittens continued to mewl, like a furry and adorable Greek chorus.

They reached Demetrius's truck parked at the curb in front of a neighboring house, and Cody stowed the animal carrier inside the cab behind the driver's seat. They removed their Critter Catchers coveralls and stuffed them in a storage bin in the truck's bed.

"Can you look up Homeless Pets and call to see if they're open?" Demetrius asked.

Cody gave a dramatic sigh but pulled his phone from his pocket.

"Thanks."

The kittens wailed as he shifted into drive and pulled away from the curb. Another job done and none on the horizon. Just another day in their lives as Critter Catchers.

And best friends.

And… what?

Lovers? Was that what they were? Or had they gone from best friends to fuck buddies?

Demetrius chewed his lower lip as he drove through town. Looking back on it all, he could see all the signs pointing to a sexual relationship brewing between him and Cody for years. But it felt as if everything had happened fast. And though they'd tried to make sure they were being smart and not risking their friendship, Demetrius couldn't help worrying it all could fall apart in a matter of minutes.

Which might happen if Demetrius didn't tell Cody about the text he had received last night. It had been from Oliver Berridge, who he'd dated almost six months. Things between them had cooled during the spring, right about the time Oliver had called him Demmy, Cody's nickname for him, during sex. Demetrius had pretty much taken two big steps back after that. Or, to put it more precisely, stopped responding to Oliver's texts and voicemails.

He'd ghosted the man, and that made him feel guilty as crap. Because he was guilty.

And he was still trying to come to terms with everything that had happened since things between him and Oliver had ended.

Everything meaning Cody. More specifically, sex with Cody. Correction, the hot as fuck sex with Cody.

Demetrius ignored the butterflies in his belly—he was kissing, sucking, and fucking Cody, they were more like airplanes than butterflies—and turned his contemplations back to Oliver's text. It had been short and vague, another reason Demetrius had yet to respond. All Oliver had written was: *Might have something that would be of interest to you.*

What the hell did that even mean? Had Demetrius left something at Oliver's apartment? Was it a booty text? He needed to work up the guts to respond and get more information before he told Cody about it

And try not to feel guilty about it in the meantime.

Cody had found the shelter's number and called. He took the phone away from his ear and shrugged at Demetrius. "Goes to voicemail. They must be busy with the animals in back or something."

"What's the address?"

Cody looked at his phone. "Take a left at Stanford."

Demetrius followed the directions to a small brick building with high-set windows and a glass door. Cody grabbed the cats—still mewling their tiny, high-pitched cries —and followed Demetrius inside. A chest-high counter divided a small lobby, behind which was a door. It stood ajar, allowing the sounds of barking and meowing to escape. As they approached the counter, both stopped and looked at each other at the sound of… clucking?

"Was that a…?" Cody asked.

"Chicken?" Demetrius nodded. "I think it was."

"Chickens at the shelter?"

"They're cute at Easter," Demetrius said, "but they grow up fast."

"Yeah, but…"

"It's a chicken?"

Cody nodded. "Yeah. I mean, I get chickens are animals and all, but…"

"It's a chicken? At the animal shelter?"

"Yeah." Cody shook his head. "People."

"They're everywhere," Demetrius said. Cody seemed to have gotten over his irritation at Lucia, and for that Demetrius was grateful.

"Hello!" Cody shouted. "Anyone here?"

"Just a minute!" A woman shouted from the back room. "No! Bad dog! Bad dog!"

Demetrius and Cody looked at each other.

"What do you think?" Demetrius asked.

"I'm getting a bad feeling."

The door behind the counter swung open and a woman stepped out. She closed the door firmly behind her, partially muffling the animal sounds. The woman had shoulder-length curly blonde hair and big brown eyes. Clumps of fur and a few feathers clung to her over-sized polo shirt. A vague sense of recognition sparked within Demetrius. Before he could even greet her, however, the woman's expression darkened as she stared at Cody.

"What?" the woman said. "What are *you* doing here?"

Cody flashed a smile and held up the carrier. "We're the Critter Catchers, and we're working with the city for animal control. We caught these kittens in a garage and wanted to drop them off."

The woman glared at him. At that expression, recognition

clicked, and Demetrius sighed quietly. This was Darcy Saunders, yet another of Cody's exes. The town was full of them, and he never knew when one of them would appear.

"We're full," Darcy said.

"Hi." Demetrius gave a small wave to attract Darcy's attention. When she turned to him, however, the power of her glare made him take a step back. "Sorry. Um, it's Darcy, right?"

She gave a single nod in acknowledgement.

"Yeah, I thought so. Right. Okay. It's good to see you again. Been a few years."

"Five," Darcy stated in a flat voice as she glared at Cody again. "Five years since his last call."

"I meant to call…" Cody started, but then his voice faded out to nothing.

"About the kittens. Like Cody said, we're working on contract with the city to manage animal control after budget cuts were passed."

"Frank and Julia were fired?"

Demetrius exchanged a look with Cody, who shrugged. "We don't know Frank and Julia, so we can't say for sure. But the space used by animal control is no longer available. Soooo…."

"There are only ten kittens," Cody added.

"No."

"They don't need much room," Demetrius said. "And they're so cute and sweet. See?"

Cody set the carrier on the counter. He waved a hand in front of the wire door of the carrier like a game show hostess.

Darcy sighed. She looked at the tiny faces peering out of the carrier, and her expression softened. Then she looked up at Cody and the anger and resentment returned in a flash.

"There's no room. We're full."

"Maybe half of them?" Demetrius suggested. "They'll be

adopted out before you know it. Lots of people are looking for kittens."

Darcy looked back at the cats. One of them stuck a tiny paw through the wires of the carrier door. Darcy sighed before turning to Demetrius again. "I hate you both. But that's not the fault of these kittens."

"You'll take them?" Demetrius asked as a cool sense of relief washed through him.

"Yes, I'll take them in." Darcy started rummaging around beneath the counter. "You're the lucky one, you know?"

Demetrius frowned. "Lucky? I'm not sure I—"

"We all think so." She pulled out a form and placed it on top of the counter along with a pen. She fixed her sad-eyed gaze on Demetrius. "You're the constant, you always have been. He's going to keep you around forever. We were his outlets, just a way to get some brief pleasure. But you." She shook her head. "You've always been his heart."

Chills rattled Demetrius, head to toe, and his heart felt a bit *squeezed*.

"What...?" Cody said in a quiet voice.

Demetrius dropped his gaze to the floor. His chest felt tight, and his lungs felt much too small to pull in the amount of oxygen he suddenly required. He couldn't seem to lift his head to look up. And he sure as hell couldn't look at Cody. Maybe not ever again.

"I'll take them all," Darcy said. "But that's the last favor I do for you. Fill out this form while I take the cats back and unload them." She paused before saying in a patronizing tone, "You'll need to sterilize this carrier before you use it again."

"Oh. Yeah. Sure. Of course," Cody stammered.

Demetrius could feel Cody's gaze on him. But he couldn't figure out how to look back. All he could do was stare at the floor.

Darcy opened the door behind her, and the animal sounds intensified. She lifted the carrier of kittens off the counter and walked into the back of the building.

"Demmy?" Cody's voice was quiet and tentative. Almost child-like. "You okay?"

"Yeah, I'm just... I guess..." He sighed and finally managed to lift his head. He glanced at Cody, but couldn't hold his gaze and had to look away toward the open door behind the counter. "I guess it's just weird now when we run into one of your exes."

"More weird than it used to be?" Cody began to fill out the form, and Demetrius was glad he stopped staring at him.

"I guess? Maybe? I don't know."

Cody was silent as he wrote. The barking and meowing and clucking seemed very loud all of a sudden, and the building very small. Demetrius kept himself busy looking at his phone as they waited for Darcy to return.

What the hell had just happened?

CHAPTER TWO

Cody was at a loss for words. He stared out his side window as Demmy drove through town. The awkwardness and tension had followed them out of the animal shelter and now seemed to ride between them like some kind of third occupant, man-spreading its legs and taking up way too much room. From the route Demmy drove, he assumed they were going back to the office. It had been so long since either of them had spoken, though, he was reluctant to break the silence and ask.

Then his stomach rumbled. A long, loud grumbly sound of hunger. He put a hand on his belly and looked over. Demmy stared at him with wide eyes and a half smile.

"Do you need to eat something?"

Cody tried to act casual. "Why do you ask?"

They both laughed, and that simple act booted the awkwardly silent third occupant right out of the truck. The sight of Demmy's smile sent a glow through Cody. All these years, he'd always tried to please Demmy because he liked making his friend happy. But since their relationship had changed, pleasing Demmy—especially physically—gave Cody even more of a rush.

Maybe it was because he had never seemed to be able to please the women he dated—or he wasn't invested enough in those relationships to work very hard toward that goal. He hadn't been able to anticipate what they needed like he could with Demmy. Many of the women claimed he didn't listen to them, while others claimed he didn't open up to them. Whatever the reason, Cody had long ago realized his connection to Demmy was stronger than any other relationship. That had been true when they'd been friends, and it seemed even more apparent now that their relationship had shifted into something more intimate.

As Demmy turned onto a street, apparently now heading for downtown Parson's Hollow, Cody thought about the things Darcy had said back at the animal shelter. She'd said *we all think so*, like she was part of some support group or something. But that was crazy to think, right?

She'd also told Demmy he was the lucky one, and Cody had to give her that one. Through all the women he dated all the years they'd been friends, Demmy had been the one constant in his life.

And now he and Demmy were having sex.

Maybe that made Cody the lucky one instead.

He drew in a deep, shaky breath. Cody wasn't good at managing the intimacy that stemmed from sex. He was good at the physical part, he had to give himself some credit there. No matter how many ex-girlfriends he'd left in his wake, he would bet that all of them would agree he was great in bed. But the closeness associated with sex seemed to bring about a change in him. He could flirt and joke and talk to a prospective sexual partner for hours, but once that line was crossed to a physical relationship, some switch seemed to flip. Maybe he considered it the end of the chase and simply became bored.

Or maybe repeated sexual encounters with the same person just became too intimate, and therefore too threatening.

Whatever the reason, it had happened many times before. But Cody didn't want it to happen between him and Demmy. He needed to work hard to make this relationship last. This was the fourth week of this new chapter in their lives, and Cody was really enjoying himself. Demmy turned him on more than he could have anticipated. He never tired of spending time with him, touching him, kissing him, and fucking him. Over the last four weeks, Cody liked to think he'd gotten really good at sucking Demmy's cock as well as rimming his ass.

Who knew all those years of dating women was leading him to this relationship with his best friend? If he could just keep from fucking it all up, things might turn out all right.

"Earth to Cody."

Demmy's voice barged into his thoughts and brought him back to the truck. They were parked a block down from Margie's Diner and Demmy had opened his door to get out. "You okay over there?"

Cody flashed a smile and nodded as he opened his own door. "I'm better than okay, you should know that. Just hungry."

As Demmy dropped quarters into the parking meter, Cody walked to Margie's and waited outside. He opened the door for Demmy and waved him inside with a flourish.

"Thank you," Demmy said with a chuckle.

"No, no, thank *you*."

Margie walked around the far end of the counter with a plate of food in each hand. She was in her sixties and dressed in her usual outfit of jeans and a white blouse splattered by a variety of sauces. Her thick black hair was pulled back into the customary bun and covered by a hairnet. Orange lipstick surrounded her big, white smile as greeted them.

"You two look like you need a big meal and a cold glass of iced tea. There's an open booth by the window there." Margie nodded in that direction. "Be right with you boys."

Neither of them needed a menu. They'd been eating at Margie's nearly all of their lives, so they knew her menu by heart.

"Please don't get the pork loin," Demmy said.

Cody pouted. "I love the pork loin."

"I don't love what it does to you a couple of hours later."

"Are you putting restrictions on what I can and can't eat? Is that where we're at now in our relationship?"

"I'm trying to prevent you from killing both of us in our sleep," Demmy said. "Please be considerate. Say no to the pork loin."

Margie hustled up to their booth and set iced teas before each of them. "You two look rode hard and wore out. Tough day? Lots of critters to corral?"

"Kittens," Demmy said. "Lots of them."

Margie widened her eyes. "Sounds dangerous."

"They were in the Widow's garage," Cody added.

Margie's eyes widened even more. "Now you're starting to scare me." She lowered her voice and leaned in over the table. "How much junk does she have in there?'

"Enough to open her own resale shop," Demmy said.

"Some people say she's got the body of her husband Earl in there, too." She looked between them. "You see Earl?"

"I don't remember seeing a body," Cody said, "but it could have been hidden behind the stacks of newspapers and bags of clothes from the forties."

"That woman," Margie said and shook her head. "Revolving yellow light or not, she's going to kill someone one day soon."

"She may have already, and we just don't know it," Cody said with a quick glance at Demmy.

Margie clicked her pen open. "Okay, boys, what'll it be?"

Cody smiled at Demmy as he said, "I'll have the meatloaf and scalloped potatoes."

"Thank you," Demmy said, then looked up at Margie. "Whitefish and steamed asparagus."

"Great," Cody muttered.

"You got something against my whitefish?" Margie gave him a hard look.

"Nope, not at all." Cody smiled. "Everything here tastes great. Especially the pork loin."

Demmy glared. "Don't you dare…"

"Don't worry. I'll be mature. Meatloaf is fine, thanks Margie."

"I think you boys were in the Widow's garage too long." Margie walked off shaking her head.

"What was that about?" Demmy whispered.

"Asparagus," Cody whispered back.

"What about it?"

"I can't eat pork loin because of the resulting smell, and you go on and order asparagus."

Demmy laughed as he looked confused. "I don't understand what the two have to do with each other."

"Asparagus makes not just your pee smell funny, but everything else that sprays from the same nozzle."

"Oh. My. God." A deep crimson blush burned across Demmy's cheeks just before he put his face in his hands. "I know we're getting to know each other, like, incredibly intimately these days, but I just never thought I'd hear you complain about the smell of my—" He looked around and lowered his voice even more. "Semen."

Cody leaned in over the table. "I know we're both still getting used to…" He waved a hand in the space between them. "This. But I think I deserve some credit here. The last four weeks I've been pretty damn adventurous when it comes to… well, cum, and where it lands."

Demmy's face turned even more red, and he couldn't seem to meet Cody's gaze. His reaction was so fucking adorable, Cody's cock took immediate notice and hardened. He would have given anything to be able to do what he wanted to Demmy at that precise moment. Especially before the asparagus arrived.

Demmy's phone gave a ping, signaling he'd just received a text message. He looked at his phone, then quickly set it face-down on the table.

"Who was that?" Cody asked.

"What? Oh, nothing important."

Before Cody could point out that he hadn't answered the question, Demmy's phone rang. He picked it up and checked the display. "It's my Mom. I'd better get it."

"Mm hmm," Cody said.

"Hi Mom," Demmy said into the phone as he managed to give Cody a stern look. "Everything okay? Oh yeah?"

Cody frowned. "She okay?"

Demmy nodded to him, then slid out of the booth and said, "Oh, really?" as he headed for the door. He stepped out on the sidewalk where he paced between a few parking meters just outside of the window as he talked.

Cody watched him as his dick pulsed with impatience. Dammit, the hold Demmy had over him was erotic and terrifying all at once.

"Well, hello handsome."

He jumped a bit and turned away from the window. A beautiful blonde waitress stood at the table, looking down at him with a smile full of sexual promise. It was Vicki Downing, one of the few women his age he had never dated.

"Vicki! Well, hello yourself." Cody's heart pounded, and his mouth went dry.

"How's the world been treating you?" Vicki asked.

"Can't complain. I'm a lucky guy."

"Yeah? I hear you're unattached these days."

Cody swallowed hard. "Oh? That's what you're hearing, huh?"

"That's right." Vicki sat in the booth beside him and pressed her leg against his. "And it just so happens I'm unattached as well."

Cody stared. Of all the fucking luck. He and Vicki Downing had been missing each other for years. And now here she was, all hot and ready to go, and Cody couldn't... Well, hell. What could and couldn't he do? He and Demmy hadn't set any parameters around their relationship. What it really came down to, he supposed, was what he should and shouldn't do.

"So what do you say?" Vicki pressed her leg harder against his, and Cody's pounding heartbeat echoed in his cock.

"You know, any other time I would not hesitate at the opportunity..."

Vicki sighed. "But?"

"But, I, um, I need to hang with Demmy tonight. He's on the phone with his mother down in Florida right now, and you know she went through that heart surgery last month. It seems she might not be recuperating as well as they'd first thought. I really can't leave him alone tonight."

A sudden burst of laughter from out on the sidewalk caught their attention. Demmy held onto a parking meter to steady himself as he threw back his head and laughed again. Cody's erection wilted, and he slowly turned to find Vicki giving him a hard look.

"Yeah, he looks real tore up about things." She slid out of the booth. "You let me know when you're ready for me to take you seriously, and I'll let you know if I'm still interested."

"Hey, Vicki—"

She walked away without a second glance. Cody practically whimpered as he watched her go, his gaze running over her perfect ass. Damn, being with her would have been amazing.

But he was with Demmy now, and sex with *him* was amazing. It was a more complicated situation, because no one other than him and Demmy knew about this new level of intimacy. When Cody considered telling people about it, he felt nervous and kind of itchy, like he might be getting a rash or sudden attack of hives. It flustered him at the very least, and quite frankly frightened him at other times.

Cody had never had a problem being friends with Demmy. He'd figured out Demmy was gay a couple of years before Demmy had officially come out to him, and Cody hadn't thought twice about it. He'd actually been kind of intrigued by the idea. Now that their relationship had become a physical one, he guessed he'd been more than a little turned on by the thought even back then.

But he hadn't pursued anything with Demmy at that time, even as he'd come to understand his own attraction to some other men. It wasn't that Demmy wasn't his type, it was that he didn't think *he* was *Demmy's* type. People had been telling him he was handsome his whole life, but he had never thought he was deep down good enough for Demmy. He had avoided getting into something physical and more intimate because he had never thought he was worthy of Demmy.

And now here they were, a month into something intense and intimate, and Cody had no idea what his end game looked like. Were they going to stay together? Would they move in together? Would they get married?

His stomach cramped at the thought. His parents and the majority of his brothers would be cool with it, as would Demmy's Aunt Amelia and his parents, but what about everyone else in town? Cody didn't think they would find a lot of hate aimed their way, but he suspected he'd get a lot of statements like, "I knew it" and "You guys finally went and made it official."

Cody wasn't embarrassed to be with Demmy, but the know-it-all reactions from the rest of the town would really try his patience. Especially people like Lucia Durant. She would savor the opportunity to smirk in his face and say something like, "I knew there was a reason."

Demmy slid into the booth across from him, bringing Cody out of his thoughts. Still chuckling, Demmy set his phone aside and looked up at Cody.

"Mom and Dad just got back from a weekend in Key West."

"Oh yeah? She's feeling better, huh?"

"A lot better. She had some funny stories about them hanging out with a group of drag queens at a bar one night."

Cody smiled. "I'm sure there was a lot to tell."

Margie approached with a tray balanced on her shoulder. She rested the edge of the tray on the corner of their table and distributed their food as well as fresh iced teas.

"There you go, boys. Anything else for you right now?"

Demmy smiled. "I think we're good, Margie, thanks."

"Enjoy."

They both quieted as they tucked into their meals. The meatloaf and scalloped potatoes were excellent, and Cody didn't miss the pork tenderloin at all. He grinned as he noticed Demmy was not eating much, if any, of his asparagus.

Things might be looking up after all.

CHAPTER THREE

Demetrius got behind the wheel of his truck and started the engine. He looked over at Cody, taking in his slouch, wide-spread legs, head reclined against the seat, and closed eyes.

"You still awake?"

"So awake I'm practically vibrating."

"Where would you like to go?"

Cody popped one eye open and looked at him. "Are you asking me if I'd like to spend the night with you?"

Demetrius shrugged and admitted, "Yeah, in a round-about way that's what I was asking."

Cody looked around, then unsnapped and unzipped his jeans. He tugged down the waistband of his red briefs and exposed his hard-on. "What's that tell you?"

Demetrius stared at Cody's cock. His mouth felt incredibly dry even as it seemed to water in anticipation of the taste. As often as he'd seen, touched, sucked, and been fucked by Cody's dick over the last few weeks, the sight of it still sent a flutter of nervous excitement through him.

"Jesus," Demetrius whispered, pulling his gaze from

Cody's cock to look around and make sure no one could see them.

"I checked," Cody said, but adjusted himself back beneath his clothing. "So did that answer your question?"

"Yep. It sure did. Your place or mine?"

"We haven't been to my place in a few days."

"Your place it is."

They were silent during the drive to Cody's apartment, but Demetrius sported an almost painful erection the entire ten minutes. It was so hard, Demetrius couldn't think about Oliver's follow up text that had come in just before his mother's call. This message had a little more detail: *You still track down monsters?*

What the hell was Demetrius supposed to say to that? *Sorry I never called you back months ago, and by the way, we don't willfully look for monsters* didn't really seem to cover it.

He parked in a visitor spot and pushed thoughts of Oliver and monsters aside as he followed Cody up the steps to his third floor exterior apartment entrance. He stared at Cody's ass the entire way, watching it tighten and release. Demetrius's cock pulsed in time with Cody's steps, and he thought those three flights were the longest in the history of stairs.

Cody opened his apartment door and Demetrius followed him inside. Before he could get five feet beyond the door, Cody slammed it behind them and grabbed Demetrius by one arm. Demetrius only had time to grunt in surprise before Cody pulled him up hard against his body. The kiss was rough and hungry, and Demetrius responded in kind. He could feel Cody's erection against his belly, and he moaned into Cody's mouth.

"I know I smell bad," Cody said between kisses. "But I'm too fucking horny to shower."

"You really worked up a stink in the Widow's garage," Demetrius said, then made a face. "We both did."

Cody sighed and pressed his forehead to Demmy's. "You're going to make me take a shower, aren't you?"

Demetrius gave him a quick kiss. "Just think of all the stuff we'll be able to do after a shower."

That seemed to decide him. Cody twisted the deadbolt on the door, took Demetrius by the hand, and led him down the short hallway to the master bedroom.

"Strip," Cody ordered, and the impatient edge to his voice made Demetrius shiver.

After Demetrius had peeled off his final sock and stood nude and hard at the foot of the bed, Cody took a moment to look him up and down.

"You're killing me," Cody said.

"Stop it." Demetrius waved his words away.

"You have no idea just how much you get to me." Cody took Demetrius by the hand and led him into the bathroom. "If we have to shower beforehand, we do it together."

"Oh no, that's a horrible idea," Demetrius said, his tone of voice conveying just how much he loved it.

Cody pushed aside the shower curtain and started the water. When he was satisfied with the temperature, he stepped into the tub. Turning, he reached out to grab Demetrius by the dick and slowly pulled him forward until he stepped into the tub as well.

Demetrius's head spun as they kissed and lathered each other. When Cody slipped a soapy finger into his ass, Demetrius gasped. He lifted his left foot and rested it on the soap tray to allow Cody a deeper reach.

"Are we clean yet?" Cody whispered into his ear and followed it up with a nibble of his lobe.

Demetrius laughed. "I don't think I've ever been cleaner."

"Time to get dirty all over again."

They dried off quickly and tumbled onto the bed. Cody pulled Demetrius against him and threw a strong, heavy leg across his hip as they kissed. Demetrius could never seem to get enough of Cody's mouth and tongue; he could kiss him for hours. But the hard length of Cody's cock proved too inviting, and Demetrius slid down to take it in his mouth. Cody rolled onto his back, sighing and moaning as Demetrius sucked him. He slowly worked the incredibly long shaft, pausing at the tip to suckle the soft, broad head. The salty taste of pre-cum urged him to move faster, but he didn't want Cody to finish quite yet. He only wanted him primed and ready.

"Fucking hell, Demmy," Cody said between moans. "You'd better slow down or I'm going to shoot."

Demetrius eased off Cody's dick and smiled as he stroked him. "Get you a little worked up?"

"You know you did, smart ass." Cody pulled him up and kissed him hard. "I think we need to share some workspace."

"Like we don't do that every day at the office."

Cody kissed him again. "I wish we could do this at the office." He shifted position on the bed, putting his feet on the pillows and his cock in Demetrius's face. Cody was level with Demetrius's dick, and he wrapped his big hand around the shaft before sliding his mouth over it.

"God, that feels so good," Demetrius said with a sigh, then took hold of Cody's cock and resumed sucking.

A short time later, Cody surprised him by shifting position once again. He pushed Demetrius onto his back before straddling his chest with his back turned. Cody pulled Demetrius's legs up and held them beneath his arms, then lifted Demetrius's hips. He ran his tongue along the crack of Demetrius's ass, pausing to press the tip of his tongue into his anus. As he rimmed Demetrius, Cody shifted his hips back so his own ass hovered just above Demetrius's face.

Demetrius pulled down on Cody's hips as he lifted his head and pressed his mouth to the tight, furrowed hole. He licked and sucked at Cody's anus, then turned his head to gently nip the firm, hairy cheeks. Cody groaned and returned the favor to Demetrius before lifting his head and spitting down into his hole. A long, slender finger pushed into him, and Demetrius groaned encouragement as his toes clenched and his cock throbbed against his belly. Pre-cum ran in a sticky stream down his torso.

"Your ass is so hot," Cody said as he pumped his finger in and out.

"Feel like sliding something bigger in there?"

"You're reading my mind again."

Cody moved off of Demetrius and leaned over to get the lube out of the nightstand. They hadn't been able to use the condoms Cody had bought on their road trip home from Florida because they'd contained nonoxynol, to which Demetrius was allergic. After not using protection that first time, they had discussed it and decided not to use them going forward. Demetrius had followed that decision up with the request that if either of them had sex outside of the relationship, they would use a condom. Cody had acted hurt, claiming that Demetrius was suggesting that he would be the one who had sex with someone else. After a bit of discussion, he had come around and agreed. Demetrius trusted Cody to keep his word about using a condom if he had sex with another person, probably more than he trusted Cody to abstain from sex with anyone else. It was a varying level of trust he was aware of, but decided not to study too closely. Cody cared enough about him to keep his word and not put him at risk, and that was what he chose to focus on.

In his previous relationships, Demetrius had always switched between top and bottom position. With Cody, he discovered the true pleasure of being a bottom and wasn't in any rush for Cody to switch places with him. It might happen one day, but even if Cody never felt comfortable enough to be on the receiving end of anal sex with him, Demetrius was enjoying himself.

With his fingers slicked up, Cody lifted Demetrius's legs and eased a finger inside him. He worked slowly, adding another finger and more lube, gently opening Demetrius up. Just when Demetrius thought he might need to tell him to get on with it, Cody drizzled lube along his cock and moved in close. The wide head eased inside, parting muscle and spreading him open.

"So fucking tight," Cody whispered. "So fucking hot."

"God you're big."

"Too much?"

"Nope. Just give me a second to adjust."

Cody paused and pulled back, then slid in once again. He went a bit deeper before pulling out and sliding back in. Deeper still the third time, and on the fourth push, he slid all the way inside. Cody leaned down for a hot and tongue-heavy kiss before he rose up, took hold of Demetrius's ankles, and started moving. It was slow at first, a few shallow thrusts followed by an even slower, deeper one. Then Cody picked up speed until he was all out fucking Demetrius. Every thrust was hard and deep, cock burrowing into him and sliding over the hard nub of his prostate. Cody filled him completely, side to side and end to end, and Demetrius knew he wouldn't last very long. He never did when Cody fucked him.

Demetrius focused on tightening and releasing his muscles in time with the thrusts, glad when he earned a heavy groan from Cody. He was on the edge and almost ready to blow when Cody tipped his head back and shouted up at the ceiling. He thrust deep, and Demetrius felt him harden even more as he came. He clenched his muscles around Cody's throbbing dick and stroked himself to his own sticky finish.

Cody rested his sweaty forehead against Demetrius's calf and looked at him as he caught his breath. "Amazing."

"Always."

Slow and gentle, Cody eased out, then collapsed beside him and threw an arm over his chest. "So good."

"Better than good." Demetrius rolled out from beneath Cody's arm. "Let me clean up a bit."

"Come back," Cody said in a weak voice, and waggled his fingers at him. "Don't leave."

Demetrius cleaned up with a damp washcloth, and by the time he retuned to the bedroom, Cody was quietly snoring. He smiled and slowly got into bed beside him, surprised when Cody sighed and pulled him close. Demetrius kissed Cody's forearm, snuggled in a little closer, and closed his eyes.

DEMETRIUS CAREFULLY SLID out from beneath Cody's arm. He sat on the edge of the mattress and looked over his shoulder. Cody lay on his side, his face handsome and relaxed in sleep. The shadow of stubble on his jaw looked sexy, and Demetrius's cock twitched in response. He located his phone on the nightstand and checked the time, surprised to find it was eight-thirty p.m. He stood up and quietly pulled a pair of sleep pants and a long-sleeved T-shirt from the drawer Cody had emptied for his use. With a final look back at the long line of Cody's body beneath the sheet, Demetrius slipped out of the bedroom and eased the door shut behind him.

After a visit to the hallway bathroom, Demetrius checked the refrigerator: a package of hamburger, a block of Monterey jack cheese, and several open jars of salsa in a variety of heat levels. An unopened bag of tortilla chips sat on the counter, and he nodded to himself. Nachos for a late evening snack. He dumped the hamburger into a skillet and as it browned he considered the text messages from Oliver.

It was time Demetrius got back in touch with him, but what should he say? He hadn't seen Oliver around town lately. Not that he had been looking for him, but he wondered if Oliver had moved. Maybe he had met someone new and moved in with him.

Before he could talk himself out of it, Demetrius grabbed his phone and tapped out a reply: *Hi there. Been a while. Hope you're doing well. We don't go looking for monsters, we just kind of find them.*

Once he'd sent the text, Demetrius turned his thoughts from Oliver to his life with Cody.

The sex earlier had been good. No, it had been great. But then again, it was always great with Cody. Demetrius supposed it had more to do with the depth of their connection than any other reason, but he wasn't going to analyze that too deeply. Not when so many other things about a deeper relationship with Cody begged to be examined.

They'd first had sex in that motel room in Charleston, South Carolina a month ago. Demetrius could remember just how nervous and excited he'd felt as he'd stood in the bathroom staring at his reflection. Those same mixed feelings still occasionally flared up since, even after they'd been together so many times. Sometimes he thought he might just be having a very long, very detailed dream, and he would wake up alone in his own bed and have to face Cody with all of these unresolved feelings.

And Demetrius had a lot of unresolved feelings for Cody.

Now that he was allowing himself time to really examine what was between them, Demetrius realized Cody's relationship countdown clock was nearing zero. In all the years they'd been friends, Cody had only dated one woman for six weeks, and that had been Zenona Baldwin, who was now a doctor at Parson's Hollow Memorial Hospital. If they could last two more weeks, at least he'd be able to say Cody had broken his dating record for him.

The hamburger was done, and Demetrius drained the grease into a coffee cup and set it aside to cool. He grated the cheese, lined up the jars of salsa and added spoons to each, then opened the bag of chips. With everything ready, he walked down the hall and eased the bedroom door open.

Cody lay on his back, grinning at him as he slowly stroked his erection.

"I was just thinking about you," Cody said, his voice deep and husky from sleep.

"I see that," Demetrius said. "I was thinking about you, too. I got stuff together for nachos."

"I love nachos."

"I know that."

"Blow job first?" Cody gripped his cock at the base and waved it back and forth. "He's really, really worked up."

Demetrius was at full mast himself. "Hell, we can microwave the nachos."

He stripped, crawled onto the bed, and went down on Cody. He savored the salty, sweaty taste of him. Since they'd already worked out a lot of their pent-up sexual energy, he took things a little slower. He dragged his mouth up Cody's length and paused to purse his lips around the head slick with pre-cum. He moved lower, lips tight around Cody's shaft.

"Oh, Demmy," Cody said with a sigh. "That's so good."

Moments later, Cody pulled Demetrius around so they lay in a sixty-nine position. Cody sucked him slow and deep, perfectly copying Demetrius's technique. As he worked Cody's cock, Demetrius gripped the shaft and stroked in time.

Their speed increased at a steady rate until both were stroking and sucking hard and fast.

Demetrius came first. He blew a deep breath through his nostrils and grunted a warning. Cody focused his attention on the sensitive head as it swelled in his mouth before releasing a flood of cum. He swallowed it down, and Demetrius groaned as he continued working on Cody's dick. Not long after Demetrius came, Cody lifted his head and cried out just before he shot his load. Demetrius swallowed it greedily, twisting his hand around the shaft as he pumped up and down. When Cody had finished, Demetrius continued sucking until Cody gasped and pulled him off.

"Too sensitive," Cody said with a breathless laugh. "It's too much."

Demetrius shifted position and kissed Cody, their tongues slowly tangling.

"We should have eaten first and saved that as dessert," Demetrius said.

"Who says we can't?" Cody kissed him again.

"A third time in just a few hours? Are you taking some kind of supplement?"

"No, but that's something I might check into."

With another kiss, Cody got out of bed and stepped into the attached bathroom. Demetrius dressed again and returned to the kitchen to heat up the food. The hamburger had cooled, but a quick spin in the microwave heated it up nicely. After he had removed the meat from the microwave, Cody came up behind and put his arms around his waist.

"A shared shower, hot sex, a nap, hot sex round two, and now nachos?" Cody lightly bit his neck. "I must have died and gone to man Heaven."

Demetrius laughed. "Not sure all men would appreciate each of those things you listed."

"Most men really like sex."

"Just not with another man."

"Then they don't know what they're missing." Cody slipped a hand down the front of Demetrius's pants to cup his cock and balls. "I'm glad I figured it out."

Demetrius closed his eyes and leaned back against Cody's tall, strong frame. "Me too."

With a final gentle squeeze, Cody removed his hand from Demetrius's pants and stepped around him to grab plates from the cupboard. They carried their nachos into the living room and sat on the couch across from the big screen television. Cody turned it on and jumped through channels until he landed on a baseball game. He glanced over at Demetrius and asked, "Is this okay to watch?"

Demetrius nodded. "Yeah. I don't mind a good ball game."

Cody grinned. "You proved that just a little while ago."

As they watched the game and ate their nachos, Cody scooted closer and pressed his leg against Demetrius's. It was just like every other time Demetrius had watched sports with Cody at his apartment, only now he was free to touch and kiss the man beside him. As enjoyable as the last month had been, Demetrius couldn't help wondering about the next month. And the one after that. And the next one, and on and on into the future.

He drew in a long, quiet breath and slowly let it out. It wasn't a good idea to try and plan too far ahead. As in love as he was with Cody—and, yes, he was able to admit that to himself, if not yet to Cody—he was trying to be realistic about the chances of their relationship surviving. He knew Cody's track record with women, and Demetrius worried that it would one day apply to him as well.

His phone buzzed and Demetrius picked it up from the coffee table. Oliver had responded, but Demetrius didn't want to read it yet. Especially not with Cody sitting right beside him.

"Who was that?"

"What?"

One of the players hit a home run, and the action distracted Cody. Demetrius sent up a quick thanks to the sports gods above. He wondered how Oliver had responded. Maybe it was time for a bathroom break so he could read the response.

"Did you ever watch me play football and want to suck me off?"

Cody's question pulled Demetrius out of his thoughts about Oliver's mysterious text messages. He stared at him for a moment, taking in the twinkle in his sexy brown eyes, the slight upward curl at one corner of his full lips, and he decided to play along.

"All the time. After your games, I would hurry home and jerk off at least twice while I thought about sitting on the bench in the locker room watching as you peeled off those tight football pants and sweaty jock."

His response hit the mark. Cody's eyes went wide and his lips parted as he stared at Demetrius. "Are you serious?"

Demetrius moved in to give him a quick kiss, then got up from the couch, picked up their empty plates, and smiled down at Cody. "What do you think?"

He turned away and walked into the kitchen. The minute he set the plates in the sink, Cody wrapped his arms around him from behind and lightly bit his neck.

"Time for dessert?" Cody whispered in his ear.

Demetrius turned in his arms to face him. "You've got quite a sweet tooth tonight."

"Shut up and follow me."

Demetrius grinned as Cody took him by the hand and led him down the hall to the bedroom. This was all too much fun to spend time worrying about Oliver and his own future.

CHAPTER FOUR

Cody slouched in his chair. With his legs spread wide and feet planted far apart, he swiveled back and forth as he stared at the back of Demmy's computer monitor. They'd been in the office for two hours without a single phone call, and he had grown more and more bored with each passing minute. Demmy, of course, had found something to occupy himself, working on something on his computer and exchanging text messages with someone. He tried to keep his mind from diving into suspicious thoughts about the texting and tried instead to think of something that needed to be done. But nothing caught his interest. He wasn't in the frame of mind for busy work.

He knew damn well that Demmy was thinking about the magic number six weeks from Cody's dating past. The run-in with Darcy the day before had thrown him for a loop. What Darcy had said to Demmy had really hit Cody hard. He knew Demmy wanted to talk about things, but was too skittish to bring anything up. And now Demmy was exchanging text messages with someone, and Cody had no idea what he might be saying.

Last night he had reverted to classic Cody moves to keep Demmy from mentioning Darcy's statement. The sex had been great, as usual, but three times pushed even Cody's limits. Now here they sat, the morning after, with plenty of time to talk, and Cody had no desire to touch on that subject. Mostly because he would have no answers for Demmy. He wasn't bored with their relationship, not even a little bit. He knew they were going to break his own personal dating record of six weeks, but after that? Cody could only hope he didn't do something stupid to push Demmy away, because he wouldn't be able to handle losing him.

Now, though, he had a driving need to break the silence and stave off his own death from boredom. Also, he really wanted to find out who Demmy was texting.

"That your mom?" Cody asked.

"Hmm?" Demmy looked at him around the monitor. "Oh. No, it's not Mom."

Cody waited, but Demmy didn't say anything more. That was interesting. "Who is it then?"

Demmy dropped his gaze, and Cody's senses went on alert. Something was up.

"It's Oliver."

Cody stared and worked hard to keep his expression neutral as emotions roared through him. He was simultaneously jealous and angry and intrigued. But he had to play it cool. He couldn't let Demmy know the extent of his jealousy or anger. He had to go with intrigued.

"Oh? What's Ollie up to these days?"

Demmy frowned. "He doesn't like to be called that."

"He's not here." Cody widened his eyes and looked under the desk. "Or is he?"

"You know he's not here. Stop acting like a child."

"Was that who texted you yesterday?"

"Yes. But it's not what you're thinking."

Cody cocked an eyebrow. "You don't know what I'm thinking."

"It involves sex."

"Fine. You sort of know what I'm thinking, but that was easy because that's my default thought process. But you don't know all of what I'm thinking."

Demmy leaned forward on the desk. "He says he has a case for us."

"Yeah? Let's go. We need the work."

"It's more of a specialty case."

Cody furrowed his brow, then understanding hit and he shook his head. "No. No more monsters."

"It sounds like an interesting case."

"So did the last three."

"We didn't willfully take on the last three monsters," Demmy said. "Well, we did work with Abigail on the chupacabra case. But that's beside the point because it wasn't actually a chupacabra."

"I don't like it." Cody shook his head. "We've been in enough danger from things that should not even exist."

Demmy nodded and rolled back out of sight behind the monitor. "I had a feeling you would feel that way. I just sent him a text to let him know we wouldn't be working with him."

"Oh. Okay. That's good. Thank you."

"You're welcome."

They were silent for a time, and then Cody couldn't take it any longer. "What kind of case is it?"

"Some urban legend in New Jersey. The Devil of Pinesville."

"Sounds very church centric. Can he call a local priest?"

"I think it lives in the woods. Lots of sightings recently."

"He live in New Jersey now?"

Demmy shrugged. "I don't know. Want me to ask?"

Cody shook his head. "No."

"Fine. End of discussion."

"Fine."

The silence stretched out for several minutes before Cody asked, "What's your take on the courtesy flush?"

Demmy looked at him around the monitor. He squinted and ran a hand through his thinning brown hair as he frowned. "What?"

"The courtesy flush," Cody said. "What's your take on it?"

Demmy sighed and rolled his chair over a bit to look at him straight on. "I don't understand the question."

"It's not a trick question. How do you feel about the courtesy flush?"

"Am I supposed to be the person engaging the courtesy flush, or the person hoping for someone else to perform it?"

"Either. Both."

Demmy considered the question. They needed some humor to get past the Ollie and monster discussion, so Cody had asked the first off the wall question he could think of. He had a bad feeling that Demmy really wanted to see Ollie again and learn more about this monster of his.

"I would have to vote in favor of it in both circumstances."

"Do you actually implement the courtesy flush when you poop in public restrooms?"

"We're getting into a weird area here." Demmy rolled out of sight behind his monitor.

Cody sat up and grinned as he leaned forward with his forearms on the desk. "You don't do it, do you?"

"I'm not talking about this any more."

Cody stood and looked at him over the monitor. "You claim to be in favor of a courtesy flush, but you don't actually do it."

Demmy looked at him with wide eyes. "What is your hang up about this?"

"I'm bored."

"Then go clean the kitchen. Or the bathroom. Or check our email inbox for any emails."

Cody made a face. "Those aren't interesting things."

A call rang through on both of their desk phones.

"There. You can answer our first call of the day."

"We're going to continue this conversation later," Cody said.

"Not if I can help it."

Cody picked up the phone. "Critter Catchers, Cody speaking."

"A skunk family is living under my deck!"

The man's voice started out shrill and rose to piercing by the last word. Cody winced and held the phone a short distance away before carefully placing it against his ear once again.

"Okay, sir. Take a moment to calm down."

"Calm down? Calm down?! How am I supposed to calm down when my dogs and my cats have all been sprayed by these things. I've had to put 'em in the garage, and it stinks in there now. My kids want to play on their swing set, but I can't let them anywhere near the backyard."

"Do you know how many skunks are under the deck?"

"I don't know, I didn't go out and take a goddamn census." The man took a moment to calm himself before he continued. "Can you please just come out here and get rid of them? I wanted to poison them, but my wife shut me down. Plus I don't want my dogs or cats to get into any poison. She recommended I call you guys."

"Well, let me see here," Cody said as he raised his eyebrows at Demmy and shrugged. Did they even want to tackle removing a skunk? "You've got multiple skunks, and that's a slightly hazardous critter, you know, with the spray and such. That's more on the premium side of our list of charges."

Demmy nodded as he typed on his computer keyboard. He clicked around a few times, then gave Cody a thumbs up.

"Fine, that's fine," the man said with a weary sigh, apparently having exhausted his manic energy. "Just come out as soon as you can."

Cody wrote down the address and the man's mobile number, then hung up. "There, you see? We don't need a monster case. We just got a job. Do we know how to handle skunks?"

Demmy stood and gave a single nod before pointing at his monitor. "I just found a website that explains how to trap a skunk."

Cody circled the desks and stood directly behind Demmy. He put his hands on Demmy's hips and rested his chin on Demmy's shoulder as he looked at the website. "Does it give a good way to remove the smell once we get sprayed?"

Demmy leaned down and clicked a link. "Yeah. Right here."

The office door opened, and Darnell "Jugs" Perramon entered. Cody's heart skipped a beat and he hurriedly stepped back, putting distance between himself and Demmy. A mixture of nervousness and regret rushed through him as he walked around the desks and forced a big smile on his face.

"Jugs! What brings you by?" Cody asked, moving in for a bro-hug.

"Enid Helen wanted to get out of the apartment for a while," Jugs said as he slapped Cody hard on the back a few times.

Cody stepped back and looked him over. Darnell Perramon, known by the name Jugs because of the size of his pectoral muscles, had attended Harriettville High School, Parson's Hollow's biggest sports team rivals. As a linebacker, Cody had often gone up against Jugs who played offensive tackle. Jugs had covered the Critter Catchers business while Cody and Demmy had been in Florida for Demmy's mother's heart surgery. During that time, Jugs had gone out on a call to remove a critter from a crawlspace. The critter had turned out to be a matted and frightened Yorkshire Terrier, and Jugs had adopted the tiny thing that same day. He cleaned her up and named her Enid Helen Perramon. And he completely spoiled Enid Helen.

"Did she tell you that?" Cody asked with a grin.

Jugs shrugged. "Not in so many words. But I can tell these things."

Cody looked him up and down. "So where is she?"

"She's snoozing in the car." Jugs looked past Cody and gave a wave. "Hiya Demetrius."

"Hi, Jugs. Good to see you."

"You, too. Got a customer to see?'

"Yeah," Cody said. "We just got the call. Something different for us."

"Oh?" Jugs looked between them. "Need an extra hand?"

Demmy briefly met Cody's gaze, then shrugged and turned away, saying over his shoulder, "Not sure you'll really want to come along once you hear about it. I'll get the coveralls and some other stuff out of the back."

The chill from Demmy's look lingered, and Cody had a feeling he knew what it was about. It wasn't the Ollie and monster discussion they'd had, or the courtesy flush conversation. It was the fact that he'd jumped back from Demmy way too fast when Jugs walked in the office. Well, more like he'd just touched a live wire. For all the passion and intimacy he felt with Demmy, Cody still wasn't comfortable revealing the new depth of their relationship to anyone else.

"Uh oh," Jugs said. "Sounds like this might be worse than a trapped deer or possum nest."

"Yeah, a bit worse than that." Cody grinned. "How do you feel about skunks?"

CODY DROVE THE TRUCK, Demmy sitting between him and Jugs. Enid Helen sat on Jugs's thighs, a pink bow on top of her head, eyes squinting against the breeze coming in the open window. Cody carried on a conversation with Jugs about what he'd been up to since they'd last talked, and if he had any promising job prospects. Jugs had been a manager at Furniture, Furniture, Furniture in Harriettville, but had been laid off over the summer.

"Nothing in the hopper yet," Jugs said. "I'm thinking about looking for something part time, and then taking system server classes, try and get myself a little more technical for those higher paying jobs."

"Sounds like a plan."

Cody had nothing more to add after that, and silence dropped over them. Cody wanted to be alone with Demmy to discuss the texts between him and Ollie, as well as his own reaction when Jugs had walked in. But he wasn't really sure what he wanted to say just yet, so he felt a guilty sense of relief Jugs had opted to come along.

For Demmy's part, he sat between them with his legs pressed tight together. He rested his hands on his thighs, gripping his phone as he followed the GPS map to the job. Cody knew Demmy was avoiding touching either him or Jugs, and he wished he could go back and change his reaction. Or, better yet, just not have snuggled up close to Demmy in the first place.

It wasn't all his fault. Well, his reaction to Jugs's arrival could have been a little more subtle, sure, but the secrecy about the change in his and Demmy's relationship was more complicated. Neither of them brought up the topic of telling others. All Demmy had had to do was suggest they mention it to Amelia, and then they could have started their "coming out" process.

Well, more like Cody's coming out process.

He shifted in the seat and sighed.

"All okay over there, big guy?" Jugs asked.

"Sure, why do you ask?"

"That was a pretty heavy sigh."

"Tired, I guess."

"Late night, huh?" Jugs grinned.

Cody focused on the road as his stomach knotted in tension. "Yeah."

"Nice. Who's the lucky girl this week?"

The desire to drive off into the ditch went through Cody like a flash-fire. That or hit the brakes hard and claim he'd just missed a squirrel or rabbit. He wanted to do something to distract Jugs from his line of questioning.

"You'll need to take a left up here," Demmy said.

Cody mentally thanked Demmy for saving him from a response. He was pretty sure he'd hear about that later, too, when they were alone.

"So you guys have trapped skunks before, right?"

"Not exactly," Demmy said.

"What's that mean?"

"We haven't actually trapped skunks ourselves," Demmy said. "But I just looked it up online, and I know a couple of techniques that have worked for other animal control companies."

Cody was glad to hear that part, because he'd had no idea how they were going to avoid getting sprayed while trapping a whole family of them.

"And what's involved in these techniques?" Jugs sounded suspicious. "I'm not going to be used as bait or a distraction or something, am I?"

"Nothing like that. It's pretty simple once we get them in the cages."

"I've heard that before," Jugs mumbled.

Cody had to admit he'd heard it before as well. He trusted Demmy, but he was nervous as well. Would Demmy let him get sprayed by a skunk if he was angry enough at him? Cody sighed as he followed Demmy's directions and pulled up in front of a nice ranch house. He guessed there was only one way to really find out. Time to get out and trap some skunks.

CODY TOOK another long drink from the bottle of water and wiped sweat from his brow. The sun was about to set, and he was eager to see if Demmy's plan would work. They'd spent a couple of hours setting up four live animal traps with marshmallows as bait before going off to get something to eat for themselves. Jugs had been with them the entire time, which prevented Cody from talking with Demmy about anything personal. Cody was glad to see Demmy's mood lighten up as the evening went on, and he started interacting more with both him and Jugs. Maybe he'd dodged a bullet this time. The question now became, would there be a next time?

They sat in lawn chairs near the back of the yard with a direct line of sight on all four traps. Enid Helen lay in Jugs's lap, her pink bow a little off center from her investigation of the strange yard. The owner, Rich Little ("No relation"), had taken his pets to a groomer to be de-skunked, and his family to stay at his in-laws' house.

He hadn't looked happy about the option, but he said as he climbed in behind the wheel, "I'd rather deal with my father-in-law's anti-everything tirades than have to wash the stink of skunk off my kids."

Cody had to give him a lot of credit. He was really taking one for the sake of his family.

"I hope you're right about this," Jugs mumbled.

"I hope so, too," Demmy said.

Cody looked down at the old towels Demmy had grabbed from the small laundry room at the office and which now soaked in a plastic dishpan filled with water.

"So, once the skunks are in the traps, we cover them with these wet towels to keep them from being able to spray us?" Cody asked.

"That's the idea. The damp towel keeps the spray and smell from escaping."

"Have you ever smelled a skunk?" Jugs asked.

"More times than I like to remember," Demmy said.

Cody chuckled. "Remember the one that sprayed underneath the air conditioner you had in the window of your bedroom?"

Demmy's quiet, genuine laugh in the fading daylight made Cody feel good, like things were back to normal. Or whatever passed for normal these days.

"Sounds bad," Jugs said, but Cody heard him snicker.

"It was really awful," Demmy said. "My dad thought he was going to have to throw the whole air conditioner unit out."

Something moved at the bottom of the deck attached to the back of the house, and Cody squinted in the waning daylight. A flash of white shifted and flickered, and then he saw a skunk emerge from a loose spot in the latticework. Cody sat up straight in the lawn chair. "Heads up," he whispered.

"I see it," Jugs whispered back. "And I think I just peed a little."

"We're getting those coveralls dry cleaned," Cody said.

"Probably going to need to do that anyway after this," Jugs said. "I just see the one." He twisted in the lawn chair to look over his shoulder before exhaling a sigh of relief. "Okay, they're not sneaking up on us from behind."

"Just sit tight and play it cool."

"Oh, I'm not moving." Jugs shook his head. "Not until one of you moves first. Me and Enid Helen are sitting right here."

"Good plan," Demmy said.

They watched in silence for a time as the lone skunk sniffed around the yard. Just when Cody was about to say something about the skunk being a solo act, three more flashes of white in the gathering darkness ambled out from beneath the deck.

"Oh shit," Jugs said almost under his breath. "We're outnumbered now."

"You're not counting Enid Helen?"

"She's a lover, not a fighter."

"She was pretty feisty when we first found her in Abigail Barcelona's crawlspace," Demmy said.

Jugs sniffed. "Those days are over. She's a class act now."

"Like in *My Fair Lady*, huh?" Demmy asked.

"I don't know that movie," Jugs said. "Is it a musical? Cause I don't do musicals."

A loud snap sounded in the dark near the deck. It made Cody jump, startled a quiet shout out of Jugs, and a bark from Enid Helen. One of the traps had closed. Cody sent up a small prayer to whatever entity guided his wayward life that the sound hadn't scared all four of the critters into spraying the shit out of each other, the yard, and them.

"Got one." Demmy's voice was quiet but confident, and it sparked a bit of a rise in Cody's cock.

Another trap shut, and then a third one.

"Just one more," Cody said and crossed his fingers.

Only the rattle of the occupied cages reached them from out of the darkness. They waited what felt like hours, but Cody figured was most likely only a couple of minutes, and then he stood up.

"I have to know." Cody looked down at Demmy and Jugs, both of them just visible in the light of the first stars.

"What?" Jugs stood up as well, Enid Helen cradled in one big arm. "You're asking to get sprayed if you go out there with one of them still loose."

"I'll be careful." Cody grabbed a couple of towels from the bucket and wrung out the excess water. "Any one else coming?"

Demmy sighed and got to his feet. "I'll go with you."

That made Cody feel good. Better than good, actually. More like relieved and touched. He knew he wasn't completely out of trouble with Demmy yet, but at least he didn't have to deal with a bunch of skunks on his own.

Demmy wrung out two more towels, pulled a flashlight from his pocket, and nodded. "Let's go."

Cody drew his own flashlight and switched it on. They'd agreed not to use the flashlights until the skunks were all caught so as not to scare them away or piss them off. But since they were venturing out among the cages, they really needed the light.

Three of the skunks were in cages. The marshmallows had been eaten, and the animals paced, tails raising slightly with each length of cage they covered.

"We need to cover those three cages," Demmy said.

Cody set the flashlight on the ground, beam pointed at two of the cages. He hefted the wet towels, one in each hand, as he kept an eye out for the one remaining skunk. "And the towels are going to keep their spray from getting out of the cage?"

"That's what the site claimed."

"Well, if it's on the internet, it must be true."

"Are you ready?"

"No."

They stood in place, towels in hand, flashlights on the ground aimed at the cages.

"How about now?" Demmy asked.

"I'd like to know where that other skunk got off to."

Frenzied, high-pitched barking erupted from behind them, intermixed with shouts of surprise from Jugs. A string of harsh curses followed, and the stink of skunk floated on the evening breeze. Moments later, Jugs rushed past them, eyes wide in the glow of their flashlights. His arms were stretched out as far as he could reach, and he held a frantically wriggling Enid Helen.

"She's hit!" Jugs shouted as he ran past. "She's hit! It got her."

"Guess that answers my question," Cody said.

Demmy nodded. "Let's go."

Cody managed to drape a towel over the first cage with no problem. As he moved to the second cage, he picked up his flashlight and directed it toward the area of the yard where they'd been sitting. Jugs's lawn chair lay on its side, but he didn't see any sign of the skunk.

Cody didn't realize how close he was to the next cage until he bumped his foot against it. He cursed as he stumbled, the flashlight tumbling from his grip as he stretched out his hands to break his fall. A pungent stink exploded around him. He gagged and turned away to draw in a breath of fresh air as he tried to stand. His feet went out from under him, and he fell flat on his stomach, face turned so he stared at the business end of the remaining skunk. He had just enough time to squeeze his eyes shut and turn his face away before he got blasted again.

"Shit!" Demmy shouted from somewhere nearby. "I got sprayed."

Cody kept his eyes closed and held his breath as he got to his hands and knees. He crawled blindly away from the skunks, lungs aching for fresh air. He ran into something and fell on top of it, rolling onto his side as he gasped for breath.

"What the fuck?" Demmy said from beneath him. "Oh, god. You… Skunks!"

Another blast of awful stink erupted around them. Cody's eyes burned, and tears streamed down his face as he coughed and gagged, trying to catch his breath. Demmy squirmed beneath him, gagging as well, and suddenly Cody was rolled to the side. He got to his hands and knees and crawled a few feet away, but the smell was everywhere. He couldn't get away from it. His nose and throat burned, as if steel wool had been packed into his lungs.

He gasped and drew in a deep breath. The searing odor filled his chest, and his stomach twisted in revolt. Moments later, everything he'd eaten came up in a burning rush. He blurted out curses between each ugly clench of his gut until nothing was left. Fuck, he hated throwing up.

A hand touched his back and ran slowly up and down his spine.

Demmy.

And from the lightness of his touch, Cody hoped Demmy had forgiven him.

"I covered the three cages," Demmy said. "Can you stand up?"

"I can't see anything. It got in my eyes."

"It's all over you. And pretty much all over me as well."

Demmy helped Cody to his feet, and they moved away from the cages. The air cleared with each stumbling step until they reached the chairs. A lingering cloud of skunk stink washed over them, and Cody gagged again and went down on one knee.

"Shit." Demmy grunted as he tried to keep Cody on his feet. "This is where Enid Helen got sprayed. Over here. Come on."

Demmy directed Cody across the yard. After they'd staggered a distance from the chairs, Cody went down on his hands and knees. He could barely see his fingers splayed in the thick grass from the tears blurring his vision.

"Fuckin' skunks," Cody managed between coughing fits.

"Stay here. I'll get the hose over here so you can wash your face and flush your eyes."

Cody put his forehead against the cool grass. He took deep, gulping breaths and kept his eyes squeezed shut. A cold wet nose suddenly pressed into his ear, and he shouted as he scrambled away.

"The skunk!" Cody shouted. "The skunk is here!"

He ran into Demmy, who put his arm around Cody as he pressed a garden hose into his right hand.

"It's not the skunk," Demmy said. "It's Enid Helen. It's okay. You're okay."

Cody thought his heart might hammer right out of his chest. He sank to a sitting position and let his head drop to his chest.

"I'm going back to the spigot," Demmy said. "Wave your hand when you're ready for me to turn on the water to the hose."

Cody felt the end of the hose and found there was no sprayer attached. He got to his knees and leaned forward, then waved his left hand over his head. The hose bucked a bit in his hand, reminding him so much of Demmy's cock he started to harden, then a gentle stream of cold water flowed out of the end. He let it run over his face and hair, and then opened his eyes as wide as he could manage so it could soothe his burning eyeballs. The cold water felt good against his fevered skin, and it seemed to be removing the worst of the burning in his eyes.

After several minutes of rinsing and scrubbing his head, face, hands, and rinsing out his mouth, Cody waved again and called out, "Okay."

The stream slowed to a trickle, and he dropped the hose. He unzipped his coveralls and stepped out of them, then used his untainted shirt sleeve to dry the water around his eyes. Blinking rapidly, he peered at the blurry world around him. A flashlight stabbed into his eyes, and he cursed as he turned away.

"Sorry, sorry, sorry," Jugs said as he came up beside him. "Have you seen Enid Helen? She got away from me."

"Dude, I can't see my own fucking hands," Cody said. "There's no way I could see your dog."

"I don't want her to get sprayed again." Jugs paused, then stepped back. "Fuck, man, you smell worse than Enid Helen."

"Yeah? Really? I did not know that. I'm glad we brought you along so you could tell me these kinds of important details."

"Dick," Jugs muttered, and Cody heard him walk away.

"I've moved the empty cage to another spot in the yard and added more marshmallows," Demmy said as he came up alongside of him. "Let's load the other three cages into the back of the truck."

"I can't see shit. I'm not going to be much help."

"Okay, let's get you into the truck first. I'll take care of the cages."

"I'm sorry." Cody truly felt bad, but there was absolutely no way he could assist Demmy.

"Nothing to apologize for. You didn't do it on purpose."

"That's for fucking sure."

Cody let Demmy lead him out of the yard to the truck. He

climbed into the open truck bed and scooted forward until he was able to rest his back against the cab.

"I'll be back," Demmy said. "Just relax."

Cody squinted and looked around. He was able to see the bed of the truck and a nearby streetlight pretty clearly, and that made him feel a little better.

Jugs and Demmy appeared at the back of the truck and slid two cages covered by wet towels into the bed. Cody pressed back against the cab.

"I hope those towels work," he said, heart pounding. "I can't take another round."

"They're working so far," Demmy said. "Just a little odor, but nothing hitting us. Right, Jugs?"

"Yep. So far, so good."

"Hey, Jugs," Cody said as they turned to leave. Jugs paused but Demmy walked off, most likely to give them some privacy. Good ol' Demmy.

Cody cleared his throat and shrugged. "Sorry I snapped at you. I'm pretty beat up here, as you can see."

"Yeah, I get it. All good."

"Did you find Enid Helen?"

"Yeah." Jugs shook his head. "That girl is a mess."

"Ugh. Sorry, man."

"My own damn fault," Jugs said. "I should have left her at home. Or in the truck."

"Did you get sprayed?"

"Not a drop." His smile gleamed in the streetlight. "It's a gift."

Cody let him walk off before muttering, "Bastard." One of the skunks rattled the bars of its cage, and Cody jumped. He sneered at the cage and said, "Fucking skunks."

Demmy arrived with the third cage in hand. He slid it into the truck bed and looked up at Cody. "How are you doing?"

"Peachy."

"You and Jugs okay?"

"Yeah, we're good." Cody hesitated, then lowered his voice. "Are we okay?"

Demmy smiled. "Smelly, but okay."

"Good."

Jugs walked up and handed Enid Helen over the side of the truck to Cody. "Smelly critters ride in the back of the truck."

"Cute," Cody said.

"You know it." Jugs got into the cab and started the engine.

Demmy used bungee cords to secure the cages, closed the tailgate, then climbed over the side of the bed and sat beside Cody. He knocked on the glass at the back of the truck's cab and called out, "Ready!"

"What about the other skunk?" Cody asked.

"I'm leaving the empty cage. We'll check it in the morning."

"What if it's a baby?" Cody held Enid Helen in his lap as he squinted at Demmy.

"They all look pretty big," Demmy said. "It'll be okay for one night on its own."

Cody put his head back and closed his eyes. What a fucking night.

CHAPTER FIVE

"Don't touch anything," Demetrius said as he slid his apartment key into the lock. "Just follow me right to the bathroom."

"You don't want me to rub my red and weeping eyes on your pillow?" Cody leaned in and blew into his ear.

Demetrius lifted his shoulder to block Cody and grinned in spite of himself. "No!"

The plastic bag of supplies Jugs had bought for them rustled with the movement. Demetrius twisted the key and opened the door, and they tromped through the living room, down the hall, and into the bathroom. He set the bag down and started to strip.

Cody's eyebrows went up and he grinned. Before he could say anything, Demetrius stuck a finger in his face. "Not right now. Okay? Just strip and get in the tub."

"Even better."

"How can you even think about sex right now?" Demetrius shook his head. "We both stink. And you can barely see."

"Don't have to see to have sex. And if we both stink, neither of us is offended."

Demetrius had to give him that one. He kept his underwear on to try and keep Cody at bay—something he never would have imagined having to do five weeks ago—then started the water and put in the tub stopper. Pulling the items from the bag, he set them on the edge of the tub.

"While I'm putting the bath together, use the eye wash." Demetrius put the bottle into Cody's hand.

"How's it work?"

"There's a cap on top. Rinse that a couple of times with the wash, and then fill it and hold it against your eye and move it around."

"Move the cap around?" Cody asked.

Demetrius shook his head as he unlocked his iPhone. "No, your eye."

"My eye? What the fuck are you talking about?"

Demetrius sighed. "Just a minute and I'll help you."

"Are you texting with Ollie again while I'm over here with skunked eyeballs?"

"No! I'm looking up the ingredients for the de-skunking wash, okay? Just stand the fuck down a moment."

He located the page he'd visited earlier and read the measurements for the ingredients of the de-skunking wash which included hydrogen peroxide, baking soda, and hand dish detergent. Since he didn't have any measuring cups or spoons with him, Demetrius doubled the amount for each ingredient he dumped into a small bucket he kept under the bathroom sink. As the mixture fizzed up, he set the bucket on the edge of the tub and turned to Cody.

He was nude, his cock bobbing at half-mast. Demetrius shook his head. "You really could have sex under pretty much any circumstance, couldn't you?"

"How long have you known me?" Cody grinned and shifted his hips back and forth to make his dick waggle.

"So many years. And so many things yet to learn. Here, sit on the toilet lid."

After some jostling and a little groping from them both, Cody sat on the closed toilet lid with his head tipped back. Demetrius helped Cody with the eye wash, a process that ended with Cody's face and torso wet with solution, and both of them laughing.

"Do they feel any better?" Demetrius asked as he dabbed Cody's face dry with a towel.

Cody looked at him and blinked rapidly. "A bit. I can see you better now."

"Good. We'll need to get you into a doctor for a check-up, but that should help with the burning."

Demetrius stepped out of his underwear and tossed them in the hamper. When he turned back to Cody, he found him staring and grinning.

"Maybe getting skunked isn't so bad after all," Cody said.

"Trust me, you don't want to touch or lick any part of me. Come on. Into the tub."

"If you're trying to get me to back off, putting me into a tub with you isn't the way to do it."

Demetrius ignored him and grabbed a couple of wash cloths from the linen cupboard. He got into the tub with Cody, pulled the curtain, and turned away to start the water. Cody ran his hand down Demetrius's spine and over the swell of his left ass cheek.

As Demetrius waited for the water to warm up, he did his best to ignore Cody's touch and focus on the task at hand. He still felt stung by Cody's reaction when Jugs had walked into the office, although he couldn't really blame him for it. They hadn't really talked in depth about telling people they had taken their relationship to a new place. And with Cody's long history of dating women, it was going to be more difficult for him on multiple levels when the truth came out.

If the truth ever came out.

When Demetrius was completely honest with himself, he wasn't sure this new relationship between them was going to last. He wanted it to, more than any other relationship he'd been in before. But when he considered all the little details, it didn't look good. Demetrius was actually surprised he and Cody had managed to last this long. Yet, from the feel of the erection against his ass, Cody wanted it to continue at least a little while longer. Whether or not that came with the stipulation of keeping everything a secret from other people still remained to be discussed. And that was a conversation Demetrius wasn't sure he was ready to have, let alone start.

This fun and really fucking hot new twist on his friendship with Cody was like a house of cards. Everything might fall apart if he said the wrong thing or reacted too strongly to a situation. Or, apparently, received mysterious text messages from his ex-boyfriend. It wasn't fair by any means, to him or to Cody, but he was enjoying the physical benefits far too much to want to risk any deep discussions. He was more than aware it would probably mean a more involved and painful conversation down the line, most likely after one or the other of them said something particularly hurtful. But that was a risk Demetrius was will… no, *needed* to take.

The water finally warmed, and he said over his shoulder, "I'm starting the shower now."

"Do I need to get my Meryl Streep in *Silkwood* impression ready?"

"Probably never going to be a more appropriate time to pull that one out."

He activated the shower and faced Cody. For a moment, all he could do was stand and stare. Cody watched him with such tenderness and affection in his bloodshot eyes,

Demetrius's breath caught. The confines of the tub made Cody's shoulders and chest appear even broader. He was, in a word, beautiful, and the way Cody looked at him made Demetrius feel beautiful as well.

Demetrius dropped his gaze to the patch of soft brown hair in the center of Cody's chest, and followed it down his just-a-bit-less-than-flat belly to the neatly trimmed bush at the base of his cock. Cody's legs were long and strong from years of football practice and regular workouts, and his heavy balls hung low between his thighs.

Demetrius's cock hardened in moments.

"I'm not too blind to see that." Cody smiled and took hold of Demetrius.

"Wash first. Play time later."

"Business before pleasure, eh?" Cody sighed and released him. He tipped his head back and held his arms over his head. "Go ahead, scrub me down."

Demetrius spread the mixture all over Cody's skin with a wash cloth. As he worked, Cody's Meryl Streep cried out, "I'm clean! I'm clean!"

"I think you missed a spot here." Cody pointed to the side of his neck. Demetrius scrubbed at it.

"This spot, too." Cody pointed to the center of his chest, and Demetrius lathered that area up.

"Maybe here?" Cody waved his hand over his belly.

"How did the skunk spray you through your coveralls and clothes?"

"It soaked in through the material. He was a powerful sprayer."

"Fine." Demetrius rubbed hard at Cody's belly. This produced giggles and bursts of laughter, but Cody didn't back away.

"Any place else?" Demetrius asked, already anticipating Cody's response.

True to expectations, Cody cradled his cock and balls in one palm. "These feel a little sticky."

"I don't think that's from skunk juice."

"Still, you wouldn't want to breathe in a noseful of skunk next time you suck my cock, would you?"

"You have a point."

Demetrius slowly and gently washed Cody's dick and balls. This elicited low and steady moans as Cody hardened in Demetrius's grip.

"Oh, Demmy," Cody said with a sigh. "What you do to me."

"And that we will finish later." He gave Cody a few more foamy tugs, then prodded him to move under the spray of the shower.

Once he had rinsed off, Cody took the wash cloth from Demetrius. With slow, sensual moves, he ran the foamy cloth over Demetrius's body. He even dropped to one knee and had Demetrius put first one foot, then the other on his bended knee so he could get between his toes. No other man had ever paid such loving attention to Demetrius's feet, or his body for that matter. And all while the smell of skunk lingered in the air.

When Cody finished, Demetrius rinsed off. He faced Cody, and they carefully sniffed at each other.

"What do you think?" Demetrius asked.

"I think I've gotten immune to the smell," Cody said. "Or it completely fried my nose."

"I agree. One more round."

After a second round of lathering, they rinsed in the now cooling water and stepped out of the shower to dry off. Demetrius wrapped a towel around his waist and got a garbage bag from the kitchen. He pulled on a pair of latex gloves he kept around for when he got serious and cleaned with bleach, and he stuffed their clothes into the garbage bag. He'd take the whole thing to the laundromat the next day, along with the coveralls. He wanted everything professionally cleaned. He didn't want that smell to get into the washers in his building.

Cody had spread a dry towel on the sofa and now sat naked on it. He smiled over at Demetrius and patted the cushion beside him. "Come join me."

"There's still some stuff to do." Demetrius struggled to keep his eyes above Cody's waist. Damn, the effect Cody had on him.

"Like what?"

"Stuff."

"You're avoiding me."

"Am not."

"Are too."

"Am not."

Cody sighed. "And you've resorted to childish arguments."

Demetrius grinned. "Have not."

Cody launched himself off the couch. Demetrius shouted in surprise and fled down the hall to the bedroom. Just as Demetrius reached the doorway, Cody snagged his fingers in the towel around Demetrius's waist and snatched it away. Demetrius shouted in protest but was laughing too hard for it to carry much weight. His laughter cut off with a squeak when Cody grabbed him around the waist and tumbled them both on to the bed.

They lay on their sides panting for a moment, Cody's big hands planted firmly on Demetrius's torso, pressing tight against him, back to front.

"I caught you," Cody whispered in his ear.

"I thought that was supposed to be my line."

"I think it applies to both of us."

Demetrius squirmed until Cody loosened his grip, and he rolled over to face him.

"You smell better," Demetrius said.

"Same can be said about you."

"We'll need to go back in the morning and check the other trap."

Cody nodded. "We can do that." He ran a finger along Demetrius's cheek. "You're not tired of me yet?"

Demetrius smiled sadly. "I thought that was supposed to be my line."

Cody scooted closer and slid an arm around his waist. "I'm sorry for what I said about you texting with Ollie."

Demetrius shrugged. "You don't want another monster case. I get it."

"I'm also sorry for my reaction when Jugs walked into the office."

Demetrius's heart galloped as his stomach tightened nervously. "Thanks for saying that."

"I guess I'm not ready to truly come out yet."

"That's okay. I don't think I'm ready for that either."

Cody's eyes widened, the whites still mapped with red. "You're not?"

"You think I want to deal with all the comments we'll get?" He slipped into a mocking falsetto voice. "Oh, I always knew you had a thing for Cody. Oh, you've wanted Cody since forever, we all could see it. Oh, you mean you two haven't been doing it all along?" He shook his head. "I'm fine with things just the way they are."

Well, maybe not *fine*, but close enough.

"What about Amelia?"

Demetrius thought about his aunt as he considered Cody's question. She was his mother's younger sister but had felt more like a mother to him because of his parents' advanced ages. When his parents had moved to Florida right after

Demetrius had graduated from college, Amelia remained in Parson's Hollow and became his only family touchstone. Demetrius considered her equal parts friend and relative, even more so after they had all fought a murderous, man-eating swamp monster down in Florida. During a tropical storm, no less. It hurt sometimes to not be able to talk with her about everything that had changed between him and Cody.

"I think Amelia already suspects," Demetrius said.

Cody considered that. "Yeah, probably."

"I think she saw what was developing down in Florida."

"Nothing like almost being killed by a swamp monster to help set your priorities straight," Cody said.

Demetrius grinned. "Did you just say I'm a priority in your life?"

"What? No. Shut up."

"You must really like me," Demetrius said. "I'm a pri-or-ity."

"You're an irritant to my very soul," Cody said, not hiding his smile.

"And you like to slide your cock in my ass."

The blunt sexuality of his statement got the desired reaction. Cody's joking expression shifted immediately to predatory. He slid right up against Demetrius in one fluid move. At that proximity, his arousal was evident not only in his hard and throbbing cock, but his wide open pupils.

"You are a filthy young man," Cody said, his voice low and deep.

"Just the way you like me."

Cody kissed him hard, pushing his tongue roughly past Demetrius's lips to claim his mouth. His hard-on pressed against Demetrius's hip as his large hands roamed his body. Cody slid his mouth to the side of Demetrius's neck, licking, sucking, and gently biting. He shifted lower, pausing to suck each nipple before paying attention to Demetrius's cock, which lay hard and flat against his belly. Cody lifted it, a runner of pre-cum stretching from the head to the soft brown hair that covered Demetrius's torso.

Opening wide, Cody took him to the root in one gulp.

"Holy fuck!"

Cody sucked him slowly, hand rising and twisting right behind his mouth. Demetrius gasped and moaned as Cody worked his full length, and he worried he would come too fast.

"Hold up a second," Demetrius said, easing himself from between Cody's lips. He sat up and kissed him softly, then turned to position himself directly beneath Cody's dick.

"I want to return the favor," Demetrius said.

"I'm all for that," Cody said, and went back to sucking him.

Demetrius opened wide and took Cody's long, thick cock into his throat. He gripped the base tight as he sucked, working that area with slow, quick strokes. Demetrius knew Cody would have him at the edge before long, and he didn't want him to stop this time. He moaned encouragement around his mouthful of dick, and moments later grunted as he emptied himself down Cody's throat.

Cody kept sucking Demetrius and thrust his hips gently, pumping down into Demetrius's mouth until he groaned and came himself. Demetrius swallowed every drop greedily, savoring the taste and intimacy of the act.

Cody lay beside him afterwards, their arms and legs entangled as they caught their breath. Demetrius loved the feeling of Cody's long, solid body pressed up against him. After all the years of friendship, of being near or next to Cody, touching him but never lingering like this, he sometimes had trouble believing things between them had shifted to something sexual. Yet here they were, naked and sweaty and full of semen.

"You are even more filthy than I first thought," Cody said.

They shared a laugh and slowly disentangled themselves. After taking turns in the bathroom, they got back into bed. Cody lay on his side and draped his arm over Demetrius's belly as he faced him.

"Sleep well," Cody said. "Don't think about that last skunk we still have to deal with."

"Bastard."

"That's why you like me," Cody said through a yawn.

"Yeah, that must be it."

Minutes later, Cody's breathing deepened. Demetrius savored the feel of Cody's arm across his body and the gentle puff of each exhalation. He studied Cody's face in the dim light of the room. It was so familiar to him, yet seemed completely different. Demetrius had never known this side of Cody, the part he'd come to think of as Sexual Cody. He'd caught glimpses of Sexual Cody over the years, when he'd been with him when he met a woman he was interested in, or the one time he'd run into Cody on a date. Glimpsed from afar, Sexual Cody had been like a mysterious relative everyone talked about but whom Demetrius had only seen photos of but never met in person.

Until a month ago.

Demetrius sighed and stared at the ceiling. Cody muttered in his sleep and pulled his arm off Demetrius as he turned his back. The space where Cody's arm had been felt cool now, and it made him shiver. He was tired physically, but his mind wasn't ready to shut down. As his mother used to say when she found him up late and staring out the window at night, his brain had too many thinks still plugged in.

He was in love with Cody, no getting around that fact. If he was honest with himself, he'd felt this way for years. But he never thought Cody would or could ever feel the same way about him. Perhaps Cody's feelings didn't run as deep as Demetrius's, and if that was the case, Demetrius could handle it. At least for a time.

But if Cody did feel as deeply for him, he might not be capable of acknowledging those feelings and accepting them for what they were. Case in point, his reaction when Jugs had shown up at the office. Demetrius's parents had raised him with a more conservative outlook than a lot of people his age, so he wasn't that comfortable with public displays of affection himself. Still, Cody's reaction had been very telling.

Demetrius sighed and folded his hands together over his chest. Too many questions with no answers. All he could do was wait and see. For the near future, he would enjoy this new-found intimacy with Cody. Not just the amazing sex, but the closeness as well. He'd never felt so important to any other man he'd dated, not even Oliver. Granted, he and Cody had decades of friendship as a foundation, so it wasn't really a fair comparison. Demetrius just hoped that when it came right down to it, Cody had some of the same deep feelings as he did.

A yawn surprised him. Maybe he'd be able to sleep after all. Demetrius looked at Cody's back, pale and broad in the moonlight coming through the sheer curtains. He yawned again, then rolled on his side with his back to Cody and slipped into sleep.

CHAPTER SIX

Cody was surprised when he awoke to find Demmy's side of the bed empty. He wanted to sleep in a little longer, but his bladder had other ideas, so he rolled out of bed with a groan and shambled into the bathroom. After a long pee, he inspected his eyes in the mirror, happy to see just a faint trace of redness. The smell of skunk was almost entirely gone. A hint of the musk lingered, but another shower with Demmy's magic mixture should take care of it.

Cody ambled naked down the hall to the living room, and then into the kitchen. Demmy had left a note for him by the coffeemaker where a half pot of still warm coffee waited.

Cody -

Left early to get some stuff done. I'll come back to pick you up after ten so we can check on the last skunk trap together.

See you then,

D

Well, it wasn't a love note, but that really wasn't Demmy's style. Still, he wondered if some of that 'stuff' Demmy was getting done included meeting up with Ollie. Cody yawned and decided to keep his jealous thoughts corralled until he at least had a cup of coffee. He looked around the kitchen as he idly scratched his chest. Waking up alone in Demmy's bed had felt strange, and even more so to be on his own inside the apartment. He had never been there before without Demmy.

He poured a cup of coffee and poked around for something to eat. After settling on a bowl of cereal, he sat naked at the small table in the eat-in kitchen and stared at the wall as he ate and sipped his coffee. His brain wasn't quite fully functioning, and the sound of his own chewing became a soothing rhythm. The padded seat of the chair was cool against his buttocks and balls, and he wondered if Demmy had ever sat naked in that same chair.

The thought made him grin, and he took another bite. Demmy wasn't the type to sit naked anywhere, not even in his own apartment.

And yet… Demmy was a lot different in bed than Cody had anticipated. Off and on over the years, he'd wondered what Demmy was like during sex. He'd kept his own attraction and the couple of times he'd kissed a man secret. But he had looked at Demmy in that light from time to time. Cody saw him not just as the best friend who put up with his shit, but someone who might be like one of those pent up pressure cookers: ready and waiting to pop.

And pop he had.

It was the most intimate relationship Cody had ever experienced, and he was pretty proud of himself for not bailing on it.

Maybe he'd grown up? Or maybe Demmy was just that important? Most likely a mixture of the two. Whatever the reason, Cody was glad for it, and he didn't want to consider what life would be like if he should do something to fuck it all up. He'd lose not only a compatible and exciting new sexual partner, but his very best friend. The thought scared him more than a little bit, and his stomach tightened uncomfortably.

He knew if things with Demmy were going to work out, he was going to have to learn to be open about his true feelings. And not just when he and Demmy were alone. But when he thought about all the people in town and how they would likely react, he couldn't quite bring himself to tell anyone. How many years would he have to deal with the smug "we knew it all along" looks? Or worse, outright hostility? Not to mention the dozens of women he'd dated and dropped who would now understand exactly why things with them hadn't worked out: he'd been gay for Demmy all along.

Cody huffed an irritated breath, then finished his cereal and drank the milk from the bowl. He rinsed the bowl at the sink and put it and his spoon in the dishwasher. He might be a slob at his own apartment, but he made more of an effort when he was at Demmy's.

Another sign this relationship was edging into a more serious area than he'd ever traveled before.

It was just after nine, and Cody pushed aside relationship deliberations as he picked up his coffee and walked back to the bedroom. He wanted to take another shower to try and wash away the last of the skunk odor, then get dressed and be ready to go when Demmy returned.

The magical mixture of baking soda and hydrogen peroxide did remove more of the smell, but Cody could still detect a trace of it when he sniffed really hard. Nothing to be done about it at that moment, though, so he applied a few extra swipes of his deodorant he kept in Demmy's medicine cabinet. He dressed in jeans and a pullover Henley, and was sitting on the couch tying his shoes when Demmy opened the door.

"Oh, you're up and ready?" Demmy seemed genuinely surprised.

"Hey, I can get up and start doing things, too," Cody said. "Where've you been?"

Demmy held up a paper receipt. "I dropped off the coveralls at the dry cleaner."

"Did Stan hate you for it?"

"Not to my face. I put them into a double layer of garbage bags and warned him about what happened. He didn't seem too upset, so hopefully he'll be able to get the smell out without the need to fumigate his business."

"I hope you gave him a really big tip."

"I will when I pick them up." Demmy frowned at him. "Wait, you said 'really big tip' without making it sound dirty. What's going on?"

Cody grinned. "I might still be a little tired."

"Did you eat?"

"Cereal."

"Leave any for me for tomorrow?"

"Do you like cereal dust?"

Demmy sighed and shook his head. "Come on. Let's go check that last trap."

"Do we have more coveralls? And towels?"

"In the truck."

Demmy turned for the door, but Cody grabbed his hand and tugged him back.

"Hey," Cody said, holding loosely to Demmy's hand as he looked down at him. "Can I get a good morning kiss?"

"Oh?" He smiled. "Yeah, of course."

The soft, sweet kiss left Cody's lips tingling. He pulled away and grinned. "Thanks. By the way, I sat naked in your kitchen chair. Okay, let's go."

"What? Which one?" Demmy asked as Cody stepped around him.

"I don't remember."

Demmy followed him out the door. "Cody, my aunt sits in those chairs! That's just not good hygiene."

"Amelia would get a kick out of it," Cody said. "Don't be such a prude."

"You're impossible."

"And yet, here we are."

"Here we are, indeed."

WHEN THEY ARRIVED at the house where skunk-mageddon had occurred, Cody's stomach felt a little upset.

"I think I have PTSD from what happened last night," he said before he got out of the truck.

"You did get blasted pretty hard," Demmy said.

Cody walked around the front of the truck and stood beside Demmy. "It feels like something awful happened here. Like the whole thing has imprinted itself on the house."

"You got sprayed by a skunk—"

"Two skunks, at least."

"Fine, two skunks. But it wasn't a mass murder, okay? The spirits of the skunks that sprayed you aren't trapped in the yard forever."

"Says you."

"Come on."

They pulled on coveralls and Demmy grabbed a couple of old towels from the bed of the truck. Cody stood with his back against the side of the truck bed, staring at the house. Demmy tugged on his sleeve and Cody reluctantly followed him to the front door. After a few minutes of ringing the doorbell and knocking with no response, they left the porch and approached the gate in the privacy fence.

"Ready?" Demmy asked with his hand on the latch.

"No."

Demmy opened the gate and stepped into the backyard. Under the tree in the center of the yard, the final skunk paced the confines of the live trap. The stale stink of its spray lingered on the air, and Cody's stomach rolled.

"It looks pissed," Cody whispered.

"You would be too if you'd been in a cage all night with just a few marshmallows to eat. I'm going to wet these towels at the hose. Will you be ready to help me out by then?"

"Check back, and I'll let you know."

Demmy spent a couple of minutes at the hose spraying the towels and wringing them out. He returned a lot faster than Cody desired, handing him one of the towels.

"What's the plan?" Cody asked. His mouth was dry, and his tongue felt too big. The cereal tumbled uncomfortably in his belly.

"We approach with the towels held up, like this." Demmy held his towel in front of him, high enough that he could just see over the edge as he gripped the corners of the narrow end.

"Like a shield?" Cody asked.

"Exactly."

"A wet cotton shield?"

Demmy sighed. "To stop the spray in case the skunk is mad about our approach."

Cody swallowed hard. "Okay." He held up his towel and tipped his head from one side to the other, cracking his neck. "Let's get this over with."

They moved slowly, Cody a little bit behind Demmy, his gaze fixed on the pacing skunk. Damn, he really did not want to get sprayed again.

"Okay, on the count of three, we move up fast and just lay the towels over the cage," Demmy whispered. "I'll take the end of the cage closest to the tree, you take the one toward the house. Got it?"

Cody took a deep breath and nodded. "Uh huh."

Demmy counted to three, then moved fast toward the cage, crouched down a bit behind the towel. Cody followed, a buzzing sound steadily increasing inside his skull. He peered over the edge of the towel as he went, gaze fixed on the cage and the skunk inside. It had its back to them, and for a moment of cold, sheer terror, Cody thought it was getting ready to spray them. But then he realized the tail wasn't up, and relief washed through him.

In moments, they had draped their towels over the cage, completely covering the bars. The skunk rattled back and forth inside, but no smell leaked out of the wet towels, and Cody let out a careful breath.

After the disaster movie that had been their first attempt, Cody was pleasantly surprised this time had not been a sequel of equally epic misfortune.

"Okay," he said, smiling at Demmy. "That went a hell of a lot better than last night."

"That's for sure," Demmy said. "Let's put the cage in the back of the truck. Then I'll leave the invoice in the mailbox."

They made sure the towels covered the entire cage, then each took an end and carried it out to the truck. Cody carefully secured the cage with bungee cords while Demmy dropped off the invoice. The skunk squealed a few times and once even growled, startling Cody into taking a step back. He secured the truck's tailgate and got into the passenger seat as Demmy slid behind the wheel.

Releasing the skunk was much easier than catching it. Demmy drove them to the same spot in Parson's Wood where they'd released the other skunks. The woods surrounded Parson's Pond, filled with dirt trails that had been carved over the slopes of the gently rolling hills around Parson's

Hollow back when Marsten's Mill had still been dealing in lumber rather than sheep's and alpaca wool like they did now. A variety of hardwood and pine trees covered the hills for miles to the north, south, and east of town, which was why they brought any captured critters there for release.

They carried the covered cage off the trail a few yards before setting it down. Demmy reached beneath the towel to open the latch and ease the door open just a bit. When they were ready, he pulled the towel off that end of the cage and dashed away to stand beside Cody back by the truck. The towel smelled of skunk, and Demmy carefully stuffed it into a garbage bag which he then put inside another garbage bag.

Moments later, the skunk nosed the cage door open and waddled off into the woods.

"Thank god that's over," Cody said.

"We earned the hell out of the payment for this job."

"Tell me you bumped up the charge for this one?"

"I tripled our usual four animal extraction rate," Demmy said over his shoulder as he went to retrieve the cage and towel. "We still have to pay Jugs, too."

"I should call and see how Enid Helen is doing."

Cody pulled out his phone and placed the call. After two rings, Jugs answered, and he didn't sound happy.

"Uh uh, not today, Satan."

"Cute," Cody said. "How are you?"

"Suffering," Jugs grumbled. "I got no sleep last night because Enid Helen kept whimpering and scratching."

"Did you use the mixture Demmy told you about?"

"Four times," Jugs said. "It got the smell out, but she didn't like it and kept squirming out of my hands. She tracked that shit through my apartment and all over my furniture."

Cody tried to keep the humor from his voice as he pictured big, brawny Jugs chasing the wet and skinny little Enid Helen around. "Sounds pretty frustrating."

"You're laughing."

"What? No I'm not."

"I hear it in your voice, Bower. You're laughing at me."

"I may be smiling at you, but I'm for sure not laughing at you."

"May as well be." Jugs sighed. "So why the call? Some other demonic critter you need help catching?"

As far as Cody knew, Jugs wasn't aware of the more unusual cases he and Demmy had been involved in, unless Jugs was a fan of some seldom-read conspiracy- and monster-theorist blogs that alluded to them without actually naming them. Cody doubted that.

"Nothing like that," Cody replied. "Just wanted to make sure you and Enid Helen were recovering."

"Yeah, we're good. How about you and Demmy? You two get cleaned up all right?"

Cody grinned as he thought about showering with Demmy the night before. "Yeah, we did. That mixture worked even better than I had hoped."

"How about your eyes? You got it in the eyes, didn't you?"

"All cleared up," Cody said. "Twenty twenty vision once again."

"Twenty twenty?" Jugs let loose a deep rumble of a laugh. "Then how'd you miss the ball so much back in the day?"

Cody sighed. "Bye, Jugs."

"Hey, you going to PayPal me for last night?"

"Yep. We'll do it when we get paid ourselves."

"All right. Let me know if you need more help. Just no skunks."

"You got it." Cody ended the call and got in the truck where Demmy waited behind the wheel.

"They doing okay?" he asked, his attention on his phone.

"He's grousing about lack of sleep and Enid Helen running away from him during her four baths." He chuckled again at the mental image of Jugs chasing his tiny dog around. "Other than that, he's up for any other work we may have."

"Yeah?" Demmy said in a distracted way. "That's good."

"Is that Ollie?"

"What? Oh, no. Just some Facebook posts about… stuff."

Demmy locked his phone and tucked it between his inner thigh and the seat before he started the truck. He looked over at Cody but met his gaze for only a brief moment. "Ready to head to the office?"

"Yeah, okay."

They were quiet on the drive back into town. Cody glanced over a few times, but Demmy didn't notice. Whatever he'd been reading on his phone had him preoccupied, and Cody knew it had to do with Ollie. He wondered how long he should let Demmy keep this latest text a secret from him. Hopefully Demmy's distracted state didn't mean he was considering helping Ollie out with this Pinesville Devil all by himself.

Dammit, Ollie the cub reporter for the *Parson's Hollow Herald* was still a pain in Cody's ass.

CHAPTER SEVEN

Demetrius stared at the computer monitor and the banking software screen. He had accomplished nothing since they'd arrived at the office over an hour before. All he could think about was the text he'd received. It had been Oliver again, this time inviting him to drive up to Pinesville, New Jersey on his own and help out with the Devil of Pinesville.

He looked at Cody sitting at his desk directly across from him and felt that familiar and still kind of scary tightening in his gut. No doubt about it, Cody really did it for him. And what would he say about Demetrius going off on a road trip by himself to meet up with Oliver? His *ex* Oliver.

Cody lifted his bored and slack gaze from whatever he'd been staring at on his own computer monitor. When he found Demetrius looking at him, however, a big smile brightened his expression. A flutter started deep in Demetrius's gut, and he quickly looked away.

"What's up?" Cody asked.

Demetrius lifted his eyebrows and gave him a glance. "Sorry, what?"

"I caught you looking." Cody leaned in over the desk and lowered his voice. "You horny?"

The burning in his cheeks pretty much gave him away. "No. I'm working."

"You haven't clicked the mouse or typed a single letter since we got to the office."

"Yes I have."

"No you haven't."

"How do you know that?"

"I pay attention." Cody leaned back in his chair and crossed his arms. "Want to talk about it?"

Demetrius frowned. "Talk about what?"

"Whatever's got you so distracted."

"What makes you say that?"

"You were all chatty this morning until we released the skunk," Cody said. "Then you got a text or something, and suddenly all communication has ceased." He sat forward and put his forearms on the desktop, hands clasped. "I'm going to assume it was Ollie again. What did he want this time? You to help him look for the monster under his bed?"

Demetrius felt trapped and flustered. How did Cody know everything? Was he always so transparent? He pushed to his feet and picked up his coffee cup before turning away. As he walked toward the small break room in the back, he said over his shoulder, "No, he didn't want me to help him look for the monster under his bed."

Cody crowded into the break room behind him, his height and broad shoulders practically filling the space.

"Why do you make me work so hard to get something out of you?"

Demetrius sighed. He knew he was acting stupid, but if Oliver had been public enemy number one before he and Cody had gotten together, Oliver's persistence in Demetrius's involvement in this case wasn't going to go over well. He had no interest in getting back together with Oliver, but he also didn't want to start a fight with Cody for no reason.

"Okay, fine. I may be a little distracted because..." Demetrius took a breath and turned to face Cody. "Do not overreact."

Cody took a step back so he could lean against the door frame. He shrugged his shoulders and let his arms hang loosely at his sides. "What? I'm cool. See how cool I am? I'm barely reacting right now, even as I'm waiting for you to continue. See? Like a cucumber."

Demetrius took another breath and let it out. "Fine. Oliver did text me again this morning when we were releasing the skunk."

Cody's smile looked artificially bright and peppy, and slightly terrifying. "Ollie? Again? I'm glad you guys can be friends now that you're done sleeping together. What did he have to say this time?"

"He asked if I wanted to work with him on my own to track down this Pinesville Devil. That's it." Demetrius pushed Cody out of his way and carried his coffee back to his desk.

Cody perched on the edge of his desk across from Demetrius, body turned so he could look at him. "All right, that's cool. That's swell. And how did you respond to Ollie? Sorry, *Oliver*?"

"I haven't yet."

Cody sat in the chair so he could face Demetrius. "I see. And when you do respond to him, what will that response be?"

"I'm not sure."

They were quiet for a moment, then Cody said, "Well, just text back and ask for more information." Then he looked away and shrugged. "That is, you know, if you want to. I'm not trying to tell you how to handle things with your ex-boyfriend."

"It's just weird," Demetrius said, getting up and pacing the area beside their desks. "I mean, it's been weeks since Oliver and I have talked or texted."

"Technically, it's been days."

"Fine. You're right. But before these latest texts, it had been weeks since I'd heard from him. And now there's our... you know... our relationship, which we have... going on here between us. And he sends me a text out of the blue, and it's kind of cryptic, and I don't know what it means." He stopped in front of Cody and looked down to find him looking up with a big smile. "What? Why are you smiling?"

"You said 'our relationship,' and it made you stammer, like it's something that means a lot you." Cody got to his feet. "You like me."

"You keep trying to get me to say that, as if I've never said it before."

"You could say it more often." Cody stepped closer. "I may act all cool and casual, but it's nice to feel liked."

"Oh, really?" Demetrius smiled, but he couldn't help wondering how Cody's tone would change if Jugs or someone else walked in at that moment. "Well, since you've been fishing for it so hard today, I like you, Cody. Okay? Does that help?"

Cody pulled Demetrius close. He smiled and leaned down to give him a long, gentle kiss. There was no tongue, no groping. Just a kiss that left Demetrius breathless and a touch dizzy.

"Oh," was all he could manage once Cody broke their embrace.

"Call Ollie." Cody made a face. "Sorry. Oliver. It's habit, I can't control it. Anyway, forget the texting and call him and get more information. If you want, I can leave the office and go get us lunch or something."

"Oh. Um, okay. And, no, you don't need to leave,"

Demetrius said, and he could see Cody was relieved at his response.

He sat at his desk and sent Oliver a quick text: *This a good time to talk?*

Not two minutes later, Demetrius's phone rang, and Oliver's name appeared on the display. Demetrius cleared his throat and swiped to accept the call.

"Hi there," he said.

"Hi." Oliver sounded anxious, and Demetrius wondered if he felt just as nervous about talking after all this time.

"How are you?" Demetrius asked.

"I'm okay, but…"

"Uh oh. But what?"

"Well, things are kind of weird."

Demetrius frowned. "Weird in what way? Are you okay?"

"Oh, yeah, I'm fine. We're both fine."

"We?" Demetrius looked over at Cody who was watching him closely. And maybe with a hint of a smile at his mention of 'we'?

Oliver sighed heavily. "Oh, yeah. We haven't talked in a while. Let me back up. Um, I didn't tell you, but I moved out of Parson's Hollow."

"Oh? You moved?" Demetrius saw Cody's smile broaden. "Did you quit the *Herald*?"

"Yeah. I wasn't getting the stories I wanted, and there was really no opportunity for advancement there."

"No, at the *Parson's Hollow Herald*?" Demetrius said with a heavy layer of sarcasm.

"Oliver chuckled. "Yeah, can you imagine? Anyway, I moved in with my grandmother in Pinesville, New Jersey. She's got a small farm up here, and it's getting to be too much for her to handle on her own."

"I didn't know your grandmother lives in New Jersey."

Demetrius saw Cody's expression brighten even more. "Is it nice there?"

"It's fine, for the most part," Oliver replied. "A lot of it reminds me of Parson's Hollow, actually. Which is why I've been texting you."

"Oh?"

"Yeah. I have a case for you guys. We need the Critter Catchers here in Pinesville."

"So what did he have to say?" Cody asked once Demetrius had disconnected the call.

"There have been a lot of sightings lately about an urban legend creature called the Devil of Pinesville. He thought of us right away, and he definitely said both of us, not just me, so I don't think it's a ploy for him to try and get back together with me."

"Okay. So what do you think?"

Demetrius clicked the mouse to wake up his computer and checked the company calendar. They had no appointments on the books. "Not a lot going on for us here in town right now. We could ask Jugs to pick up anything that comes in so we can drive up to Pinesville and check things out."

Cody nodded slowly while Demetrius spoke. "What's this Devil of Pinesville all about? I don't really want to get involved with another swamp monster, right?"

"I'm with you on that. I don't even know where Pinesville is located," Demetrius said, turning to his computer. A few clicks later, he was looking at Google Maps. "It's small."

"Smaller than Parson's Hollow?" Cody walked around the desks and leaned in over Demetrius's shoulder. "Jesus, look at all that forest right next door to it."

"That's the Wharton State Forest." Demetrius clicked on

the highlighted name and read the information aloud. "It's the largest forest in the state of New Jersey, encompassing nearly 115,000 acres of land known as the Pinelands."

"It's not swampland, thank God," Cody grumbled. "But anything could be living in there."

Demetrius smirked. "Getting nervous, big guy?"

"Yes. And you should be, too, if you know what's good for you." He dropped heavily into his desk chair. "Why the fuck do we keep getting these monster cases? We don't have a retro cool van and a talking Great Dane."

"No, but we've got a lot of bills coming due and no jobs on our calendar." Demetrius typed and clicked on the map until he found directions to Pinesville. "It's a six hour drive from here. We can do that easy."

"Sure, it's easy to drive to your doom."

"Come on, look what we've dealt with already. How can this be worse than a wolf man, or a drug altered dog, or a fucking swamp monster made of logs and moss?"

"I'm afraid we're going to find out." Cody rubbed his hands over his face. "Look, I don't like going into something blind. Can we at least call Ollie back and ask for more information?"

Demetrius knew Cody was right. He should have asked Oliver for more information, but he'd been nervous and awkward talking with him again.

"Yeah. Do you want me to call him back and put it on speaker?"

"Think you can trust him not to slip an 'I miss you' into the conversation with me in the background?"

"I'm pretty sure he can restrain himself."

Demetrius unlocked his phone and accessed the recent calls. He tapped on Oliver's number, then the speakerphone option. As the line connected, he set the phone down so it straddled both of their desks.

"Hey there," Oliver's voice sounded clear and happy to hear from him again. "I didn't think you'd call back so soon."

"Is this an okay time?" Demetrius asked. "Can you talk?"

"For you, any time is a good time."

Demetrius waved off Cody's arched eyebrows that practically disappeared into his hairline.

"Good," Demetrius said. "I've got you on speakerphone, and Cody is here with me."

"Oh, okay. Hi Cody."

"Hey there, Ollie. I hear they asked you to leave the state."

Oliver sighed as Demetrius stared at Cody who shrugged back.

"Not exactly what happened," Oliver said. "I'm living with my grandmother and helping her out around her farm. I'm also writing for a few different blogs, trying to build up my portfolio."

"Helpful and productive," Cody said. "Shame you had to move to Jersey for it."

"Anyway…" Demetrius said as he glowered at Cody. "Before we can commit to this job you called about—"

"I'd call it a case rather than a job," Oliver said.

"Okay. A case. Either way, we were hoping to get some more information about it."

Oliver let out a breath. "It's easier to show you the physical evidence, but I'll tell you an abbreviated version. Have you ever heard of the Devil of Pinesville?"

"Nope. Neither of us has heard of it," Demetrius said.

"It's this legendary creature that supposedly lives in the Wharton forest. It's based on a legend about a creature that's part goat, part bat, and part man. It was blamed for some cattle and sheep mutilations in the late 1700s, then again in the 1800s. Over the years, people have claimed to have seen it on dark roads and in farmers' fields and on top of abandoned houses. Some photographs have been circulated over the years, claiming to be of the devil, but they're always blurry or taken at night, and most have been labeled fake. All of these years, there's been rumors and sightings but never any physical evidence."

"Until now?" Demetrius asked.

"Well, maybe."

Cody stared at Demetrius, his expression still and unreadable. "What's maybe?"

"My grandmother saw the Devil the other night. It was out in one of the fields around the farm, and she went after it with her shotgun."

Demetrius raised his eyebrows. "Oh?"

Oliver chuckled. "You'll have to meet Grandma Eileen to really appreciate her."

"So, this Devil," Cody said. "Why the sudden need to catch it? It's been out in that forest for centuries, and no one's wanted it caught like you're suggesting."

Oliver cleared his throat. "Since the beginning of the year, several hikers in the forest have gone missing."

"Okay, good talking to you, Ollie," Cody said. "Good luck with the monster in your woods."

"It wouldn't be a lot of out of pocket for you guys if you do come," Oliver said. "You can stay here at my grandmother's place for free, and she'll feed you. She's a good cook. All it would take is time and gas money. A few days of looking around and talking to people, and then give us your opinion. If you don't find anything like what you've seen in the past, you can go right back home."

"Let us talk it over," Demetrius said. "I'll get back to you."

"I do hope you'll come," Oliver said, lowering his voice. "And that even applies to you, Cody, if that helps any."

Cody shook his head as he blatantly avoided meeting Demetrius's gaze.

"I'll call you back later," Demetrius said.

They said their goodbyes, and Demetrius ended the call.

Cody leaned back in his chair and crossed his arms tight over his chest as he finally turned his head to stare across the desks at Demetrius. "You're out of your fucking mind if you think I'm driving to New Jersey and hiking through the biggest forest in the state to look for another fucking monster. We just barely lived through the last monster, in case you don't remember."

"We have nothing going on here," Demetrius said. "It wouldn't hurt to go and take a look around. We could get our business name out there, maybe get some business."

"It's a six hour drive!" Cody almost shouted. "How would that help us here?"

"Word gets around!" Demetrius almost shouted back. "And if this is something paranormal, it would mean a lot of exposure for us. If people here in Parson's Hollow know we can tackle something that big, they'll be calling non-stop for us to manage their pest control."

"Did the wolf man, or the chupacabra, or the fucking swamp monster give us a bump in business?"

"The wolf man did," Demetrius shot back. "For a couple of months."

Cody put his hands on the desktop and pushed up to his feet. He fixed Demetrius with a steady, scrutinizing look. "What's this really about?"

"I don't know what you mean."

"Is this about some kind of goodbye sex with Oliver and not some misguided attempt to increase our business?"

"What?" Demetrius got to his feet as well. "I'm not interested in Oliver. Okay? I'm with you." He heard how intimate and possessive that sounded and panicked. Words tumbled out of his mouth as he attempted to fix what he feared Cody might see as clingy. "For now. I mean, right now, we're together. Dating. Seeing each other. Whatever it is. And I'm not looking around for anyone else, okay? I'm not hoping Oliver wants to get back together." He took a breath and forced himself to consider his next words, finally settling on something he thought Cody might be feeling as well. "I think we work well together. And because of that, I think we could do a lot of good for people."

Cody's temper seemed to cool at that. "Oh?"

"Yes. You heard what Oliver said, people have gone missing. Remember down in Florida when we took the police to the place where the swamp monster had piled all those bones? Those victims were being missed by someone still living, and though it was awful, they finally got some closure. And we stopped that thing from killing anyone else."

Cody sighed. He moved out from behind his desk to pace, his furrowed brow and downcast gaze indicating the intensity of his struggle.

As Cody weighed his options, Demetrius pulled up a satellite map of Pinesville. He checked out the downtown area, and then he zoomed in on some of the farms on the outskirts. Much of the farmland butted right up against the Wharton forest. The trees of the forest grew close together, the only real open spaces caused by small lakes and narrow rivers and streams. A few roads wound through the trees, and Demetrius wondered with a chill just how dark those roads were at night.

"You made some good points."

Demetrius looked up at Cody beside the desk. "Yeah?"

"Yeah." Cody took a deep breath and let it out. "I will probably regret this, but let's do it."

"You're sure?"

He nodded. "I'm sure."

"Good. I'm glad to hear that. I'll call Oliver back and let him know. When do you want to leave?"

"The sooner we leave, the sooner we get back, right?"

Cody looked grim as he said it, and Demetrius appreciated how difficult his decision had been.

"So tomorrow?"

"I'll call Jugs and ask him to cover any calls that come in," Cody said. "We'll owe him a lot of money by the time we get back."

"Let's just hope we have money to give him."

Before Demetrius could call Oliver, his phone buzzed with a text from his aunt Amelia, inviting them to dinner.

"Amelia's invited us to dinner."

"Well, that'll be a nice wrap up to the day," Cody said. "Tell her I'm double hungry."

Demetrius sent the response, then decided to simply text Oliver rather than call, and sent that message as well. Oliver responded within a couple of minutes, telling him he was happy they decided to come. He sent another text immediately after with the address to his grandmother's farm, then followed that up with a final message that made Demetrius squirm a bit.

It will be good to see you. I've missed you.

He hesitated, then wrote back: *See you tomorrow.*

It was a bit of a cop out, but he thought it got his point across. With the secrecy around his involvement with Cody, he wasn't sure how to explain to Oliver he wasn't looking to get back together. He could say they just weren't a good match, or something similar, but that seemed a little cold. But if he let Oliver know he and Cody were now a couple, he could only imagine his reaction.

He sighed and pushed his phone to the other side of the desk. Opening a browser, he typed in PINESVILLE DEVIL and started going through the weird history of the goat-bat-man creature they'd just agreed to investigate.

What was he thinking?

CHAPTER EIGHT

Savory aromas filled Amelia's house, and Cody's stomach rumbled the minute he followed Demetrius through the front door.

"Hello you handsome men," Amelia called from the kitchen, and they headed in that direction. She stood in front of the stove, carving slices from a massive pot roast and laying them out on a serving platter. Her silver hair was cut into a bob, and a T-shirt and jeans showed off her generous bosoms and hips. She was in her late sixties but didn't act or dress like it.

"Amelia, your house smells like Heaven, and you look like an angel." Cody put his arms around her from behind and nuzzled her neck as he snagged a piece of meat from the platter.

"Oh, you stop that picking right now, you rascal," Amelia said, giggling at his nuzzles and whacking the back of his hand with a wooden spoon. "Cottonwoods!"

Amelia used the names of trees in lieu of profanity, and Cody liked to see which variety he could get her to say next.

He yelped at the smack on his hand and pulled it away, shaking out the sting.

"Good hit, Amelia."

"Thank you. Now go set the table." She peered over her shoulder at them both. "We have things to discuss."

Cody looked at Demmy who shrugged in response.

"What kind of things?" Demmy asked.

"Things we'll get to over dinner. Go set the table."

Cody grabbed some plates from the cupboard while Demetrius gathered up the utensils. They moved into the dining room and put out the place settings.

"What's she want to talk about?" Cody whispered. "Are we in trouble?"

"I don't know. Did we forget to do something for her?"

"She's your aunt," Cody said. "You're supposed to keep track of that stuff."

"She may as well be your aunt, too, with all the food she's fed you over the years."

"Stop squabbling like chickens in there and come help me carry in the food!" Amelia called from the kitchen. "I swear, you two are like a couple of old women sometimes."

Demmy walked in the kitchen ahead of Cody and said, "He started it."

"Did not!"

"Did too!"

"Oh for the love of birch trees, can it!" Amelia started to hand the platter of meat to Cody, then set it aside out of his reach. Instead, she handed off a bowl of green beans and gave him a gentle shove toward the doorway.

Cody set the bowl of beans on the table and sat in his usual spot. Demmy brought in a bowl of mashed potatoes which he set out of Cody's reach before returning to the kitchen. Cody stood and grabbed the bowl of potatoes, then froze as Amelia entered the dining room carrying the platter of meat.

"Caught you red-handed, you big sneak," she said.

Cody grinned. "You look beautiful today, Amelia."

"So any other day I look ugly?" She sat and smirked as she unfolded her napkin.

"Ha, she got you on that one," Demmy said as he brought three glasses of iced tea to the table.

"Yeah, yeah." Cody tried to sound annoyed, but he couldn't help smiling at Demmy when he sat across from him.

"What did you want to talk with us about?" Demmy asked.

"Let's serve up the food before it gets cold."

The scrape and clatter of serving utensils on plates was the only sound for a short time. Just when Cody was about to ask if it was time yet to talk, Amelia took a long drink of iced tea and set down her fork down. She rested her elbows on the table to either side of her plate and folded her hands before her. After giving each of them a long, searching look, she fixed her gaze on Demmy.

"I'm going to ask you some questions you might think very personal, but I have my reasons." She looked to Cody. "Both of you."

Cody's stomach seemed to shrivel up. What if she asked if they were more than friends? What if she point-blank asked if they were having sex? He didn't know what he would say to that direct of a question, and he wondered how Demmy would react. They'd been skirting the discussion themselves for a while now. Were people in town talking? Had they been asking Amelia about them? Was he acting differently toward Demmy when they were out in public?

"Okay," Demmy said, drawing the word out. "Go ahead."

Amelia nodded once and looked between them again

before focusing on Demmy. "What do you pay a month in rent?"

"Oh. Rent?"

Demmy looked relieved as he sat back and glanced at Cody. Cody felt himself relax a bit as well and took another bite of roast. The flavors danced on his tongue, and he savored the taste.

"Right, for your apartment," Amelia said.

"I pay eight hundred."

"Good. Okay." Amelia looked at Cody. "And you?"

"My place isn't as classy as Demmy's," Cody said. "I pay seven fifty."

"So over fifteen hundred a month between you both," Amelia said. "Plus your utilities."

"Right." Demmy leaned forward. "What's this about?"

"Well, you know I've been seeing a nice man I met at the senior center," Amelia said.

"Right, Otis," Demmy said.

"Otis, yes. You've met him several times. Anyway, we've been seeing a lot of each other lately, and he's got a nice condo in the independent living section of Parson's Pines." She looked at Cody. "Where your grandmother stays in the elder care section."

Cody nodded and swallowed his mouthful of food. "That's right. He's in the Golden Aspens group?"

"That's the one." She smiled and looked between them. "He's asked me to move in with him."

Demmy's eyebrows went up. "Really?"

Amelia blushed, and that reaction made Cody feel so good tears blurred his vision. She looked happy and excited and, well, in love.

"I think that's great," Demmy said. "He's a good man, and he really cares for you."

He got up and pulled Amelia out of her chair to give her a

hug. Cody did the same, and they were all laughing as they sat back down again.

They went back to eating, but not before Cody noticed a touch of sadness in Demmy's eyes. Cody was pretty sure it was because they had yet to tell anyone else they were a couple, even Amelia, although she most likely already knew. That subtle sadness that tinted Demmy's happiness for Amelia made it very clear to Cody how this relationship was affecting him.

But he couldn't find the words to say anything just yet. Not even to Amelia.

"You going to put your house up for sale?" Demmy asked around a mouthful.

"It's paid for, you know," Amelia said. "And the property taxes are very low. I was thinking I might keep it for an investment. And see if maybe the two of you wanted to move in."

Cody dropped his fork. He looked from Amelia to Demmy and back again. "What?"

Amelia smiled. "Yes. There's two bedrooms, so you each could have your own room. And I wouldn't charge you any rent. You'd just have to pay utilities and the property taxes and keep the place up. Maybe do a bit of remodeling, if you were so inclined." She popped a bite of roast into her mouth and looked between them as she chewed.

"No rent?" Demmy asked. "Are you sure?"

"Of course I'm sure, my dear," Amelia said. She sighed and set her knife and fork down again. "Look, after that horrible business we all went through down in Miami, I've decided to stop putting off being happy." She focused her gaze on Cody, and he shifted in his chair.

"I'm not getting any younger, you know. My knees have been bothering me something fierce, and these basement steps are tough on laundry day. Otis's condo is one level with a laundry room and three bedrooms. It's got a pool and hot tub at the community building, and we can eat one meal a day in the Parson's Pines dining room." She smiled as she looked between them. "I've lived alone for far too long. And I don't care what anyone thinks about me being with Otis, or me living with Otis. He is a good man who treats me well, and we have fun together. I'm going to take advantage of it while I can. And I can help out my two favorite nephews." She smiled as Cody raised his eyebrows. "Yes, I consider you my nephew, Cody. You're family, my dear." She looked back at Demmy. "If I can help you both out in the meantime, then even better. You two are the closest I have to children of my own."

"Aunt Amelia, I don't know what to say." Demmy looked from Cody to Amelia and back again.

"Well, give it some thought," Amelia said. "Maybe a couple of days to talk it over and let it simmer? But if you could let me know by next week, I would appreciate it." She waved her fork in the air as if to clear up a misunderstanding. "Now, I know you have lease agreements with your current apartments to let play out, but you could move in ahead of time and maybe find sub-letters or just pay the rent until the lease is up. Either way, give me your answer next week."

She reached out and picked up the platter of meat, then held it out to Cody. "More roast?"

"YOU PUT YOUR FEET UP, AMELIA," Cody said as he gently escorted her to the recliner in front of the TV. "We'll take care of the clean up."

"You boys are too good to me," Amelia said. "But don't think you're getting out of here without dessert."

"Have you ever known me to skip dessert?" Cody

switched on the TV, then placed the remote in her hand. "You relax."

He returned to the kitchen where Demmy stood at the sink. He wore bright pink dishwashing gloves, scrubbing plates and utensils. Cody grabbed a dishtowel from the drawer and dried the dishes Demmy had already washed.

"What do you think?" Cody asked in a low voice.

"Of her offer for us to live here?"

"No, of the pot roast," Cody said. "Of course the offer."

Demmy glanced at him as he set a plate in the rack. "It's very generous of her."

"Yeah, but that doesn't tell me what you think of it."

"Well, what do you think of it?"

Cody was quiet. What did he think of it?

"See?" Demmy said. "Not so easy to just come up with a decision, is it?"

"Fine." Cody scowled. "You proved your point."

"Let's talk about it later," Demmy said. "We've got a six hour drive to Pinesville tomorrow. We'll have plenty of time to talk about it then."

"Pinesville." Cody felt a twinge of he didn't know what deep in his belly at the thought of it. Their other unusual cases they'd pretty much stumbled into. Now they were willfully going somewhere outside of their own hometown to try and catch a monster. This really changed the rules of their business, and Cody wasn't sure he liked that.

"You still want to go?"

No, he really didn't. But it seemed like Demmy wanted to.

"Do you want to go?"

Demmy frowned. "Are you turning the questions around on me like I just did to you with Amelia's house offer?"

"Kind of sucks, doesn't it?"

Demmy sighed, then was quiet as he scrubbed at the roaster. It took several minutes for him to get the baked on bits off with a scouring pad. When he had finished and handed the scrubbed and rinsed roaster to Cody, he leaned against the counter and looked at him.

"It's kind of scary, to be honest. I mean, this time last year, I wouldn't have put much stock in Oliver telling us about the sightings and hikers gone missing. I would have thought there was some other explanation."

"And now that you've seen some monsters up close, you're a little nervous about it?" Cody said.

Demmy nodded. "Yeah. Now that I know there are things that go bump in the night—or roar and try to eat you—it makes me cautious."

"You're having second thoughts?" Cody asked, with a glimmer of hope.

"No, not really. Because I think about how we beat the monsters we have seen, and I have to admit, it kind of gives me a thrill to think about looking for this Pinesville Devil." The excited glow in his expression and light in his eyes made Cody want to pull him close and kiss him hard. "And we work really well together, you have to admit that."

Cody lowered his voice. "In and out of bed?"

Demmy blushed, and his smile broadened. "Oh yeah."

"Glad to hear that." Cody set the roaster aside and muttered sort of under his breath, but not really, "Especially if we're going to be seeing Ollie."

"Are you jealous?" Demmy grinned. "You are! You're jealous."

"It's really difficult to take you seriously when you're wearing those gloves."

Demmy flipped him off with a bright pink covered finger. "Next time, you wash the dishes and I'll dry."

"I'm thinking with the money we'd save on rent, we could install a dishwasher," Cody said as he opened cabinets and peered inside. "Who needs all these baking sheets?"

"We haven't agreed to move in yet, remember. And Aunt Amelia will still own the house."

"But it would be a nice improvement. I'll get her to agree to it."

"You can get people to agree to a wide range of things," Demmy said.

Cody squeezed Demmy's ass cheeks. "I can be pretty convincing."

"Easy, tiger. Amelia's right in the other room."

"I know, I know." Cody stepped close and put his hands on the counter, his arms to either side of Demmy as he pressed his steadily lengthening cock against the swell of Demmy's ass. "Where are we sleeping tonight?"

"We need to pack for our trip."

"That didn't answer my question."

"I'm thinking we should sleep in our own beds."

Demmy faced him and draped his gloved hands over his shoulders. Cody felt the wet drip of soap suds down his back, but he didn't care. All he focused on was Demmy's erection grinding against his own.

"We both need to pack enough for several days, and then get some good sleep. You know monsters like to prowl around at night, so we won't be getting a lot of sleep once we get there."

"You are way too practical." Cody kissed him and flicked his tongue over Demmy's lips. "You need to loosen up."

"Oh, you've loosened me up in quite a few ways, believe me." Demmy turned away and resumed washing dishes. "You'll be okay for one night."

"Can we at least FaceTime and jerk off together?"

Demmy laughed and lifted one shoulder in a half shrug. "Why not? That might be fun."

Cody leaned close and whispered into his ear, "Not as fun as my cock sinking into your ass."

Demmy let out a long breath and lowered his head as he supported himself on the counter. "You're a very bad man."

"I believe you meant to say that I'm very good at being very bad."

Cody chuckled and turned away. He stepped to the kitchen door and looked into the living room. Amelia's head was turned to the side, eyes closed and lips parted.

"Amelia's sound asleep," he said.

"Aw, really?" Demmy pulled off the gloves and peered over Cody's shoulder. "She did a lot of work on this meal."

Cody pulled him back to the sink. "Let's leave her to sleep and take some dessert to go. We'll go back to your place and have some fun; then I'll go to my apartment and pack and sleep with a lonely hard-on all night."

Demmy smirked as he shook his head. "You are too much."

"Not for your hot ass."

Demmy grinned and blushed, and when Cody put his hand on his crotch, he found Demmy's cock hard and ready to go.

"Just think, if we lived here together, we could just go into the bedroom and get started."

"Now you're just being creepy," Demmy said. "My aunt is asleep in the other room."

"Come on, let's go. Leave her a note, and I'll get us each some dessert."

Demmy sighed, but nodded. "All right. But wash whatever utensils you use to serve up the dessert. I don't want to leave anything for her to do."

A Boston cream pie sat on the top shelf of the refrigerator. Cody lifted it out and set it on the table. It was a work of art, and he wanted to eat half of it in one sitting. Amelia was good to them, and he loved her as much as his own family. Hell, more than a few of them.

"Holy shit, that looks amazing," Demmy said from just behind him.

"She is incredible."

"That she is. I kind of feel guilty about taking the dessert and leaving."

"I know." Cody looked at him. "Do you want to stay and wait until she wakes up?"

As if on cue, Amelia snorted quietly in her sleep from the other room. It took every ounce of Cody's will power to keep from laughing out loud, and from the looks of it, Demmy struggled to keep his own laughter contained.

"All right, she answered for us. Let's take a couple of big pieces, because she would have made us eat big pieces anyway." Demmy opened a cupboard and retrieved a couple of larger Ziploc storage containers.

As Cody cut the dessert and transferred the pieces to the containers, Demmy sat at the table and wrote a note.

"Tell her we'll be out of town for a few days," Cody said.

"I am."

"Tell her we're going to see Ollie."

Demmy sighed. "She doesn't need to know that."

"You embarrassed about Ollie?"

"It's just too much information for a quick note!" Demmy replied in an agitated whisper. "There. I thanked her immensely, told her we took dessert and will be out of town for a few days for a job in Pinesville."

"Nothing about Ollie?"

"You're impossible."

"That's why you like me."

"That makes no sense. Put the dessert away."

Cody put the dessert away, then washed the server and set it in the dish drainer as Demmy wiped down the Formica topped table and tile counters. Cody set the note on the table, they picked up their dessert, and quietly slipped out the door.

Once Demmy pulled out of Amelia's driveway, Cody gazed at his dessert through the opaque plastic wall of the storage container. "This is calling to me."

"If you eat that now, you'll be asleep in twenty minutes. That means no sex for you tonight."

Cody stared at him. "Are you saying I can't have my dessert and eat it too?"

"Ugh, that was bad. And you can eat your dessert, just later when you're back in your own apartment."

"Hmm. Can we FaceTime while we eat our desserts so I don't get lonely?"

Demmy laughed. "Sure. Why not?"

"Good." Cody leaned back and looked at Demmy's profile in the setting sun. Things were good. Very good. Why did he have a feeling they weren't going to be for much longer?

CHAPTER NINE

Demetrius drove along the Pennsylvania Turnpike as Cody slept beside him. Cody's truck had a full tank and rode better than his own, so they'd opted to take it for the trip. He didn't mind driving, though he wished he'd gotten more sleep the night before. Once they'd returned to his apartment, they had had sex and then Cody had convinced him to take a small bite of Amelia's Boston cream pie. That had led to them eating an entire gigantic serving before they could stop themselves. Demetrius had known the sugar crash would hit Cody in minutes, so he'd rushed him back into his clothes and out the door with the other serving of dessert, sending him home to pack.

Cody had made it home safely but had crashed on his couch after eating the remainder of the Boston cream pie. He had gotten no packing done, so when Demetrius had knocked on his door that morning, Cody had answered with extreme bed-head and a line across his cheek from the seam of a couch cushion.

They'd left an hour and a half later than Demetrius had planned, but thirty minutes earlier than he'd anticipated. So, all things considered, they were ahead. Cody had talked to Jugs the night before as he'd eaten the second serving of dessert, and Jugs had agreed to man the office while they were gone. Because they weren't sure where Jugs fell on the paranormal belief scale, Cody had told him they were attending some kind of animal control seminar to learn better techniques for handling skunks.

If only.

Instead, Demetrius was driving them toward a small town menaced by something as yet unexplained. And they were going to stay with the grandmother of his ex-boyfriend, while not letting that ex-boyfriend know he was currently involved with his best friend and business partner, because they weren't ready yet to tell people.

This trip might not have been his best idea.

Cody mumbled something in his sleep, and Demetrius glanced over. It wasn't hard to fall in love with Cody. Demetrius could admit now he had fallen for Cody years ago, but continually fooled himself into thinking otherwise. And he knew most of Cody's ex-girlfriends had loved him at some point. Except maybe for Lucia and Zenona, but Demetrius couldn't be certain. As easy as it was to love Cody, it was just as effortless to be exasperated with him. Or even angry.

Yet, Demetrius could not imagine his life without Cody by his side. Or, thanks to the change in their relationship, in his bed.

He sighed and considered Aunt Amelia's offer. It was astoundingly generous of her, and would save them both thousands of dollars. But Demetrius wondered if Aunt Amelia might not be trying to get him and Cody together as well as give them a financial boost. She could be a bit of a schemer, and Demetrius wouldn't put it past her to play matchmaker. She'd been pretty insistent about Cody being in love with Demetrius that night on his parents' patio, just before the swamp monster had taken her off into the Everglades. Since then neither of them had really broached the subject again, which meant Amelia had been dwelling on it all these weeks, and probably thought he and Cody needed a push to get together.

If only she knew. Although he had to give her credit: Amelia knew a lot of things Demetrius never expected her to.

A glance at the clock had him shifting in his seat. They were halfway to Pinesville, and his ass was getting tired. He would need to stop soon and walk around a bit. Maybe wake Cody up and have him drive the rest of the way so he could get some sleep.

Five miles later, a gas station billboard showed a good price on unleaded, so he decided to stop. As he approached the exit, he started saying Cody's name over and over in a quiet voice. Cody snorted and blinked awake. He looked around in confusion a moment, then stared sleepily at Demetrius.

"We there yet?" Cody asked, his voice scratchy.

"Halfway. I'm stopping for gas."

"Good, I could use some caffeine."

"Think you could drive for a while?"

"Sure, I'm good to go." He stretched his mouth wide in a tremendous yawn.

Demetrius pumped the gas as Cody went inside to use the restroom and get some drinks. He returned with a large plastic cup filled with soda and a bag of snacks.

"I got you a couple of bottles of that tea you like," Cody said.

"How big is your drink?" Demetrius asked.

He grinned. "Just enough to keep me alert."

"It looks like a gallon of pop."

"Might be a little more."

"Remember your sugar crash from the Boston cream pie last night?"

Cody smiled and sighed. "It was dreamy."

"Just don't drive us off the road."

"Would I do that?"

The pump clicked off, saving Demetrius from coming up with a response. He replaced the nozzle, grabbed the receipt, and went inside to use the restroom. When he returned, he got into the passenger seat and fastened his seat belt. Cody smiled over at him as he sipped from the straw of his drink.

"You ready?" Cody asked.

Demetrius shook his head as he smirked. "Remember there's a speed limit, Captain Sugar Rush."

"Speed limits are for the lesser folk."

The sound of the road soon lulled Demetrius into a doze. He awoke a little over two hours later just as Cody was leaving the highway. Demetrius yawned and rubbed his eyes before sitting up in his seat and looking around as they pulled into the downtown of Pinesville, New Jersey. They cruised the area a few times to learn the layout, each of them reading out restaurant and store names as they drove past.

Downtown Pinesville consisted of two parallel streets, Main Street, of course, and Forest Street. The stores and restaurants on Main Street appeared to be the more established businesses, and the buildings were a variety of two- and four-story brick. Homes that had been converted to businesses made up the majority of commerce on Forest Street, and Demetrius picked out a few medical and health services signs along with specialty shops. At the far end of Forest Street, on the way out of town in the direction of Wharton Forest, were a couple of gift shops with Pinesville Devil cutouts in the window.

Cody noticed them, too, and said, "Looks like they don't mind doing some business off their local monster."

"Looks that way."

"Seen enough of the downtown?" Cody asked.

"Yeah. Let's find the farm."

Demetrius checked the map app on his phone and relayed directions. Five miles later, Cody turned into a long gravel driveway that wound through tall hardwood trees with leaves just beginning to change. Sunshine winked between the branches as birds sang and flew from branch to branch.

"It's like a damn animated movie," Cody grumbled.

"Yeah," Demetrius said. "Complete with a monster at the end of the road."

"You really know how to creep me out."

"It's a gift."

"I hope you kept the receipt."

Cody rounded a bend in the driveway and a house came into view through the trees. It was smaller than Demetrius had expected. Oliver had referred to his grandmother's property as being a small farm, and Demetrius had imagined a two-story house with shutters at numerous windows and a big wrap-around porch. Instead, he found himself looking at a small cottage with what looked to be a loft bedroom in the peak that made up the second-story. A very small but covered porch barely had room for two rocking chairs and a low plastic table.

Behind and to the right of the house stood a massive barn. The bright red paint was faded and peeling in some spots, but the roof looked sturdy. A number of chickens pecked at the ground as they meandered around the open barn doors, and a sheep bleated somewhere. Cody stopped the truck in front of the house and turned to smile at him.

"You ready?" Cody asked.

"I think the more appropriate question is, are *you* ready?"

"Most likely, the appropriate question would be, is Ollie's grandmother ready?"

Demetrius laughed. "Good point. Let's hope her heart is strong."

They got out of the truck and approached the house. Before they reached the porch steps, the front door opened and Oliver stepped outside. He looked the same as Demetrius remembered: thin and wiry, with small round glasses perched before his blue eyes. His sandy red hair was longer, but it looked good on him. Oliver's smile was broad and genuine, and Demetrius felt a tug of affection.

"You found us out here in the sticks," Oliver said as he walked down the steps.

"The magic of GPS," Demetrius replied.

Oliver opened his arms and hugged Demetrius tight. It felt familiar and warm, but Demetrius was glad to realize it was nowhere near as tempting as one from Cody. He returned the hug and caught a steely look from Cody when he stepped back. Well, yet another fun conversation they would get to have later.

By then Oliver had turned to face Cody. He smiled and stuck out his hand. "Hi, Cody. Thanks for coming all this way."

Cody smiled back as he shook Oliver's hand. "Seeing as how you missed out on the last monster we met up with, I guess it was about time to get you involved again."

Oliver looked between them with wide eyes, his hand still gripping Cody's. "*Another* monster case?"

Demetrius shrugged. "Yeah. And we almost didn't make it out of that one."

Oliver finally released Cody's hand. "What the hell is it about you two and these cases?"

"Wish we knew, Ollie." Cody gave him a tight smile. "If you don't mind, could you point me to the little farmer's room? It's been a while since our last stop on the turnpike."

"Oh, yeah. Get your bags, and I'll show you where you'll be sleeping. Then I'll introduce you to my grandma."

As they leaned inside the truck's cab from opposite doors, Cody looked across at Demetrius and said with raised eyebrows, "That was a nice, familiar hug between the two of you."

"If you were ever nice to him, he might have given you a hug, too."

"Not my point."

"Oh, really? Guess I missed your point." Demetrius had his duffel bag by then and stepped back from the truck, slamming the door behind him.

As Oliver led the way to the barn, he told them a bit about the farm.

"It's forty acres, and my grandma keeps a pretty big garden out behind the house. You'll be able to see it from the window of your room. It's all fenced in to keep the deer and rabbits and other animals out. We take the produce into town every Saturday morning and sell it at the farmer's market. She leases out a couple of the fields, and that plus the farmer's market brings in good money, but it's all a lot of work."

The chickens scattered before them, and Demetrius asked, "Fresh eggs, too?"

"Oh yeah." Oliver made a face. "I hate chickens."

"I'm with you about that," Cody said, nervously eying the birds as they passed.

Oliver led them into the barn and along the aisle between stalls. Most were empty, but two horses occupied a couple of stalls across from each other.

"That's Tarzan and Jane," Oliver said, indicating each horse as he spoke its name. "They like to be able to look at each other, so we put them in opposite stalls."

"That's sweet," Cody said. "We bunking in one of these empty stalls?"

Oliver grinned. "Nope. Grandma had the hayloft fixed up a while back for one of the family reunions she hosted. It's even got a bathroom."

"Sounds fancy." Cody's voice was low and the sarcasm heavy.

A very narrow flight of steps had been built in the back corner of the barn, and Oliver went up first. Demetrius heard Cody's duffel bag thump against the bannister posts as he brought up the rear, and he could already imagine what he would have to say about the steps. At the top, drywall had been put up at the back of the hayloft to cordon off a wide room. A window in the drywall let in a nice breeze with the faint hint of manure.

Six single beds had been set up in rows with a small table between each. At the side of the room closest to the stairs, more unpainted drywall created an area for a toilet and a very cheap vanity with a sink. It would have allowed for more privacy if not for the lack of a ceiling and an old sheet that could be draped across the doorway.

"I know it doesn't have all the comforts of home," Oliver said.

"None of the comforts of home," Cody muttered so only Demetrius could hear him.

"But there's an electrical outlet beside each bed," Oliver continued. "So you can charge your phones. All the beds have fresh sheets, I saw to that myself. And there are a couple of extra blankets on the shelves at the other end of the room. It's starting to get a little cooler at night now."

From somewhere outside the barn, a gravelly woman's voice shouted, "Oliver! Who's fucking truck is this?"

Oliver blushed and smiled nervously. "And that would be grandma. I'll go down and explain, again, that you're here, and that you'll be staying in the loft."

"She sounds…" Demetrius hesitated as he searched for a word. "Lively."

Oliver grinned. "You have no idea." He waved to the row of beds. "Get settled and then come on down to the house, and I'll introduce you."

Demetrius smiled as Oliver slipped past, and he watched him scurry down the steps. He turned without meeting Cody's gaze and looked at the rows of beds.

"It kind of has that minimum security prison feel to it, doesn't it?" Demetrius said.

"Can we go back to that courtesy flush conversation from a few days ago?" Cody asked.

Demetrius finally looked over and found him standing by the bathroom, holding up one end of the sheet that acted as a door. "Fine. I'm sorry, okay? I didn't know we'd be staying in a barn."

"Ollie conveniently left out that little tidbit," Cody said. "I'm definitely going to have to give some serious thought to my Yelp! review of this place."

Demetrius sighed. "Which bed do you want?"

"I need to try out the mattresses first," Cody replied. "That's going to take some time."

"Well let's go meet Oliver's grandmother, and then we can come back up here and you can test drive all the mattresses."

Cody smirked. "I like the way you said that."

Demetrius shook his head. "Come on."

CHAPTER TEN

Cody followed Demmy down the stairs and through the barn. The horses snorted as they passed their stalls, and Cody got the feeling the one Ollie had called Tarzan was a biter. He just had a look about him.

The chickens were right underfoot the minute they left the barn, and Cody barely held in a completely non-masculine shout of surprise and fear. He really hated chickens.

"You okay?" Demmy asked. Damn it all to hell if he wasn't smirking.

"I'm fine," Cody snapped. "You're going to owe me big for this trip."

"If it brings us a bump in business, consider us square."

"I don't know…"

Before Cody could say any more, the screen door on the back of the house banged open. A short, spry woman with her hair pulled back into a long silver braid stepped out onto the very small slab of concrete that acted as a back porch. She wore a man's red and blue plaid quilted barn coat with the sleeves rolled up several times, a pair of faded and patched jeans, and bright yellow Wellington boots.

"Oh my…" Demmy whispered.

"She's a colorful gal," Cody whispered back.

"Which of you is which?" the woman hollered at them.

Cody raised his hand. "I'm Cody Bower, ma'am."

She snorted. "Ma'am? You may as well have just called me a bitch to my face. I'm Eileen." She looked at Demmy. "You're Demetrius."

"That's right," Demmy said, eyes wide and his tone just a little shy of being a question.

Eileen stomped down the two concrete steps and approached, the Wellingtons squishing and squashing with each step. Her gaze was fixed on Demmy, and she marched right up to look into his face. She was a full head shorter than Demmy, which meant she was about two feet shorter than Cody himself. If she wasn't such a force of nature and more assertive than his high school football coach, he might have laughed.

"You're skinny," she said.

"Oh, um…" Demmy threw a quick look at Cody, then focused again on Eileen. "Thanks?"

"It wasn't a compliment." Eileen moved to stand in front of Cody and craned her head back to look up at him. "You're a tall one. You a gay, too?"

Cody's eyes went wide and a sudden cold spot spread across his chest as his cheeks heated with a blush. "W-What? Why…why would you ask me that?"

"Grandma!" Ollie had rounded the front corner of the house. "I've been looking for you."

Eileen waved at him over her shoulder without taking her gaze from Cody. She had brilliant green eyes Cody figured got her a lot of attention in her younger days. Hell, they probably still did.

Before Cody could formulate an appropriate response to her blurted question, Ollie came up alongside her.

"I see you've all met," Ollie said.

"Which one were you shacked up with?" Eileen asked.

Once she stopped looking at Cody, he found it a little easier to breathe. Cody avoided looking at Demmy, though it took great effort. What the hell was going on?

"We didn't live together," Ollie said with a heavy sigh. "I told you, we dated for a few months." He gestured to Demmy. "Demetrius and I dated." He waved toward Cody. "Cody is Demetrius's best friend and business partner. They've known each other since elementary school."

"Right," Demmy said. "Over twenty years."

Eileen blew a short raspberry. "I've got underwear older than that." She looked between them again. "What makes you two think you can track down the Devil?"

"We've got experience with animals like this," Demmy said.

Cody was glad Demmy had taken the lead with Eileen. He still felt stunned by her question, and, to be honest, her overall personality. He needed a little longer to process everything about the farm, Eileen, Pinesville in general, and maybe himself.

"Yeah?" She squinted one eye and crossed her arms. "Like what?"

"I told you about the wolf man case," Ollie said.

Eileen nodded but didn't look away from Demmy. "Right, okay. So you nabbed a wolf man. How'd you do it?"

"Silver bullets," Demmy said, and gestured at Cody. "It was Cody's idea."

Eileen turned her intense gaze on Cody once again. "From what I hear, you thought my grandson might've been the wolf man."

"Grandma…" Ollie said.

"We did suspect him, at first," Demmy replied. "But then

we realized the wolf man's true identity, and we took care of it."

"You killed it," Eileen said.

Demmy nodded. "We killed it."

"Feel bad about it?"

"I didn't feel good about it," Demmy said, and Cody detected a slight hitch in his voice. "The wolf man was only part wolf, and I felt badly for killing the man who had been bitten. He hadn't chosen that for himself, and it ended up killing him."

"Sounds like he deserved it." Eileen looked between them before taking a step closer to Demmy. "From what I understand, he killed several people."

"That's right," Cody said, pulling her attention from Demmy and feeling that sharp, green-eyed gaze drill right into him. "And because of that, we did a good thing. But it came at a cost."

"You two sound like some kind of liberal animal lovers." She looked at Ollie. "I thought you said they were tough?"

"They are tough. I worked with them to track down the chupacabra."

She made a face. "Kimmy Cabra? That another one of those damn Kardashians?"

A quick bark of a laugh slipped out before Cody could help it, and he tried to cover by pretending to cough.

"No," Ollie said. "It's a scary kind of dog-like creature."

Eileen looked back at Demmy. "Did you kill it, too?"

Cody could see Demmy was quickly wearing down under Eileen's scrutiny. He needed to step in and give Demmy a chance to catch his breath.

"The chupacabra turned out to be a family dog that had been subjected to scientific drug testing," he said.

"That doesn't answer my question."

"The dog died from injuries it received while protecting its former owner from…" He hesitated, trying to come up with a good explanation for what had happened to Reed Wilkes, whose anabolic steroids had had a very adverse reaction to the drugs introduced by the dog's bite.

"A very bad man," Demmy finished for him.

Cody smiled at him. "Right. Thanks."

Eileen made a "hmph" sound. "All right."

"And the swamp monster," Ollie added. "I just found out about that one."

"Right. A carnivorous monster made from moss and logs that tried to kill us down in the Everglades," Cody said. "So, as you can see, we've had some experience with your less ordinary creatures."

"Sounds like probably more experience than those two stuck on themselves women who've been running around my property trying to track the thing down." Eileen shook her head. "All right. So you're all settled in up in the loft?"

"Yes, we are," Demmy replied. "Thank you."

Cody fixed Ollie with a stern look as he asked Eileen, "There are two women working on this case, you say?"

Ollie looked at him, and when he discovered Cody staring, quickly dropped his gaze.

"Oh yeah, some other animal control company." Eileen looked over her shoulder at Ollie. "What do they call themselves?"

Ollie cleared his throat and looked down at his feet. "Um, Critter Ridders."

"What?" Demmy asked.

"Yeah, that's it." Eileen looked at Demmy. "Critter Ridders. They handle all the animal control stuff around Pinesville. Pest elimination. What's the name of your company?"

"Critter Catchers," Demmy replied. "We catch and relocate the animals."

"Ha! That's sweet. So you think you're going to catch the

Devil of Pinesville alive and simply move it to a different place?"

"That's always our intention," Cody said. "With most of our cases, at least."

"Didn't work so well for you with those monsters, did it?" Eileen asked.

"Well, we never set out to kill a critter," Demmy said.

Except maybe the wolf man, Cody thought. Because that thing had been evil to its core. And old man Klemper had been a nasty piece of work himself. But he wasn't about to say that in front of these two.

Eileen was still smiling as she turned her back on them and set off for the house. "Come on inside. Let's get you fed and talk about the Devil."

As Eileen squished and squashed in her Wellingtons back to the house, Cody stepped up close to Ollie.

"Critter Ridders?" Cody asked.

"I'm sorry," Ollie said. "They started working the case a few days ago, but they're really abrasive, and they haven't handled a job like this before. I didn't care about that until Grandma saw the Devil out in her fields a couple of days ago. That changed everything, and I wanted someone with experience to come in and get this thing figured out before something happened to her or to someone in town that I know."

He looked right at Demmy, and Cody had to stop himself from grabbing Ollie and giving him a hard shake.

"I wanted someone I trusted," Ollie said.

Demmy smiled. "That's why we're here. Come on, you can tell us the details over dinner."

"I'm glad you guys are here," Ollie said, turning toward the house. He looked at Cody over his shoulder and said, "Both of you."

Cody managed a smile that was only slightly sarcastic. Demmy walked beside him, blatantly not looking at him.

Oh yeah, this trip was getting off to a great start.

OLLIE COOKED pork chops in a large cast iron skillet as Eileen sat on one side of the kitchen table and Cody sat beside Demmy on the other.

"It's been here as long as I can remember," Eileen said. "Some stories say it was the thirteenth child of a satanic priestess. Some claim it's been here longer than the town or even the Indians before us."

"Native Americans, Grandma," Ollie corrected as he flipped a chop. Cody's mouth watered from the aroma of the food, and he hoped to hell Ollie's cooking tasted as good as it smelled.

"Yeah, yeah." Eileen waved a hand at him over her shoulder, then fished a crumpled pack of Virginia Slims from the pocket of her barn coat along with a neon orange plastic lighter. Once the cigarette was lit, she continued, pausing now and then for a puff and squinting her right eye against the smoke.

"Back when I was a girl growing up in town, the Devil was something our parents used to scare us into going to bed or coming home by curfew. They'd say, 'The Devil of Pinesville knows if you stay up too late,' or, 'The Devil of Pinesville is hungry for bad children.'" She shook her head. "And they'd always say it like that: The Devil of Pinesville. It wasn't the Pinesville Devil, it was The Devil of Pinesville.

"There were the usual sightings and livestock killings that went along with a monster legend. Rumors would start about the police being called out to a farm near the edge of the forest for a dead cow or some missing sheep. Those of us in town never saw these mutilated cows or sheep, mind you, but that didn't stop people from talking about it. There were hikers who went into the forest and didn't come out, and campers who swore something had prowled around their tent at night, something other than a bear or a wolf or even a goddamn deer."

"Did anyone ever take pictures of it?" Demmy asked.

"Oh hell yes, lots of 'em." She took a long, final hit off the cigarette and stabbed it out in a glass ashtray as she blew smoke out of her nostrils. "But it was always at night, and the Devil never stood still, of course. There always seemed to be just enough motion to be too blurry to see any details. When I got older, I never gave the Devil much thought. I started dating a boy who lived in town and married him a few months later."

"Ollie's grandfather?" Cody asked.

Eileen smiled, but it looked a little sad. "That's the one. Oliver Berridge."

"Aw," Demmy said, and smiled at Ollie's back. "You're named after your grandfather?"

"Yeah," Ollie said and smiled at Demmy over his shoulder. Cody tamped down the sudden rush of jealousy, and focused on Eileen again.

"We bought this house and land with money we'd both saved up and what we got as wedding gifts. We had two children, a boy and a girl."

"So the boy was Ollie's father?" Cody asked.

"That would be him. We named him William after my father, and the girl we named Belinda after my Oliver's mother." She drew out another cigarette and lit it. "When William was five and Belinda was three, Oliver was killed in a farming accident." She waved her hand toward the window over the kitchen sink, the cigarette between her fingers trailing smoke through the air. "Right out there in the fields. Tractor quit on him, so he got off to try and fix it. He'd left it in gear, though, and it rolled right over him. Killed him on the spot."

"Jesus," Demmy whispered. "I'm so sorry."

Eileen shrugged. "Just getting you caught up on what's what around here. I remarried not long after. I had two children to raise, and I couldn't manage the farm all alone."

"I'm going to remind you that you said that," Ollie said with his back to them as he worked at the stove.

Eileen said in a loud enough whisper that Ollie could still hear her, "Someone's been wearing his sassy pants ever since he moved in with me."

"He still has those?" Cody added, and he and Eileen shared a grin.

"I can hear you," Ollie said, not looking around. "And I'm cooking your food."

"Dammit," Cody muttered.

"Long story short, I married a year after Oliver died, but it didn't last. That was Frank Westerhaus, and after seven years we divorced. He moved in with some trollop in town he'd been cozying up to. He died about two years ago. I went to the funeral and checked her out. Talk about not aging well. Dealing with Frank's snoring, drinking, and bad breath probably wore her down over the years. Guess I dodged a bullet on that front. After the divorce, I kept myself to myself until the kids were in high school. William joined the football team, and Marvin Answell was the coach."

She paused to tap the ash from her cigarette, a small, secretive smile on her lips. And was Cody imagining things, or did he detect the barest hint of a blush in her cheeks? Then again, it could have been wind. Or sunburn.

"We met the first time I dropped William off for practice, and he called on me here at the house the very next day. That man had big shoulders, big hands, and size thirteen shoes." She sat back and grinned as she looked between Cody and

Demmy. "You know what they say about the size of a man's feet?"

"Grandma!" Ollie said with a gasp.

Eileen let out a lively cackle of a laugh before she took a final hit from her second cigarette and ground it out beside the first. "Well, it's all true. I can attest to that."

She got up and joined Ollie at the stove. As she inspected the food and they bickered back and forth a bit, Cody looked at Demmy, glad to see his wide-eyed stare reflected in Demmy's expression.

"Before you go off thinking I'm just an old woman who's running on and on about her memories with no point to make, I want to assure you I do have a point." She set a plate of thick, sizzling pork chops on the table and stood looking down at them. "And my point is, I've lived either in this town or on this farm all my life. I've heard tales of the Devil ever since I can remember. But that's all they were: tales. Until this week when that thing showed up out in my field. I've seen a lot of things in my many years on this Earth, but I've never seen anything even close to that. So believe you me when I tell you that all them other sightings over the years might be made up, or maybe just a few of them were. I may have laughed about them in the past, but I ain't laughing now."

"Tell us about that night," Demmy said.

"Grab a chop. I've got stuffing in the microwave."

Cody and Demmy each forked a pork chop onto their plates. They waited until Eileen had set a big glass bowl of instant stuffing in the middle of the table and she and Ollie had taken their seats before picking up their silverware.

After a few minutes of silence while they all scooped up stuffing, which Cody found surprisingly moist and good, and he had never been a fan of instant stuffing, and cut into their pork chops, Eileen started to speak.

"I was sitting here at the table, not doing much, I think I

was playing Words with Friends with some smart-ass kid in Idaho. That's when I heard a hell of a racket out near the barn. The sheep were going balls out crazy, and it sounded like the horses were going to kick down the stall doors. I pulled on my Wellies and trucked myself outside."

She paused and put her elbows on the table, then clasped her hands over her plate and fixed her eyes on a spot between Cody and Demmy as she thought about what she had seen.

"It was big, I can tell you that. It was half behind the barn, so I wasn't able to get a real good look at it at first. More just a big shadow moving around back there. The sheep were practically scared out of their wool, I could tell that much. They had pressed up against my side of the fence so hard I thought some of them might break a leg. As I got closer, it flapped big wings and flew up to the barn roof." She shook her head as she looked between them. "Moon was out that night, so I got a pretty good look, even with my old eyes. It had a goat's head, and its eyes flashed in the moonlight, like a cat's or something. It had big wings that looked like bat wings. At least a six foot wingspan, probably more. Long front legs with claws at the end, and big back legs too. It looked down at me, then just took off. It circled the house a couple of times before it flew over the forest and disappeared."

"Wow," Demmy said.

"At least, right?" Ollie said.

"Did you see it?" Cody asked him.

"I was in town having a drink with a friend," Ollie replied.

"His newest friend." Eileen looked over at Demmy. "Not as handsome as you, but he doesn't need a paper bag on his head."

"Grandma!" Ollie said, nearly choking on his food.

"Well, it's true." Eileen gave a casual shrug.

"You seeing someone, Ollie?" Cody asked, more than a little relieved.

"It was just a drink. We haven't seen each other since."

"That's too bad," Cody said, feeling disappointed not just for Ollie.

Eileen looked at him and Demmy. "So what do you boys think? Am I crazy?"

Cody smirked. "Not about the Devil of Pinesville."

Eileen gave him a wry grin. "Seems like you've got a pair of sassy pants yourself."

"You have no idea," Ollie said.

Demmy chuckled, and Cody shot him a dirty look, which he ignored as he looked across at Eileen. "Would you mind showing us some other places tomorrow where people have recently seen the Devil?"

"I can do that," Eileen said with a nod. "And I'll introduce you to my friend Mabel who works at the police station so she can tell the boys in blue about you two, maybe keep them from giving you a bother if they find you asking questions and poking around."

"You think they'd do that?" Cody asked. "Give us a problem?"

"They get tired of the lookie-loos and them monster hunter guys that cruise through town every now and then. Can't say as I blame them, either. Some of those people are weirder than the monsters they're hunting."

They talked more about the Devil as they finished eating, but came up with nothing really useful. By the time they'd helped Eileen wash the dishes and clean up the kitchen, it was a little after eight.

"Do you guys want to go into town and get a drink?" Ollie asked. "Maybe talk to a few of the locals?"

Cody looked at Demmy who shrugged and nodded. "That sounds good."

"We can take my car," Ollie said. "Think you could park

your truck closer to the barn? That way I'll be able to get in and out of the driveway easier."

Demmy had the keys with him and Cody stood on the front porch and watched him pull the truck out of sight as Ollie disappeared around the corner of the house to get his car. Eileen stood next to him, arms crossed against a chill in the night air.

"I never really believed the stories all these years," she said in a quiet voice. "Not deep down, you know? But when I saw it up on the barn glaring down at me, I didn't know what to think. I was amazed and terrified at the same time."

"I get that," Cody said. "I really do."

"A swamp monster, huh?" she asked.

"Yep." He nodded. "Damnedest thing I've ever seen. It was just logs and moss, and it nearly killed me and Demmy's aunt."

"Hell of a thing," Eileen said. "How'd you kill it?"

"We didn't kill it, not really. A group of alligators brought it down."

"Gators killed it?" Eileen shuddered. "Not the easiest way to go out."

"It didn't look that way to us." Cody looked around. "How far away did Ollie park?"

"There's a garage out back of the barn. He should be coming around soon." She took a deep breath and let it out. "The Devil of Pinesville after all these years. It's a hell of a thing."

"That it is, Eileen. That it is."

CHAPTER ELEVEN

Demetrius sat in the backseat of Oliver's Honda Civic coupe, with one foot on either side of the transmission hump. He leaned forward between the seats and listened as Oliver told Cody about his decision to move in with his grandmother.

"I came up for a visit from Parson's Hollow, and the place was kind of a mess, you know? Expired food in the fridge and pantry. Dirty dishes in the sink, and some even sitting in the oven. The fields looked bad, and the animals weren't as well cared for as usual. I decided she needed me up here more than I needed my job in Parson's Hollow, so I gave my notice that week and moved soon after."

"You're a good kid, Ollie," Cody said.

"You are a good person, Oliver," Demetrius said. "How's the blog writing business paying?"

"Not much, actually. But I'm living rent free with Grandma which has given me the opportunity to work on articles for a variety of blogs. Got some great comments on them, and my number of shares are going up. I'm hoping that'll help me get noticed by the bigger sites."

"Get any crackpots commenting?" Cody asked.

"Oh yeah, they crawl out of the woodwork."

They'd reached the edge of town by then, and Demetrius saw a number of businesses with the lights off and gates pulled down over the doors. A coffeehouse was still open, of course, along with a smattering of restaurants and diners. In the middle of the block was a bar, beer signs flashing like beacons and the name written over the door in green neon: O'Shaunessey's.

"Town bar?" Cody asked as they passed it.

"Yeah, but I want to take you somewhere else," Oliver said. "It's just outside of town."

"You're not going to just drop us off and leave us as a sacrifice for the Devil, are you?" Cody asked.

Oliver heaved a deep sigh. "You're always two steps ahead of me, Cody. I hope you won't hold a grudge."

Demetrius smirked as Cody chuckled a bit uneasily. They left downtown along the narrow asphalt strip of First Street, and thick woods quickly gathered close to either side of the road. It was full dark, and Demetrius shivered as he peered out at the deep shadows between the trees.

"Gotta admit, I'm starting to get nervous," Demetrius said. "Maybe Cody was right?"

"You guys have always been scaredy cats," Oliver said. "The bar's just up ahead. It's a more agreeable crowd than O'Shaunessey's."

Oliver rounded a bend and a long, low building appeared at the side of the road. A large parking lot was half-filled with all manner of vehicles: trucks, SUVs, compact cars, motorcycles, even a couple of RVs. The large lighted sign close to the shoulder of the road called out the bar's name to all passers-by.

"The Brutal Poodle?" Cody said, turning to look back at Demetrius. "Were you guys into bondage?"

"What? No!" Demetrius said. "I mean, I didn't think we were." He looked at Oliver's profile. "Were we?"

Oliver laughed. "No, Demetrius, we weren't into bondage. And that's not what this bar is about. It's an all orientations, genders, and levels of income kind of place. The name's just something fun." He parked next to a lifted pickup and shut off the engine. "But don't go into the basement or past the bathrooms in the back hallway, just in case."

"O-okay," Demetrius said, drawing the word out as he opened the back door.

He followed Oliver through the parking lot, Cody right beside him.

"I feel like I should have dressed a little better," Cody said, and looked down at the long-sleeved Henley he wore over a University of Pittsburgh T-shirt, and his well-worn Levis.

Demetrius liked it when Cody dressed down. And the jeans fit Cody really well. Like, really *really* well.

Oliver led them past a group of men and women standing off to one side of the door smoking and talking. He pulled open the door and stepped into The Brutal Poodle. Demetrius followed, with Cody behind him.

A New Order song from the eighties was blasting on the sound system, something he'd heard before but could never remember the title. Bizarre something or other, he thought. The dance floor was packed with men and women, and people stood two deep along the bar and sat at tables scattered throughout the place. They wound their way around people standing and seated, Oliver greeting someone every now and then. He discovered an empty table near the back of the club, and they each took a chair.

"Nice place," Cody said over the music, grinning at Demetrius. "A step or two up from the Hollow Leg."

Demetrius smirked as he thought about the old bar on the outskirts of Parson's Hollow. It was held together with duct tape, stale beer, kitchen grease, and old cigarette smoke, but it was comfortable and familiar.

"Yeah, it's got a little more shine on it than the Leg," Demetrius replied.

"You guys still go out to that dive bar?" Oliver asked. "Oh, you want to get a pitcher of beer?"

Demetrius looked at Cody, and they shrugged.

"Sure," Demetrius said.

As Oliver looked for a waiter, someone behind Demetrius caught his interest and he quickly dropped his gaze.

"Dammit," Oliver said.

"What?" Demetrius started to turn, but Oliver grabbed his hand tight.

"Don't look!" Oliver said, his voice low and harsh.

"Um…" Cody's gaze shifted between Oliver's hand gripping his, to Demetrius's eyes, and back again.

"Who's this? Fresh meat?"

Demetrius looked up to find a woman with a wide face, bright smile, and long dirty blonde hair pulled back into a ponytail. A loose fitting camouflage fleece zip up hoodie covered a bright yellow T-shirt, and the cuffs of her black jeans were tucked into the tops of mud-splattered cowboy boots.

"Friends of mine from Parson's Hollow," Oliver replied, releasing Demetrius's hand.

"Yeah?" She bumped her hip against Demetrius's shoulder. "Where's Parson's Hollow?"

"Um, a little west of Pittsburgh," Demetrius replied. He turned in his seat and held out his hand. "I'm Demetrius."

"Tonya." Her grip was strong, and when she released Demetrius's hand, she reached across the table to Cody, who introduced himself.

"So what brings you to Pinesville?"

"Just a visit," Oliver said before Demetrius or Cody could respond.

"I see. So, you two an item?" Tonya flicked her gaze between Demetrius and Cody.

"Demetrius and I used to date, and he and Cody are friends. Like I said, just a visit."

"So no attachments, huh?" Tonya smiled.

"Here you are!"

Another woman appeared at Tonya's side. She was beautiful and athletic, with long red hair that lay loose around her shoulders. When she smiled, Demetrius was struck by her white and perfect teeth.

"Hey," Tonya greeted her. "I was just chatting up a couple of Oliver's friends."

"What handsome friends you have, Oliver," the new arrival said. "Are they together?"

"That seems to be the question of the night," Cody said before Oliver could speak.

Demetrius looked across the table at him. From Cody's smile and expression, he could see he was attracted to Tonya's friend. And Demetrius couldn't blame him, she was beautiful. But Demetrius didn't know how to feel about it. Or rather, how he *should* feel about it. Because he knew how it made him feel, and that was a little bit threatened. But he didn't know if he had a right to feel that way.

"And what would the answer to that question be?" The woman circled around behind Oliver to stand between him and Cody.

"They're friends," Oliver said. He leaned over and put an arm around Demetrius's shoulders, giving him a quick squeeze. "Demetrius and I dated while I lived in Parsons's Hollow. Cody is Demetrius's best friend and business partner."

"Oh?" Tonya looked down at Demetrius, who was

distracted by the sudden tension he felt in Oliver's arm around his shoulders. "What kind of business?"

"It's called Critter Catchers," Demetrius said. "We do pest and animal control around Parson's Hollow."

"Oh, really?" Tonya and her friend exchanged a look, then Tonya turned back to Oliver. "Is that why they're here?"

"No, that's not why," Oliver said, pulling his arm from around Demetrius. "They just wanted to come up for a visit, that's all."

"What's going on?" Cody asked, looking between the women, and settling his gaze on the one standing beside him. He lifted his hand and said, "Cody Bower, by the way."

She gave him a cool smile as she shook his hand. "Madison Keene. Tonya and I have our own business as well here in Pinesville. It's called Critter Ridders."

Cody gave Demetrius a wide-eyed look, then turned back to Madison. "You're the Critter Ridders?"

"That's us." Madison released his hand and looked between Cody and Demetrius. "You've heard of us?"

"I might have mentioned you two when they arrived earlier," Oliver said. "Because you're in the same line of work."

"That's it?" Tonya asked. "Not because of that reward for proof that the Devil exists?"

Understanding dawned on Demetrius. A reward was being offered for proof of the Devil's existence, and the Critter Ridders wanted to be the ones to collect it. How interesting Oliver hadn't mentioned any reward money when he'd invited them to drive up.

Cody had apparently caught on to all of it as well, because he gave Madison a perfectly believable look of confusion. "The Devil of Pinesville? That sounds like the title of a bad movie."

"So you don't know anything about it?" Madison asked.

Cody shrugged and gave Demetrius a quick look before returning his attention to Madison. "Nope."

Madison did not look convinced. Tonya still stood between Demetrius and Oliver, and she said, "You drove a long way if you came from the other side of Pittsburgh. You and Oliver must be pretty close friends."

"Ollie?" Cody looked over at Oliver, flicked his gaze to Demetrius for a moment, then looked up at Tonya. "We're as close as a double yolk egg."

"That might be an exaggeration," Oliver said. "But Demetrius and I are still close."

Demetrius felt Cody's gaze on him and knew he'd have to explain later that Oliver was lying. Until he'd received Oliver's text the day before, Demetrius hadn't heard from him in months.

Madison squeezed Cody's shoulder. "So that means you're unattached?"

"I could ask you the same question," Cody said.

"Oh, she's attached all right," Tonya said, "but we give each other some room to breathe."

"Yeah," Madison said, not taking her gaze off Cody. "And I haven't taken a deep breath in a long time."

"Oh, really?" Cody laughed, and Demetrius noticed he avoided looking at him as he blushed.

"Wow, that hurt," Tonya said. "Maybe he can give you a ride home, too."

Tonya did an abrupt about-face and stomped off into the crowd.

"Oh fuck," Madison said with a sigh as she looked after Tonya. She gave Cody's shoulder a squeeze, and then smiled at Demetrius. "It's been nice to meet you two." She looked back at Cody. "Very nice."

"Good riddance," Oliver mumbled as Madison went off in search of Tonya.

"Wow," Cody said, watching over Demetrius's shoulder as Madison walked away.

"Yeah, wow." Demetrius fixed his gaze on Oliver, who had turned away to survey the crowd.

"Oliver?" Demetrius said.

"I'm looking for a waiter," Oliver said. "What's a guy have to do to get a drink in this dive?"

"Oliver," Demetrius said in a more stern tone.

Oliver finally looked at him. "Yeah?"

"What did Tonya mean when she asked if we were in town for the reward?"

"Reward?"

"Dude, answer the question," Cody said. "What's this reward stuff about?"

Oliver sighed and turned in his seat to face them again. "A cable channel documentary series has taken an interest in the recent sightings of the Devil. It's one of those myth or monster investigative series."

"I've seen a few of those shows," Cody said. "They try to prove Bigfoot or the Yeti or the Loch Ness monster exist. Sometimes they send in their own team, other times they just provide assistance to local monster hunters."

"Right."

"Are we your local team, Oliver?" Demetrius asked.

"I wasn't going to keep it from you," Oliver said. "I was going to tell you about it when we started looking around more seriously."

"Uh huh," Cody said, sitting back and crossing his arms over his chest. "Or you were going to wait until we found some proof and then left town before you got in touch with the producers."

"No, I wouldn't do that."

"I need a drink." Cody shot up out of his chair and stomped off into the crowd.

"I really was going to tell you about the money," Oliver said. "I swear."

"I believe you," Demetrius said. "But you're going to have to win Cody back."

"Yeah." Oliver looked after Cody. "Unless he decides to switch sides."

Demetrius looked over his shoulder and felt like he'd been punched in the gut. Cody hadn't made it to the bar. He stood swaying on the dance floor with Madison. His big right hand rested on her hip, and he smiled down at her as she swiveled her hips against him.

"Oh," Demetrius managed to say. His stomach clenched, and he feared he might throw up his dinner.

"He moves in quick, doesn't he?" Oliver said. "Same ol' Cody."

"Yeah." Demetrius looked away and blinked against a sudden sting of tears. "Same ol' Cody."

"Do you want a drink?" Oliver asked. "I'll go to the bar and get us something."

Demetrius shook his head and avoided his eyes. "No, thanks. But you can go ahead if you want."

"Nah," Oliver said. "I'm not in a party kind of mood anymore. This was probably a bad idea to come out here. Think you can convince Cody to drop Madison so we can leave?"

Demetrius drew in a deep breath and kept his gaze on the tabletop. "Oh, I don't know…"

"You know what, you're right. He could just get a ride home from her in the morning, couldn't he?"

"Um. Yeah. I guess you're right." It took a lot of effort for him to not turn and look at the dance floor.

"Oh, wait. Looks like we'll be able to ask him ourselves," Oliver said. "He's coming back to the table. Probably going to tell us he's going home with Madison."

An uncontrollable trembling had started low in Demetrius's belly and spread to his chest and limbs. He felt cold and light-headed. Was this normal?

Cody took his seat once again and let out a heavy breath. "That Madison is quite a woman."

"Yeah, we saw that," Oliver said.

"Oh?"

Demetrius felt Cody's gaze on him, but he didn't look up from his study of the tabletop.

"I thought you were coming back to tell us that she would give you a ride back to my grandma's house tomorrow morning," Oliver said.

"Oh, no. I didn't even see her out there when I got up," Cody said. "Right, Demmy?"

Demetrius finally looked Cody in the eye. He saw the concern in his expression, and it warmed him a bit. "What?"

"Me getting hijacked by Madison on my way to the bar," Cody said, his gaze steady and intense. "I didn't plan that. She grabbed me as I cut across the dance floor. Before I knew it, we were dancing. But that's it. Nothing went any farther. I didn't get her number or give her mine."

"Wow, you have changed," Oliver said.

Demetrius smiled and nodded as he continued to look at Cody. "Yeah, you have."

"I guess I have."

"How about we take off?" Oliver asked. "Demetrius and I have both lost our interest."

"You want to leave a place called the Brutal Poodle before ten o'clock?" Cody said.

"Pretty much," Oliver said.

"Well I guess I'm ready, too." Cody met Demetrius's gaze again. "I'm looking forward to that single bed in the loft."

Demetrius grinned and stood up. "Yeah, me too."

"They are comfortable beds," Oliver said as he led the way to the door. "Even though it looks like a prison camp."

As Demetrius followed Oliver to the exit, Cody crowded up close to his back and whispered in his ear. "Nothing happened. I swear."

Demetrius nodded without looking around. When Cody brushed the swell of his ass with his hand, Demetrius let out a small, shivery breath.

At the car, Demetrius opted to let Cody have the front passenger seat again. It was primarily because he was so tall, but Demetrius also wanted a chance to sit in the dark backseat and process what he'd felt at the sight of Cody dancing with Madison. Up front, Oliver and Cody talked about the Brutal Poodle and some of Oliver's blog posts, their quiet voices the perfect backdrop to his internal musings.

Seeing Cody dancing with Madison had struck Demetrius in a way he hadn't expected. It wasn't just jealousy. While that had been a part of his reaction, the core of his feelings had been sadness. Cody had been dancing close with Madison without a care in the world about who was watching. Oh, he'd felt badly about possibly hurting Demetrius, but he had no anxiety about being seen with her; he'd been able to lose himself in the moment.

Would Cody ever be able to act that way with him? Would they ever get to a point where Cody was able to claim their relationship honestly and without hesitation?

Demetrius was jarred from his thoughts by Oliver slamming on the brakes and shouting, "Fuck!"

If the seatbelt hadn't held him in place, he might have ended up in a heap between Oliver and Cody.

"What happened?" Demetrius asked, craning his head side to side as he tried to see out the windshield.

"What an asshole," Cody said.

"Who?" Demetrius fumbled with the release for his seatbelt. "What's happening?"

He struggled out of the shoulder harness seatbelt and slid over so he could see between the seats. A man staggered back and forth across the road, his head swiveling as he looked into the woods on either side. The man seemed completely unaware of them sitting in the car a dozen yards away.

"What's he doing?" Demetrius said. "Is he looking for someone?"

"He may be high," Oliver said.

"One way to find out," Cody said, opening his door.

"Shit," Oliver muttered before he turned to look back at Demetrius. "You're getting out, too, I imagine."

"Yep." Demetrius got out and leaned down to look back in at Oliver. "Come on. You're a reporter, for God's sake."

"Fine."

Oliver followed as Demetrius stood behind Cody and listened as he spoke to the man.

"Hey buddy," Cody said. "Hey there."

The man stopped in his tracks and slowly looked at Cody. "Hey. Are you Carl?"

"Carl?" Cody shook his head. "No, man, I'm Cody."

"You're not Carl?"

"Nope. I'm Cody. Hey, are you all right?"

"Where's Carl?"

A quiet rustle from the dark between the trees to Demetrius's right made them all look that way.

"Did you hear that?" Cody whispered.

"Yep," Demetrius whispered back.

"Is that Carl?" the man said, also in a quiet voice.

"I'm going to call the police," Oliver said.

Demetrius nodded. "Good idea."

"What's your name, buddy?" Cody asked.

The man blinked rapidly as he tried to focus. "Carl?"

"No, that's who you're looking for," Cody said. "What's *your* name? What does Carl call *you*?"

"Henry. I'm Henry." He peered into the woods where they'd heard the rustling sound.

Demetrius heard Oliver talking quietly on the phone behind him. He looked over his shoulder along the empty road back toward the Brutal Poodle, and then beyond Henry into the darkness. They were very isolated on this road, and difficult to see in the darkness.

"Maybe we should get him out of the road?" Demetrius suggested.

"Yeah, good idea. I really don't want to touch him, though." Cody lowered his voice. "He's got some strong b.o., and he's covered in what I can only hope is mud."

"I see your point. Maybe we can lure him to the shoulder and get him to sit down?"

Cody stepped back and waved for Demetrius to proceed. "Be my guest."

"Great." The smell coming off the man hit him like a punch in the gut, and he turned his head aside to cough.

"Told you," Cody said.

Demetrius saw Oliver standing behind Cody, no longer on the phone. "Do you recognize this guy?"

Oliver shook his head. "I've never seen him before."

"I think it took Carl," Henry said, looking off toward the woods again. A chill went through Demetrius as he looked at the woods as well. Nothing but darkness looked back. At least, nothing else he could see.

"Hey, Henry?" Demetrius waited until Henry managed to focus on him. "How about we get you out of the road?"

"The road?" Henry's eyes went wide. "Are you it?"

"What?" Demetrius turned to Cody and Oliver who both looked back at him. When he faced Henry again, he saw the small size of his pupils. They should have been a lot bigger being out in the dark. He was high all right. "Am I what?"

Henry staggered back a couple of steps. Over his shoulder, Demetrius saw a police car round the bend, light bar flashing red and blue along the trees as it sped toward them. Henry slowly lowered himself to a crouch a bit offside of the yellow line, and looked up at Demetrius.

"Are you the Devil?" Henry whispered.

Demetrius jumped when something big crashed off into the woods to his right just as the police car slowed to a stop on the opposite shoulder. The pulsing lights drenched the scene in reds and blues as a shiver shook Demetrius down to his bones.

CHAPTER TWELVE

Cody felt surprisingly well-rested for sleeping in the loft of a barn and going without sex the night before. After a quick breakfast that morning, he'd driven the four of them out to a trail that led to a campground where people had spotted the Devil. And so they had started hiking. With his longer strides, Cody had gotten pretty far ahead of the others, and he stopped to look back the way he had come. Demmy, Ollie, and Eileen approached a few yards back, trampling the bracken, fallen leaves, and sucker saplings that had sprouted up along the narrow footpath.

None of them would ever be called subtle.

The woods stretched out in all directions, and Cody appreciated the beauty of it, with the colored leaves and the dappled sunlight and the birds singing and flitting around. Nothing bad could ever live here among the trees, unless Henry knew where it was.

Although, if pressed to give an honest answer, Cody really didn't feel like Henry could have given a coherent response to any question, at least not in the condition he'd been in last night on the road. And the police had had no better luck with Henry than they had.

"Break time?" Demmy asked as he came up beside him.

Cody grinned. "I just finished my break."

"Okay, Grizzly Adams. How about letting us city folk catch our breath a minute, huh?"

"Fine," Cody said with mock exasperation, then muttered, "City folk," just loud enough for Demmy to hear.

"We stopping?" Eileen stood looking around with her hands on her hips. "Guess I could use a cigarette."

"Don't start a forest fire, Grandma," Oliver said.

"Now why the hell would I want to do something like that?" Eileen asked after taking a long drag of her smoke.

"I didn't say you'd want to. Just warned you not to."

Demmy took a swig of water and asked, "What's the possibility of us finding anything out here?"

"Honest answer?" Cody asked.

"Of course."

"I'm afraid we're going to find everything we're looking for out here."

Demmy raised his eyebrows. "Big, strong Cody Bower is afraid?"

Cody raised his eyebrows as well. "Big, strong Cody Bower has learned what happens when we go off into the woods looking for something unusual."

"We're just checking out a campground," Demmy said. "That's all. What can be so dangerous about a campground?"

"Well, first of all, we're walking through the woods to get there," Cody said. "Why isn't there a damn road that would have let us drive right up to it?"

"Is he griping again about there not being a road to this place?" Eileen asked, smoke drifting all around her face.

"It doesn't make any sense," Cody said.

"It's for camping!" Eileen practically shouted. "It's setup

for people to hike through the woods and then pitch a tent. There's no road because you're not supposed to take a car to get there. You're supposed to hike with your tent rolled up in a back pack and your pots and pans hanging from the straps and clanging around. Have you never been camping?"

"I've camped before," Cody said with a growl. "And I was able to park my car right next to my tent."

"When did you ever camp?" Demmy asked.

"I've camped," Cody said. "I've camped plenty."

"When? And with who?"

"Whom," Oliver said.

Cody smirked as Demmy shot Ollie a look. Maybe things between Demmy and Ollie were really, truly over and he could let his guard down.

Yeah, right.

Eileen stood smoking with her back against a tree, and Cody said, "While you're catching your breath around that cigarette, why don't you enlighten us on the reason you suggested this particular campsite for us to poke around."

"It's where the Devil was sighted about a month ago. You didn't figure that out by now?"

"Just making sure it wasn't to see the pretty leaves," Cody said.

"They are nice though," Demmy added.

"Pinesville is a big draw this time of year for the color tours," Ollie said.

"Lots of hikers and campers?" Cody asked.

"Yeah. And there are some bed and breakfasts in town and out in the rural areas."

Cody looked to Eileen. "How much farther to the campsite?"

"Probably another hour." She crouched down and buried the cigarette butt in a shallow hole she'd dug in the dirt.

"Have the police been involved in the Devil sightings?" Demmy asked.

"First time I've talked to the police here was last night," Ollie said.

"Oh!" Eileen smiled at Ollie. "I heard something about your strange man."

Ollie frowned. "He's not *my* strange man."

"Yeah, yeah," Eileen said, waving him off. "Let's get walking again, and I'll tell you about it."

Cody took the lead as Eileen delivered her news. "I'm pretty close with Mabel who works as an administrator down at the police station. She said the officers couldn't get a straight answer out of your road wanderer last night. He just kept asking about Carl, but not much more. They took him to Pinesville General to be examined, and they found needle tracks up and down both arms."

"Needle tracks?" Cody looked over his shoulder at her. "Heroin?"

"Yep. According to Mabel, there's been a lot of that kind of stuff going on around here," Eileen said. "Anyway, they're letting him sleep it off at the hospital, but he's going to be charged when he's released."

"Heroin is very popular around Parson's Hollow, too," Demmy said. "It's an epidemic all across the country. They haven't been able to find out more about Henry's friend, Carl?"

"No," Eileen said.

They fell quiet after that as they walked along the narrow, overgrown path. Cody figured no one had been out here for a week, at least, gauging from the ferns and tall grass that grew amid the roots and dirt of the path. Eventually, they topped a low rise and looked out into a clearing of half beaten down grass and half hard-packed dirt. A hand water pump stood in the center of the clearing, with eight fire pits in a ring around it. From what Cody could see, the fire pits were the tops of metal barrels that had been stuck into the ground and extended half a foot above the dirt.

On the other side of the clearing stood a single tent. It billowed gently in the breeze, the bright blue material faded by sunlight.

"Oh, someone's camping out here," Ollie said.

Cody squinted at the tent. Something was off about it, but he couldn't tell what.

"Something's not right," Demmy said in a quiet voice.

"You think so, too?" Cody whispered.

"Yep." Demmy said to Eileen and Ollie, "Let's wait a minute or two before we leave the trees."

"What's wrong?" Eileen asked, keeping her scratchy voice pitched low in imitation of them.

"Not sure," Cody said.

The wind ruffled the tent again, and that was when he saw it. Cody heard Demmy gasp quietly beside him.

"It's torn," Demmy said.

"Yep. Saw it."

"Torn?" Ollie stuck his head over Demmy's shoulder, and Cody had to restrain himself from giving Ollie a sharp elbow in the gut to get him to back off. "Oh. The back of it is torn. Almost shredded."

"The Devil."

Eileen's voice was calm and quiet, and it creeped Cody out so much he shivered even though the day was mild and the sun was shining.

"You think there are people in there?" Ollie whispered. "Bodies?"

"One way to find out," Cody said, but he remained rooted to the spot.

"It could be a crime scene," Demmy said. "If we all go over there, we could be trampling on evidence."

"The Devil would have flown in on its big bat wings," Eileen said. "It wouldn't have come in across the ground."

"I'll go," Ollie said.

"Okay," Cody said without hesitation.

But Demmy frowned at Ollie. "Why you?"

Ollie shrugged. "I live here in town, so if there is a body in there, I may not be as much of a suspect as you two, being new to town and all."

"Works for me," Cody said.

"You're sure?" Demmy seemed more than a little protective of Ollie, and Cody tried not to let himself feel rankled by it. Demmy was just concerned about his friend. That was it.

"Yeah, I'm sure. It's the middle of the day, what could happen?" Ollie tried for a laugh, but it sounded weak.

"But if there is a body in the tent, it could be pretty gruesome," Demmy said.

"I'll be fine. Remember I found one of the bodies left by the wolf man."

"Yeah, I remember."

"Time's wasting," Cody said. "We still need to walk back, and I don't want to be out after dark."

"Yeah, okay." Ollie stepped out of the trees and stood on the edge of the clearing, clenching and releasing his hands.

"Be careful," Eileen said.

Ollie looked over his shoulder at her. "I will." He looked at Cody. "Keep an eye on her, okay?"

"I'll keep both eyes on her."

"Well, keep one on me, too," Ollie said. "Just in case."

"You'll be fine," Cody said. "Like you said, it's the middle of the day."

Ollie flashed a nervous smile at Demmy and set off across the clearing. Eileen and Demmy stood to either side of Cody, all of them silent as they watched Ollie slowly walk away from them. When he reached the hand pump in the center, he looked back over his shoulder. Demmy gave him an encouraging nod and a thumbs up, and Cody had to fight to not roll his eyes.

"You be careful, boy," Eileen whispered. Cody heard the concern and love in her voice, and his attitude toward Ollie softened. Not much, but it did shift a bit.

"He's doing good," Cody assured her. "He'll be fine."

Ollie stopped suddenly, and Cody's heart pounded as he squinted at the tent, and then looked at the woods all around the clearing, searching for any kind of threat. He didn't see anything himself, but maybe Ollie had heard something.

"What is it?" Demmy called quietly.

"There's a back pack inside the tent," Ollie said. "I can see it through the opening."

"Anything else?"

"Can't tell." Ollie slowly crouched down and picked up a long, thin stick.

"That's not much protection," Cody called.

"I'm not using it for protection," Ollie said without looking back.

He moved forward again, step by slow step, the stick held out in front of him like a sword. When he was a few feet in front of the tent, he reached out with the stick and moved the flap open so he could peer inside.

A figure burst out of the trees behind the tent. It moved in a flurry of motion, swaying branches, and shaking leaves. Ollie jumped and ran back toward them as they all let out shouts of surprise.

"Oliver?" the figure called.

Ollie stopped and turned. The new arrival wore camouflage coveralls and a matching hat with netting that covered its face. Eileen bolted from the trees, heading for Ollie's side, and Demmy took off as well, hot on her heels. Cody let out an irritated huff before he followed.

"Who is that?" Ollie called.

Cody came to a stop right behind Demmy who stood beside Ollie. Eileen was on Ollie's other side, and they all watched as the figure struggled a bit with the netting around its face before it managed to get both it and the hat off. It was Tonya, the woman they had met at the Brutal Poodle and who had gotten more than a bit upset over Madison's flirting with Cody.

He and Demmy hadn't talked much at Eileen's place the night before. Demmy had said maybe five words as they got ready for bed. When Cody had come out of the bathroom, he'd found Demmy tucked into one of the single beds with his back turned to the one where Cody had dropped his bag. Nothing more had been said, either that night or the following morning.

And now Tonya was in front of them, about to bring the whole thing back up again.

Fucking Critter Ridders.

"Tonya?" Ollie lowered the stick and took a couple of steps toward her. "What are you doing here?"

The trees rustled off to their right, and another figure dressed in similar style appeared.

Madison.

Staring right at Cody.

Oh boy.

"Well, look who's here," Madison said. "And you brought Ollie's grandma."

"I've got a name," Eileen said.

"Grandma Moses?" Madison asked in a sweetly sarcastic tone.

Cody stepped between the two women. He turned his brightest smile on Madison and asked, "What brings you two lovely ladies this far out in the woods?"

"Probably the same thing you're doing here." Tonya stared with wide eyes down at the tent. "Oh my god."

"What?" Madison asked. "What is it?"

"The back of this tent is torn to shit."

Madison moved up beside Tonya, and she stared as well. Cody noticed the startling green of her eyes, and how her red hair tumbled perfectly out from under the camouflage hat and over her shoulders.

Dammit, what the hell was wrong with him? He avoided looking at Demmy as he said, "Ollie noticed that, too."

"It's been here," Madison said, then snapped her gaze up to Cody. It was filled with such cold anger, he took a couple of steps back. "Did you know about this already? Is that why you're out here?"

"I brought them out here," Eileen spoke up. "I've heard talk around town that people have seen and heard strange things out here."

"There's something inside," Tonya said, her voice low.

"I saw a back pack in there before you came out of the woods," Ollie said.

"Oh." Tonya leaned down and parted the shredded back of the tent. Her face went pale and she looked up at Madison beside her. "You'd better use the satellite phone to call the cops."

Madison peered into the tent and pulled out a phone with a thick plastic case from a deep coat pocket. "Oh shit. Yeah, don't touch anything else."

"What is it?" Demmy asked. "Is it a body? Blood?"

"Come take a look," Tonya said.

All four of them circled the tent and stood around Tonya. Cody stood behind Demmy and rested a hand on his shoulder, needing to feel connected to him. He leaned in closer and peered over Demmy's shoulder into the tent as Tonya held the torn fabric open.

An icy dread filled Cody's chest. The backpack Ollie had seen lay at the other end of the tent, right in front of the opening. Closer to the rear, where they all stood grouped together, were two sleeping bags, wadded up in a tangled heap. Between the sleeping bags lay a man's arm, severed at the shoulder.

"Oh," Ollie said in a soft voice. He walked back to the center of the camping area and pumped some water to splash on his face.

"Aw hell," Eileen said, turning away.

"Could it have been a bear?" Demmy asked, leaning back against Cody.

"Cops will find out," Tonya said, dropping the tent fabric.

"Have you seen anything like that before?" Cody asked.

"Nope," Tonya said. "Have you?"

Cody glanced at Demmy, then looked back at her. "No."

The lie came easy and, in Cody's mind, was more than necessary. He didn't want the Critter Ridders to become competitive.

Tonya moved off to talk quietly with Madison, leaving Cody and Demmy alone at the back of the tent.

"You thinking what I'm thinking?" Demmy asked in a low voice.

"Yeah, we're going to be bunking with Eileen and Ollie a little longer than we'd anticipated."

"Fucking monsters," Demmy said with a sigh.

"Fucking monsters," Cody repeated, looking into the shadow-drenched woods.

CHAPTER THIRTEEN

Demetrius paced from one end of the line of single beds to the other. He clasped his hands behind his back and stared at the floor as he walked back and forth. Thoughts spun through his mind, collided, and splintered off into a number of different directions. His stomach rumbled, and he checked the time on his phone. Almost four thirty in the afternoon. They'd been so busy talking with the police out at the campsite, they hadn't gotten a chance to eat lunch.

"How are you not dizzy yet?" Cody sat on his bed with his back propped up on a pillow.

Demetrius stopped at the foot of Cody's bed and looked at him. "It's a real thing. The Devil of Pinesville is a real monster."

"You're surprised by this?"

"Once it would be nice if it was some greedy land owner in a rubber suit or something."

"Your *Scooby Doo* is showing."

"Yeah, I know." Demetrius sat on the edge of his bed right beside Cody's.

"This arrangement makes me think of our trip to your parents' condo," Cody said.

Demetrius looked at him. "Really? Oh, yeah. Two single beds."

"Knock, knock." It was Oliver, calling up the loft steps as he ascended. "I hope you're both decent."

"Unfortunately," Cody grumbled.

Demetrius raised his eyebrows at Cody, then turned toward the steps as Oliver came up. "How are you and Eileen doing?"

Oliver shrugged. "We're okay. She's loading her shotgun and having a beer." He sat on the bed closest to the bathroom. "So what do you guys think?"

"I think we're all in a heap of trouble," Cody said. "But that's just me."

"I think you may be right," Oliver said.

"It's a miracle." Cody lifted his hands up to the barn roof. "Ollie agrees with me. Call the papers. No, wait." He pointed at Oliver. "You can write a blog post and sell it to the highest bidder."

"Ha ha," Oliver said with a sneer. "But, seriously. Did you guys see many details about the… about that arm?"

"Just that it looked like a man's arm," Demetrius said. "Did you see something more?"

Oliver sat on the edge of the bed beside Demetrius.

"Make yourself at home," Cody muttered.

Oliver looked between them before setting his gaze on Demetrius. "I watched the cops put the arm into an evidence bag. It looked like there were needle marks in the elbow."

Cody slid his legs over the side of the mattress and sat on the edge of the bed. He had one foot planted between Demetrius's feet, their knees almost touching. "Like the guy you almost ran over on the road last night?"

"Henry, right." Oliver frowned. "And I didn't almost run

him over. I stopped well away away from him. Like, yards away."

"If you say so." Before Oliver could respond, Cody continued. "Could there be some kind of pattern here? Heroin users getting high in the woods and stirring up the Devil?"

"Maybe," Oliver said. "I just don't know."

Demetrius looked at the floor as he considered Oliver's information. Cody's big foot between his own smaller feet was weirdly intimate and erotic, and he pushed aside the dirty thoughts that had sprung to mind. "I wonder if that arm belonged to the guy Henry was looking for. What was the name he kept calling out?"

"Carl," Cody said.

Demetrius could see so much hovering in Cody's gaze and expression. Subtle clues about his current state of mind. Cody was worried about what they had learned so far. It seemed there was a monster out there, and it had killed someone. Or it had appeared to have killed someone.

Cody might also be concerned about their relationship. But Demetrius couldn't focus on that at the moment.

"Right, Carl." Oliver's voice brought Demetrius back to the conversation.

"What about the Critter Ridders?" Demetrius asked. "Could they know more than they're letting on?"

"It's possible."

"Think they can be trusted?" Cody said.

Demetrius worked to keep his expression neutral, but he wondered what Cody had meant by his question. Could the Critter Ridders be trusted to tell them the truth and work with them, or could Madison be trusted to keep a quick tryst secret? He'd seen the spark between Cody and Madison. He wanted to trust Cody, he really did, but he had known him a very long time and heard many of the thoughts he'd had about the women he'd dated over the years, as well as Cody's schemes to break things off with them.

But to accomplish what they needed with the Devil and possibly win that reward from the cable channel, they might have to team up with the Critter Ridders.

"Trusted?" Oliver shrugged. "I don't really know them all that well. I've talked with them a few times at the Brutal Poodle, and then a couple of jobs Grandma hired them for here on the farm. They removed a family of skunks from under the barn. And have kept the rat population under control."

"Did they get sprayed by skunks?" Cody asked with a grim smirk.

Oliver shook his head. "Nope. Not once."

Cody scowled. Demetrius wondered if Cody's competitiveness stemmed from a business perspective, or something more personal. He remembered Madison's expression as she'd seen Cody out in the woods, and something small and scared tightened inside his gut. If the two of them had been alone out there, would something have happened between them? And given Cody's dating history, was it fair of Demetrius to expect Cody to not date women now that they were seeing each other? Would Cody be okay if Demetrius dated other men? Was that really even the same kind of thing? And who was he to think he was the magical being who could keep Cody satisfied for the rest of his life?

His heart pounded and his face flushed. The rest of his life? What the ever-loving fuck had brought that thought to mind? They'd only been together a month, and here he was thinking of marriage? With Cody?! Was he trying to set himself up to get his heart broken?

"Demmy?"

Cody's voice brought him out of his contemplation, and he blinked as he stared at him.

"Sorry," he managed to say, as somewhere inside his brain he was screaming. "My mind drifted a bit. What were you saying?"

"You tired?" Oliver asked.

"I am, actually. Didn't sleep well last night, and it's been kind of a long day already."

"New place," Oliver said, gesturing to the beds lined up along the loft. "You don't sleep well in a new place. I remember."

Demetrius took note of Cody's tightened expression. Well, at least Cody still felt some jealousy about Oliver. He had that going for him.

"Yeah," Demetrius said with a grin and a shrug. "Just like always. I'll sleep better tonight."

"I'm sure you will," Cody said, his voice low and with a gruff edge that sent a tingle up from Demetrius's toes and into his groin.

"Do you guys want to go to the Critter Ridders's office and talk to them?" Oliver asked. "See about any leads they might have on the Devil?"

"Would they even talk to us with that reward money hanging over all of this?" Cody asked. "And, by the way, just how much reward money are we talking about here?"

"$250,000."

"A quarter million dollars?" Cody said, and looked at Demetrius. "Did he say a quarter million dollars?"

"That's what I heard." Demetrius looked at Oliver. "That's a lot of money."

"There've been a lot more sightings lately," Oliver said.

"How many other people are in town looking for this thing?" Cody asked.

Oliver shrugged. "I don't know. I've seen some groups with vans full of video equipment and other groups with just home video cameras and their cell phones and stuff. There have been a lot of new faces around town since the reward was announced."

"Funny how all of this just failed to get mentioned when you invited us up here," Cody said. "What's your game, Ollie?"

"There is no game, all right? I just thought..." He huffed out a breath and got up to stand at the foot of Cody's bed. "I thought since Grandma saw the Devil out by the barn, we'd have an easy time proving it existed. And that the money would really help her pay off the years of property taxes she owes on this place."

Demetrius saw Cody's expression soften a bit, and knew it was time for him to step in.

"Okay, let's put that all aside for the time being. What about Tonya and Madison? Do you think they'll work with us?"

Oliver thought a moment. "Maybe. Now that the Devil has killed someone, they might welcome some fresh insight on the case."

"Allegedly killed someone," Demetrius said. "And we're not even sure the Devil exists yet, remember. No one's managed to get a clear picture or video of it."

"That we know of," Cody said. "One of those crack investigative teams might have it all in the can and be emailing a digital file to the cable channel as we sit here trying to come up with a plan."

"I'm sorry, okay?" Oliver practically shouted. "I was wrong. I should have told you about the money right away. But you have to believe I would never have cheated you out of it."

Cody shook his head as he remained silent.

"Let's go into town and talk to Tonya and Madison." Demetrius looked at Cody, trying not to put any weight behind his gaze. "Do you agree?"

Cody shrugged and appeared only slightly interested in the idea. "Yeah. It's worth a try. But if they knew anything more than us, I figure they'd have already killed the thing and strung it up in the middle of downtown."

"We can ask if they've had any calls from their customers about Devil sightings," Oliver said. "Not sure if they'll share that with us, but you never know."

"Let's give it a try." Demetrius pushed to his feet.

Oliver looked relieved. "Great."

"Hey, Ollie, give us a minute, will you?" Cody asked. "I want to talk with Demmy, then take a leak and maybe change my socks after all that hiking earlier."

Oliver hesitated before he nodded. "Yeah, sure. Just come on down to the house when you're ready." He turned away, then stopped and looked back. "I really wouldn't have cheated you guys out of the money. I hope you believe that."

Demetrius didn't even look at Cody. "We believe you. It's okay."

Oliver started down the steps, but stopped and looked back. "Oh, can you drive? My car is low on gas."

Cody sighed. "Fine."

Oliver went down the steps and Demetrius stayed on his feet and crossed his arms as he looked down at Cody with raised eyebrows. "You want to change your socks?"

Cody unlaced his boots. "Yeah. My feet got sweaty from all our walking. You know I get overheated easily."

"That's an understatement."

Cody kicked off his boots and they thudded to the wooden planks like size twelve bunker buster bombs. He peeled off his socks and dropped them on the floor, then wiggled his toes. Demetrius smiled as he looked at Cody's feet, noting the familiar dark hairs along his toes and the broad, pale size of them. Not that he had a fetish or anything, but Demetrius did think Cody had nice feet.

"Hey."

Demetrius looked up. The skin at the corners of Cody's eyes looked tight, and a couple of worry lines had appeared on the bridge of his nose.

"Crazy stuff out there, huh?"

"Yeah. I didn't… I didn't expect to see a severed arm."

"You doing okay?"

"Yep. How about you?"

Cody nodded. "I'm hanging in there."

"You going to be able to forgive Oliver?"

Cody sighed. "Yeah." Then he muttered, "Fucking Ollie." He opened his mouth, closed it, opened it again, but finally closed it.

Demetrius stepped up to his bed and kept his back to Cody because he didn't think he could stand to see his expression as he said, "Those Critter Ridders are a real piece of work, huh?"

"That they are." Cody's voice was flat.

Demetrius rummaged through his duffel bag. He wasn't looking for anything in particular, he was just keeping his hands busy. He heard Cody rustle around in his own duffel bag, grumbling to himself about socks and their tendency to hide on him, but a small, nervous part of Demetrius's mind refused to listen. As he kept his attention on own his duffel bag, all he could manage to do was repeat the questions he'd asked himself countless times since he and Cody had first kissed: Could or should Demetrius expect Cody not to date other people now that they were together? Was he being at all realistic in thinking Cody would be satisfied with just him?

The questions were endless and exhausting.

"You ready?"

Startled out of his thoughts, Demetrius saw Cody on his feet and staring at him. Damn, had he been lost in thought that long?

"Everything all right, Demmy?"

"Yep. Good. All good." Demetrius zipped his duffel and straightened up. "I'm ready if you are."

Cody gave him a long, searching look, then a quick nod. "I'm ready."

Demetrius flashed a quick smile before turning to the steps and leading the way down into the barn. He thought about the look Cody had just given him, weighing the meaning behind it. Was it the last look preceding a farewell? Or maybe something else, like Cody had just come to some kind of conclusion, but didn't have time to discuss it?

Or did it not mean anything at all?

He pushed those thoughts aside and stepped out of the barn. The chickens squawked as they scattered, and Demetrius heard Cody curse the birds behind him. Oliver waited beside Cody's truck, and Demetrius pushed his thoughts and insecurities out of his mind for the moment. No time to figure it all out now; they had more important stuff to worry about.

CHAPTER FOURTEEN

"**W**hy would we want to share any information with you three?"

Tonya's voice was quiet, but rough. Cody shifted his weight and uncrossed his arms, trying to keep from saying something that would definitely not win Tonya over.

And he worked hard to avoid looking at Madison, even though he could feel her staring at him.

"Look, someone's dead now," Ollie replied. "It's more serious than that stupid reward."

"Can I get that in writing?" Tonya asked.

"If that will help you share information with us, fine," Ollie said.

Tonya's eyebrows went up as Cody barely managed to suppress a grunt of surprise. Demmy stood beside him, hands clasped behind his back as he watched the back and forth between Tonya and Ollie.

And Madison sat in an office chair a few feet to Tonya's left, her gaze fixed on Cody.

It was… Interesting. No, more like nerve wracking. She was attractive. Cody would have to be dead not to see that.

And he had enjoyed a bit of ginger now and then over the years. But where any other time he might give Madison the attention she sought, this time felt different. Demmy was here, for one. And now that he and Demmy were together, Cody felt more of a responsibility for his actions.

"Cody?"

It was Ollie's voice, and Cody blinked and looked around. The other four were all looking at him.

"Yeah, I'm here," he said.

"You sure?" Tonya asked. He saw her give Madison a steely side-eye. "Wouldn't want anyone getting distracted during this important conversation."

From the corner of his eye, Cody saw Madison look away from him and at Tonya. "What? I'm listening."

"Just making sure, honey," Tonya said with a cold smile.

"Okay, dear," Madison said.

"So, there's nothing you want to share with us?" Demmy asked. "Nothing at all."

Tonya shook her head. "Not at this time."

"Waste of time. Come on," Ollie said, and turned for the door.

Cody let Demmy follow Ollie before he turned to go himself. He stopped at the door and paused to give the office a long once over. It was a small space, even smaller than their own office back in Parson's Hollow, but it was brightly painted and had comfortable chairs for customers.

He looked from Madison to Tonya and flashed a cool smile. "Ours is bigger."

Cody could practically feel Tonya flipping him off as he let the door close behind him.

"Did you really have to instigate?" Ollie asked.

"Yes, he did," Demmy replied for him.

"Instigate? Me?" Cody tried his best to look innocent. "I was just stating a fact."

"Okay, so they're going to be no help," Demmy said, and looked at his phone. "It's six o'clock now. How about we get some food and talk about our next move?"

"That sounds good," Ollie said. "I know just the place."

THE DOWNTOWN AREA of Pinesville was almost identical to Parson's Hollow. It was so similar, in fact, Cody had to keep reminding himself he was away from home as he followed Ollie and Demmy along the sidewalk. They passed a convenience store and pharmacy that looked very much like Parson's Pharmacy in size and layout. A couple of store fronts down, they passed an Italian restaurant that could have been a replica of Antonio's back home.

"I know we're not in Parson's Hollow," Cody said, "but it sure as hell feels like we're in Parson's Hollow."

Ollie smiled at him over his shoulder. "I felt that same way when I first moved here. There are a few differences, though."

They all jumped at the sound of a long, loud car horn. A big, older model pickup truck with a few blisters of rust showing through its odd green color moved slowly down the street. Behind it crept a line of cars, looking to Cody like the angriest, most put-upon parade he'd ever seen. The driver of the middle car in line leaned out of the window, shouting, honking, and waving his fist.

They watched as the pickup truck puttered by. The driver was an old, grizzled man who smacked his lips and clutched the steering wheel with pale, bony hands.

"Holy crap," Cody said.

"You have a Widow Monroe," Demmy said. "Only he's a widower."

Ollie sighed. "Yeah. Imagine my elation at discovering the menace of the Widow Monroe had spread to Pinesville.

That's Wilbur Hartley, otherwise known as Old Man Hartley. I think he's even older than the Widow, if you can believe that."

Cody watched the truck move away in what he suspected might have just been idling speed. "Oh, I think I can believe it."

"Say what you will about the Widow Monroe," Demmy said. "But she saved our lives when she ran over Reed Wilkes."

"Didn't even put a dent in her Sherman tank of a car, either," Ollie said. "Come on. A diner a couple of blocks down serves good food."

"It's not called Margie's, is it?" Cody asked, even though he really wished that it was true. He also wished Margie herself was inside, ready with a big smile and plates of savory food.

"No." Ollie stopped to pull open a door and waved his hand beneath the diner name painted on the glass as he smiled. "Welcome to Polly's Place."

Polly's Place was nothing like Margie's. Where Margie's Diner had a counter with stools along one wall, booths along the opposite, and a few tables in the middle, Polly's Place was all booths. The booths extended along both walls and down the center of the space. The center booths allowed diners to slide onto the bright yellow vinyl benches from either side. Ollie led them to an available booth in the center of the diner. A little more out in the open than Cody would have liked, but they didn't have much choice. He sat beside Demmy and, feeling the need for connection, spread his legs wide enough so their knees touched. Demmy didn't move his leg away, so that made him feel better.

A young woman wearing an apron approached. She was tall and slender with a bright smile.

"Hey Oliver, good to see you," the woman said as she

handed out menus. She looked at Cody and Demmy. "Who's this?"

"Friends from out of town," Oliver said.

"Yeah?" Her smile widened. "Welcome to Polly's Place, handsome."

Cody smiled as he looked up from his menu. "Thanks."

"I was talking to your friend," she said, gaze fixed on Demmy.

"Who?" Demmy looked up, surprised himself. "Me?"

"Oh." Cody's face burned. Ollie laughed and just managed to avoid Cody's kick, the bastard.

"That was awesome," Ollie whispered, loud enough for all of them to hear.

Cody glared. "Okay, Ollie."

"Ollie?" The waitress smiled and looked at Oliver. "That's cute."

"Yeah, yeah," Ollie said, glaring back at Cody. "It's not my name."

"Oh, you'd better get used to it," Cody said. "I'm spreading it all over town."

"Ass," Ollie said.

"Got one, and it rocks, thanks." Cody saw the waitress tip her head as she checked it out. From her expression, at least she was impressed with that part of him.

"Can we please get some waters for now?" Demmy asked. "We'll need a little more time."

"You take all the time you want, honey. My name's Sonia if you need me. I'll come back and check on you all in a little bit. Sit tight."

She moved off, and Cody made sure to keep his cold, angry gaze fixed on Ollie's face instead of watching her walk away. Ollie stared right back and must have figured out Cody's intention, because without shifting his gaze, he said, "Looks like Cody's trying to change his ways,

Demetrius. He didn't even stare at Sonia's ass as she walked away."

Cody glared a little harder. "I think there's more than one Devil in Pinesville."

"Cute," Ollie said.

"That's enough," Demmy whispered. "Both of you."

"He started it," Cody said.

"Well I'm finishing it." Demmy groaned and put his menu up like a fortress. "You made me go into Dad mode. Ugh."

"Double ugh," Ollie said, and stuck his tongue out at Cody before looking down at his menu again, although he apparently couldn't help one last jab by saying, "Sonia's got good taste."

"Dude…" Cody started.

"Stop," Demmy said, pointing first at Ollie, then at Cody.

Cody couldn't help his grin. "Or what?"

"You going to turn this booth around?" Ollie added.

Cody had to smirk at that. Dammit.

"If I have to," Demmy said. "Now figure out what you're going to order."

"So we can tell your girlfriend what we want?" Ollie asked.

"Oliver…"

"Demetrius…."

"Oh, Demetrius?" Sonia said as she placed plastic cups filled with ice water in front of each of them. She never took her gaze off Demmy, and that sweet and slightly predatory smile never wavered. "That's a strong, masculine name."

A flash-flood of jealousy surprised Cody. He'd expected to feel a twinge of jealousy while watching Demmy interact with Ollie, but not when a woman hit on him. When Demmy blushed, he looked so damn cute Cody wished he could kiss him right there in the middle of Polly's Place. He'd put his hands on either side of his face and hit him with a deep, tongue-heavy kiss that would let Ollie, Sonia, and anyone else who might be watching know that Demmy was not available. Demmy was his and his alone.

Oh, hell.

That strong of a reaction over Demmy being on the receiving end of a simple flirtation? Cody closed his eyes as his breath caught in his chest, and his heart pounded.

This was it. This was what he'd been missing all along. All those years of dating only to break up weeks later. He'd finally found everything he'd been looking for his whole life. And he had been right beside him all these years.

Sure, Cody had known he loved Demmy. With a friendship as long as theirs, he couldn't avoid loving him. But he hadn't realized until this very fucking minute that he was *in love* with Demmy. That Demmy was everything to him, and he really needed to come out and tell him so before he fucked this up for good.

Because if Cody had learned anything from his years of dating experiences, it was that he was really, really good at fucking things up.

"You taking a nap?"

Ollie's voice burst into Cody's thoughts. "Maybe," Cody said with a snarl. "Thanks for ruining it."

"Boys..." Demmy said absently as he continued to look over the menu.

"Asshole."

"Fuckwad."

"So, who's ready to order?" Sonia still stood by the table with her pad and pen ready. She smiled at Demmy and cocked her head. "How about you, handsome?"

Demmy blushed again, and Cody had to put his hands between his knees and press his legs tight together to keep from grabbing him and pulling him into an embrace. Why couldn't he have realized all of this back in Parson's Hollow when he had had all the time in the world to sit down and talk about it?

"I'll have the grilled chicken and steamed vegetables with garlic mashed potatoes," Demmy said.

Cody smiled and looked down at his own menu. That was Demmy: raised by older parents and taught to eat a heart healthy diet from a young age.

Ollie ordered something that Cody didn't bother to listen to, and then it was his turn. He smiled up at Sonia and said, "Meatloaf and garlic mashed potatoes."

"You got it." Sonia took their menus, tipped Demmy a wink, and headed toward the kitchen.

"So, what's our next step?" Ollie asked.

"We need to find out where the majority of the most recent sightings have been happening," Demmy said. "Maybe then we can pinpoint a central location where we could find the Devil."

"I'm sure a lot of calls have gone into the police department, but I don't know anyone on the force," Ollie said.

"What about Eileen?" Cody asked. "Didn't she say she was going to introduce us to someone she knew who worked at the station?"

"Yeah, what was that name?" Demmy looked at Ollie. "Martha?"

Ollie thought a minute, his forehead creased in concentration. Then he brightened and said, "Mabel. She's an administrator at the police station. Let me call Grandma and see if she can find out any information." He looked around. "There might be some interested parties in here. I think I'll go out to the truck to call, so no one overhears me." He held out a hand. "Can I have the keys?"

Cody stared at him.

"Cody," Demmy whispered. "He's not going to drive off

and leave us." He looked over at Ollie as if suddenly second guessing himself. "Right?"

"Of course not," Ollie said. "I just want to make sure no one listens in on my conversation." His hand was palm up on the table, and he waggled his fingers impatiently. "Come on, Cody. You can't seriously think I would drive off in your truck."

The restaurant was packed with men and women in hiking clothes that looked pretty expensive. A few of the diners had camera bags on the floor by their feet. Apparently everyone else had had a long day of searching for the Devil and come to Polly's Place for a big meal.

"Fine," Cody said with a sigh as he sat back in the booth so he could slide his hand into the front pocket of his jeans. He pulled out the keys and dropped them into Ollie's hand. "Don't change the seat position. Or the mirrors. Or my radio station."

"Oh for fuck's sake." Ollie closed his hand on the keys and slid out of the booth. "I'll be right back."

"I'm going to use the restroom," Demmy said, and he was out of the booth before Cody could say a word.

"Dammit," Cody grumbled. He stared at his hands curled into fists on the table. Demmy was the answer to every question, and they might be in a much better place at the moment if he'd understood everything years ago. He didn't know if this meant he was gay or bisexual, but a label was the least of his concerns. What he needed to figure out, and pretty damn quick, too, was how and when to tell Demmy about his feelings. If he could manage it, he wanted to wait for the drive home to give them plenty of time alone to talk. He just hoped that wouldn't be too late to tell Demmy how he really, truly felt.

A rush of warmth went through him, and he smiled. He was in love. Actually *in love*. With his best friend, no less. It wasn't very original, but he didn't care about that. All that mattered was Demmy and him and their future together. Hopefully, Demmy would feel the same way.

Sonia approached the booth with plates in each hand and one balanced on her arm. Demmy was right behind her, and Cody smiled. Maybe Ollie would stay away for a few minutes, give him and Demmy some privacy.

"Hot stuff, coming in," Sonia said as she set a plate before Cody. She saw Demmy slide in beside Cody and smiled. "See? I was right."

Demmy smiled and blushed again. He was so damn easy.

Sonia set down the other two plates. "Anything else I can get for you gentlemen?'

Cody looked at Demmy when he said, "No. I think we've got everything we need."

"Enjoy." Sonia walked off.

"Smells good," Demmy said as he picked up his fork. He looked over his shoulder toward the front of the diner. "I hope Oliver gets back before his food gets cold."

"Yeah."

Cody could barely smell the food, and his appetite had shriveled up. His tongue felt huge inside his mouth. They needed to talk, but Cody had no idea where to start. It wouldn't be fair to tell Demmy how he truly felt when Ollie would just barge in on the conversation, but maybe he could allude to it somehow? Let Demmy know things were good between them, at least where Cody was concerned?

He licked his dry lips as Demmy ate a few steamed vegetables. He could do this. This was Demmy, his best friend Demmy, and he could talk to him about anything.

"We should probably talk," Cody said.

Demmy frowned at him around a mouthful of vegetables. He swallowed and asked, "Talk about what?"

"Something important."

Demmy stopped chewing and gave him a steady look. "Is this about Aunt Amelia's offer to let us live in her house?"

Hell, Cody had completely forgotten about Amelia's house. And how fucking perfect would it be to move into a house with Demmy? Live and sleep and fuck there with him. Good god, he really was in deep. "Um, well, yeah, that's part of it."

"Part of it?"

Demmy's phone buzzed where he had set it on the table. Cody clenched his jaw to restrain himself from shouting in frustration as Demmy looked down at the text message displayed on screen.

"It's from Oliver."

"What?" Cody looked over his shoulder and out the front window of the diner. His truck sat idling at the curb in front of the restaurant. "What the hell?"

"He says to get our food to go," Demmy said. "That we need to leave right now."

"Now?"

"Yeah." Demmy waved to get Sonia's attention.

"But…"

Cody sat back and crossed his arms. Sonia brought the carryout boxes, scooping the food into them as Demmy paid, leaving Sonia a generous tip that Cody figured she more than earned. What a sweet talker.

Minutes later, Cody followed Demmy out the door and into the cab of his truck, scowling as he carried their boxes of food in a plastic bag.

"Why are you driving my truck?" Cody asked with a growl as he set the bag on the floor between his feet.

"Because I know the streets better," Ollie snapped back. "Buckle up and hang on. There's some shit going down that we need to see first hand."

Before Cody could ask another question, Ollie hit the gas.

CHAPTER FIFTEEN

A hard bump jostled Demetrius against Cody.

"Sorry," Demetrius said.

"My pleasure," Cody said. "Easy on the truck, Ollie. The extended warranty doesn't cover off-roading."

Demetrius adjusted his position and sighed. Why couldn't Cody and Oliver just get along? Cody always had to call Oliver out about something.

"You're such a city boy. This isn't even close to off-roading. We're on a trail."

Then again, Oliver sometimes provoked Cody.

"Is it paved?" Cody asked with a sneer.

"All dirt, per the dust plumes behind us."

"Then we're not on a true road," Cody said. "Slow it down."

Demetrius took in Cody's profile, his tense jaw and the squint of his eyes. He'd started to bring up something back at the diner before Oliver had sent his text. It had been somehow related to Amelia's offer of her house, but he couldn't exactly ask any follow up questions right now.

But it was curious. Cody had looked so serious. And even

now Cody was tense and impatient. His demeanor might have to do with the jarring drive along the trail in his truck, especially with Oliver at the wheel, but it could also stem from whatever he'd wanted to talk about at the diner.

Another hard bump made Demetrius let out a loud, "Umph!" as insight exploded and sent tingles through him.

What if Madison looked better and more socially acceptable to Cody? Maybe the four weeks he and Cody had been together had been enough to show Cody he wasn't meant to be in a gay relationship. Amelia's offer might have been the final nail in the coffin for their relationship.

Demetrius felt a little sick, and wasn't sure if it was from the rough ride or his thoughts about Cody.

He couldn't look at Cody, not even when he put a hand on the dash and leaned forward to bark at Oliver.

"That's it! Stop the truck *right now*!"

"We're almost there!"

"NOW!"

Oliver slammed on the brakes, and the truck slid to a halt. He grumbled as he put the gear shift into park and jumped out of the door. Cody pushed the passenger door open and stepped out. Demetrius watched them sneer at each other as they passed in front of the truck. Cody got in behind the wheel and glared across Demetrius at Oliver as he adjusted the position of his seat and the mirrors.

"Oh for the love of fuck, just drive, will you?" Oliver said.

"I told you not to change the seat position."

"This is important," Oliver said. "Way more important than the position of your damn seat."

"Seat *and* mirrors," Cody said.

Oliver blew out a frustrated breath and looked out the side window.

"Come on," Demetrius said to Cody. "Let's go."

"You taking his side, Demmy?"

"I'm not taking anyone's side. But Oliver feels this is important, so I think we should respect that."

"Thank you." Oliver glared at Cody.

"Fine."

Cody started driving, much slower than Oliver had been before. "Where are we going?"

"It's a little farther up this trail," Oliver said. "A mile, maybe less."

"Another campsite?" Demetrius asked.

"It didn't sound like a campsite from what Mabel said," Oliver replied. "But she was whispering so no one would hear her telling me to come out here." He leaned forward to root through the bag of food. "Man, I'm hungry. Oh, bless Sonia. She gave us plastic cutlery."

"No eating in my truck," Cody said.

"Dude, how many rules do you have about this truck?" Oliver asked.

"So many." Cody frowned as he looked in the rearview mirror. "Someone's coming up behind us."

Demetrius turned at the same time as Oliver and found himself in very close proximity with his face. He smiled and scooted back a bit. "Sorry."

Oliver grinned. "No problem."

"Any idea who that is?"

"It's another truck," Oliver said. "Hard to see through the dust we're throwing up."

"They're coming up fast," Cody said. "Here's a turnoff, do I take it?"

"Yeah, bear left at the fork."

The road split at a dense pack of birch trees, and Cody angled off to the left. As they moved deeper into the woods, the evening was quickly giving way to night, and Demetrius wondered just how long they would be out here.

"Going to be full dark soon," he said.

"Great," Cody mumbled.

They rounded a bend, and Cody hit the brakes hard. Two big police SUVs sat just off the side of the trail. An officer stood at the front of the lead SUV and waved them forward. When Cody pulled up alongside the man, Oliver powered down his window.

"Hi officer, what's going on?"

"Just some minor police business. Drive safe now."

"Does it have anything to do with the Pinesville Devil?" Oliver asked.

The officer laughed, but Demetrius thought his humor looked strained. "You one of those out of towners trying to get rich and famous?"

"Nah, I'm Oliver Berridge. I'm Eileen Answell's grandson."

"Oh yeah, I've seen you around town." The cop grinned and shook his head. "Your grandma is a real pistol."

"That's for sure," Oliver said, grinning back. He leaned a little farther out of the window and lowered his voice. "So what's the story out here? More missing hikers?"

The officer's expression tightened. "Can't say." He waved for Cody to move along. "Have a good evening."

"Okay, officer," Cody said with a quick wave. "We're leaving. Sorry for the intrusion."

Cody drove off along the trail and Oliver put his window up.

"Dammit," Oliver said. "I bet whatever is going on back there has everything to do with the Devil."

"We weren't going to find out anything from him," Demetrius said. "But you gave it a good shot."

"How soft are the shoulders of these trails?" Cody asked.

"Guess it depends how much rain we've had. Those police trucks seemed okay parked off the trail like they were." He leaned forward and looked at Cody with wide eyes. "Are you going to pull off the road so we can get out and make our way back through the woods?"

"Oh crap," Demetrius said with a sigh as Cody smirked.

"You're not as dumb as you smell," Cody said.

"Cute."

"Lots of people think I am," Cody said. "Isn't that right, Demmy?"

"That's the word on the street," Demetrius said. He really had no idea how to respond to Cody in this situation. He didn't seem to want anyone to know they were a couple, but he kept trying to pull compliments from him.

Dammit, why was everything so complicated?

"Here, this looks like a good place." Cody eased the truck off the trail into an open spot between two big trees. He cut the engine and turned in his seat to face them. He moved in close, placing his hand on Demetrius's thigh as he leaned over and popped open the storage compartment in the dash. Demetrius breathed in Cody's familiar smell as the heat from his hand soaked into his thigh and warmed a spot low in his belly.

Dammit, Cody could get to him like no one else.

"I know there's a couple of flashlights in here somewhere," Cody muttered. "Ah, found them."

He gave Demetrius's thigh a gentle squeeze, then pushed himself upright and smiled at him. "Let there be light."

"Only two?" Oliver asked.

"That's usually how many people are in my truck," Cody said. "You can walk between us."

"Just don't run off and leave me out here."

"Would I do that?" Cody flashed a tight smile and stepped out.

"Ass," Oliver muttered.

"I won't let him leave you," Demetrius said, following Oliver out of the truck.

Cody took the lead, and Oliver fell in line behind him with Demetrius bringing up the rear. They didn't need the flashlights yet, but Demetrius knew it wouldn't be long.

They walked in silence for a time, all of them trying to be as quiet as possible. After several minutes, they heard voices through the trees, and Cody held up a hand as he came to a stop. He turned and put a finger to his lips. Demetrius and Oliver both nodded, then all three of them doubled over and slowly moved from tree to tree until they were a few yards from a small group of police officers milling about inside a small clearing.

Demetrius leaned around the side of the tree and squinted in an effort to see better through the gloomy woods. He caught bits and pieces of conversation, but none of it made much sense. Some words stuck out, like "wasted" and "vicious" and "bloody," but there was no common thread he could use to tie them all together.

He looked around and caught Cody's attention, and then he shrugged and shook his head. When he pointed at Cody, he received the same response, and Oliver mimicked him as well. None of them knew what the police were discussing.

The sound of a car alarm ripped through the quiet of the woods, the horn blasting every couple of seconds. Demetrius spun around and pressed himself against the tree. He knew the sound well because it was Cody's truck making the noise.

"What the fuck is that?"

The cops had heard it too, of course, and Demetrius's heart fluttered hard as he gripped the tree behind him. Should he run for the truck or stay out of sight? He looked over at Cody and relaxed when he made a downward motion gesture with his hand: stay put. Cody repeated the gesture to Oliver, and they all stood with their backs tight against the tree.

Heavy footsteps approached. The cops were heading

toward them through the woods, and right for Cody's truck. Shit, what were they going to do? They would get caught and put in jail for disturbing a crime scene or some other bullshit charge.

Cody waved in the quickly dimming daylight to get his attention. He made a circular motion with his finger and pointed to the tree at his back, telling him to circle around the tree as the officers passed them. Demetrius nodded and took several deep breaths to try and calm down as the officers approached. He hoped this worked. He really didn't want to go to jail.

Luck was with them, at least for the moment. The officers trampled through the undergrowth between the trees Demetrius and Cody had hidden behind. This allowed both of them to slowly circle the tree and keep out of sight as the cops moved past. Oliver was off to Cody's other side and out of the officers' sight.

Demetrius knew they would only have a few minutes to see what the cops were protecting. After that, they would have to come up with a quick story to explain why Cody's truck was parked off the trail nearby.

Cody set off at a quick jog, and Demetrius and Oliver fell in line behind him. The sun had completely set, light quickly fleeing the woods. The dimness played tricks on Demetrius's vision, making him think he saw figures moving off in the gloom, and he had to restrain himself from turning on the flashlight and shining the beam in that direction.

"Where is it?" Oliver asked in a rough whisper. "Where were they at?"

"Here, I think," Cody said, coming to a stop.

Demetrius came up beside him and looked around. He had to squint to be able to see much of anything. Nothing seemed amiss, and he frowned.

The truck alarm cut off, and the woods around them sounded suddenly very quiet.

"Oh, shit," Oliver said with a gasp, hurrying forward to crouch at the base of a tree. "Get a light over here."

Cody ran over and Demetrius followed. Putting his hand over the flashlight lens, Cody flicked it on and spread his fingers a bit to let out a small amount of light. Oliver crouched next to what appeared to be a digital video camera. It looked pretty beat up, and if Demetrius wasn't wrong, there were splashes of blood on the sides.

Oliver's eyes were wide in the muted glow of the flashlight. "I bet it was being used by one of those documentary teams."

"Looks like they got their up close and personal footage," Cody muttered.

Demetrius heard voices behind them and glanced over his shoulder. "They'll be coming back soon. What do we do?"

"I really want to see what kind of footage they got," Oliver said.

"You can't take it," Demetrius whispered. "That's evidence!"

"Three cocks among you, and all I see are pussies."

Demetrius nearly shouted at the sound of another voice. He spun around and saw two figures step out of the trees behind them. Even in the dark he had no trouble recognizing Tonya and Madison.

"What the fuck?" Cody turned and hit them with the muted beam of his flashlight. "Did you fuckers set off my truck alarm?"

Tonya grinned in the glow of light. "Welcome to the big leagues, small town."

"Pinesville is actually less populated than Parson's Hollow," Oliver said.

"Can it, Ollie," Tonya said with a sneer.

"We need to get out of here," Madison whispered. They could hear the cops returning.

Oliver grabbed the video camera and held it against his chest.

"Oliver!" Demetrius was shocked.

"I have the camera now," Oliver said with a defiant jut of his chin. "If you don't take us back to your truck and to your office to view this video footage, I'm going to run straight to those cops and hand it over."

Tonya stomped a foot and turned in a circle. "You asshole! They'll throw you in jail."

"I don't care. As long as you won't get to see the video, it'll be worth it."

Demetrius looked back the way they had come. He could see flashlight beams weaving back and forth as the cops returned.

"They're coming!" Madison whined.

"Ugh, fine!" Tonya shook a fist at them. "I'm not going to forget this. Come on. We parked back this way."

The women turned and moved off into the woods. Demetrius exchanged a quick look with Oliver and Cody before they all followed.

CHAPTER SIXTEEN

Cody would swear Tonya intentionally hit every pothole and bump in the road as she drove them back to the Critter Ridders office. He, Demmy, and Ollie all rode in the camper-covered bed of the pickup truck. Tools and equipment rattled around them and Cody's ass was sore from bouncing on the metal truck bed by the time they arrived.

Ollie clutched the video camera to his chest the entire way. He looked scared, and Cody could sympathize. He didn't like to think what was going to happen to his truck out there in the woods. At best, it would be impounded.

From the cab he heard an occasional bit of conversation between Tonya and Madison, but more often the pop and static of a police band scanner.

What felt like hours later but was probably less than thirty minutes, the truck screeched to a stop, throwing them against each other. Madison opened the back of the camper and lowered the tailgate. She flashed a tentative smile before moving out of sight.

"Here we go," Demmy whispered before he slid out of the truck.

"Come on, Ollie," Cody said. "Let's go find out what those guys saw out in the woods."

"I can't believe I stole evidence from a crime scene," Ollie whispered as he stepped down to the parking lot.

Cody squeezed his shoulder and grinned. "I may have to change my opinion of you, Ollie."

"Is that all it takes?"

"Pretty much."

"Come on, you two," Tonya called from where she held open the door to the Critter Ridders office. "Stop making goo goo eyes at each other and get your asses in here before we're all arrested."

"She's such a soft-spoken lady," Ollie said under his breath.

Cody couldn't help smirking as he followed Ollie into the office.

Ollie got busy looking at the camera while Tonya and Madison stood at the other end of the office whispering back and forth.

"Before we look at this video, I have a couple of questions I'd like answered." Demmy's voice had a hard edge to it that made Cody's eyebrows go up.

"Oh you do, do you?" Tonya crossed her arms and stared.

"Yes. First of all, have you been working with any of the other teams that have come here looking for the Devil because of the reward?"

"No, we haven't," Madison said, waving off Tonya's angry hissing. "They deserve some answers, too."

"Have you been following us?" Demmy asked.

Madison shook her head. "No."

"Then how did you happen to be at the campsite earlier today and out on the trail tonight?"

Cody answered before Madison could. "They've got a

police scanner." He looked between the two women. "That's how you've known where to be."

"That's right."

"For the love of…" Tonya stomped a foot. "I can't even with you right now. Why don't you just lie spread eagle on the desk and let him fuck you in front of all of us?"

"Why are you so jealous all the time?"

"Because men and women flock to you! Look at you! You're gorgeous!" Tonya clenched her jaw, her lips pressed into a tight line.

"Um…" Demmy said as he nervously cracked his knuckles. "Sorry. This is awkward and all, but I think Oliver is all set?"

"Almost," Ollie said, so focused on the camera's controls he totally missed Demmy's practical plea for help. He did straighten up and look over at Madison and Tonya who had turned their backs to each other. "Do you have an HDMI cable I can use to connect to one of these computer monitors?"

"In the bottom drawer," Madison said. She wouldn't look at any of them, just stared at a blank wall.

"Did you set off the alarm on Cody's truck?" Demmy asked, either not reading the mood of the room or not caring.

Tonya glared at him. "Seriously? You're still playing this game?"

"Almost done with the questions," Demmy said. "Sooner you answer, the sooner I'm done."

"Yes, I did it," Madison said. "I got on the front bumper and bounced a few times."

Cody had to admit he would've liked to have seen that, then he felt guilty about it.

"What else do you know besides what we've all seen together?" Demmy asked, then looked over at Tonya. "It's my last question."

"I'm so happy for you," Tonya said with a sneer as she

glared at Madison's back. "For you and little Miss Answer Box over there."

"We don't know anything else," Madison said with a sigh. "We think the severed arm belonged to some guy named Carl, from what we've heard on the scanner."

Demmy looked over at Cody.

"What was that look about?" Tonya took a step closer. "That name means something to you. Come on, she answered your questions. It's your turn now. Fess up."

"The night we left the Brutal Poodle—" Demmy started.

"Last night," Ollie added, leaning over the desk in order to connect a cable to the back of a monitor.

Demmy looked surprised. "Wow. You're right. Feels like a week ago. Okay, so last night after we left the Brutal Poodle, we found a guy wandering around the road in the dark. He was really out of it and kept asking if we'd seen Carl."

"Who was he?" Madison asked.

"His name was Henry," Ollie said. "He has needle tracks in both arms."

"Like that arm in the tent," Tonya said.

"There's been a lot of heroin overdoses in this area since the beginning of the year," Madison said. "The police have had to create a task force dedicated just to that. They have no idea how the stuff is getting into town."

"From what I hear, overdoses are swamping the hospital, too," Ollie said.

"We have a friend who's a nurse in the ER," Tonya said as she nodded. "She's told us some pretty awful stories."

"So is all of this somehow related to the recent bump in sightings of the Pinesville Devil?" Demmy asked, looking between Tonya and Madison and Ollie. "Or is it just a coincidence?"

"The Devil of Pinesville," Ollie corrected in an absent-minded sounding voice.

"When did these sightings really start ramping up?" Cody asked.

"February, I think," Ollie said. He sat in the desk chair and waved toward the monitor. "This is all set, if we're ready to view it."

Tonya and Madison crossed the small office and stood a few feet apart, one to either side of Ollie. Cody shared a glance with Demmy before they stood between the two women. Cody made sure he let Demmy stand next to Madison.

"Let's see it," Cody said.

Ollie hit a button on the camera and images appeared on the monitor. Slow pans of the woods at some point during the early afternoon, gauging by the sunlight.

"Is there sound?" Demmy asked.

"Hit the power button on that speaker to your right," Madison said.

Ollie pressed the button and the sounds of the woods filled the room: birds chirping, wind in the trees, insects buzzing, and the sound of footsteps as the cameraperson moved slowly along a narrow footpath.

"That looks like the trail we took to the campsite," Cody said.

"Maybe," Ollie said. "But there are a lot of trails out there. Could be any one of them."

They watched in silence as more footage of woods came and went, with cuts in between. Finally, one shot showed a group of people, two women and three men all dressed in black with bright orange vests over their clothing. Each of them carried a variety of equipment. They were smiling and laughing and joking with one another, and Cody felt a little sick as he considered the fact that all of them might now be dead.

"Where are we going next?" the cameraman asked the group.

One of the women looked at the camera. "Come on, Don. Haven't you shot enough footage of us? Save some battery for the Devil."

"I have six spare batteries in my bag," Don said. "You're the navigator, Karen. Where are we going next?"

Karen pointed down the path. "Based on Ray's interviews in town, we're heading to one of the campsites deeper in the forest." She paused in the middle of searching for something in her backpack to look up at the camera. "I don't remember the name." Karen looked over her shoulder. "Ray!"

A young kid with a light scruff of beard spun around, a big smile on his face. "Yeah?"

"What's the name of the place we're hiking to?" Karen asked.

"Mariner's Ridge," Ray said as he loped across the grass and stood a few feet in front of the camera. He stared into the lens and widened his eyes as he said in a spooky voice, "We're going to Mariner's Ridge because everyone who's camped there in the past six months has heard or seen things they can't explain. Mwahahahah." He opened his mouth wide and moved in close so it looked like he was going to swallow the camera.

"Gross, Ray," Don the cameraman said, and the picture went black.

Demmy smirked at Cody. "I think you and Ray would get along great."

"Me, too."

Tonya muttered something under her breath that sounded suspiciously like, "Adolescents," but Cody couldn't be sure. Before he could ask her to repeat herself a little louder for the class, the video switched scenes. It was more deep woods, but late in the day based on the weaker daylight. A large vehicle rested in the middle of a stand of trees. Vines and moss had grown over it, and the sides were dirty and stained green from years of exposure.

"What is that?" Demmy asked, leaning in and squinting at the monitor.

"It looks like a trailer," Ollie said. "Like a camping trailer you tow behind a truck."

Demmy had moved close enough for his face to be right alongside Ollie's. If they turned to look at each other, they would almost be kissing. Cody suddenly realized his left hand had curled into a fist, and he forced his fingers to relax.

Fucking Ollie.

"Oh. Weird." Demmy straightened up again and Cody was able to focus on the video. "Who would just leave a trailer out in the woods?"

Like an echo, someone off camera said, "Who would leave a trailer out here in the woods?"

"Pretty fucking creepy," Don said as he panned the camera in a slow three-sixty. The five others in his group all stood close to each other. They looked nervous and creeped out, and, Cody thought, for good reason. That trailer resembled a crime scene from a horror movie.

"Who's going to knock and see if anyone's home?" Don asked as he focused on the group again.

"I'm not going near that thing," Karen said, her arms crossed tight over her chest. "I got us to this point. Sticking my head into a haunted camper is not on my bucket list."

"You haven't gotten us to Mariner's Ridge yet," Ray said without taking his eyes off the trailer. "We're about a mile out from there."

"Come on," one of the other men said. "We're wasting daylight. Let's turn away from the spooky trailer and get to Mariner's Ridge. We'll get a fire going and make camp like we'd planned."

Cody looked at Tonya and Madison. "Have you been out to Mariner's Ridge yet?"

Madison shook her head. "No. We haven't even thought of it, actually. Well, I haven't anyway. Have you, Tonya?"

Tonya didn't take her gaze from the monitor as she shook her head. "No. We never heard about any sightings out that far."

"Any way to see how long ago this video was made?" Cody asked, looking at Ollie who sat staring at the monitor. "Ollie?"

He looked up, blinking. "Huh? Oh, the date? Um, there's usually a date and time stamp. I would have to check."

"What are you thinking?" Demmy asked.

Cody shook his head as he looked back at the monitor. "Not sure yet."

The video had changed again. Apparently, Don had placed the camera on a tripod, because six people stood in view. Don stood a few inches taller than the others and had a stocky build. His dark beard hung down to his chest and a black knit hat covered what appeared to be a shaved head. A campfire flickered and crackled between the team and the camera, providing illumination, and a couple of tents were visible off to either side.

"We've made camp here at Mariner's Ridge," Don said to the camera. "It's pretty damn cold out tonight. Forecast is calling for frost, which is a bit of a surprise. Luckily we all brought more than enough socks, right guys?"

"Get on with it, Don," said the man who had encouraged the team to keep walking back at the trailer. "Stop messing around."

Don smiled in the camera's direction. "Ned is a little overtired because he missed his afternoon nap." Ned ignored him, and Don continued. "Like I said, we're getting ready to eat some dinner. We'll set up some night vision trail cameras with motion sensor activation around the camp, and I'll have this camera with me at all times." He gave Ned a pointed look. "And not for pornographic reasons."

"Gross, Don," Karen said. "Come on, let's eat."

Don pointed a remote control at the camera, and the scene ended. A blip of static flashed across the monitor, before a close up of Don's wide-eyed face within a green glow filled the screen.

"Night vision," Ollie said.

"We're hearing something outside the tent," Don said in a whisper. "There have been sounds deeper in the woods for a while now. Not sure what they were, but they sounded like—"

An explosion of sound and shaking images made them all jump. The tent wall behind Don tore away and high-pitched screams blared through the tiny computer speaker. Ollie hurriedly turned down the volume as they all stared at the monitor.

The camera swung back and forth, the night vision casting the world into an eerie green glow. Trees rushed by as the picture spun back and forth. Nearby someone was screaming. The camera spun and spun, and the picture changed from tree trunks to branches and leaves. Crashing sounds and a grunt of pain interrupted the screams.

"God, no! God, no! Help me!" Don's screams off camera heightened in pitch and fear.

"Jesus," Madison whispered.

"Karen! Ned! Help m—"

Don's voice cut off as the camera whirled in a slow circle, showing a narrow trail cutting through the forest dozens of feet below in that weird green glow. At a certain spot in the rotation, near the top edge of the monitor, Cody could see what looked like the remains of a tent. He didn't see any sign of the others who had been with Don, and he didn't hear a sound, not even crickets or frogs.

Then a long, deep, rumbling growl sent gooseflesh up Cody's arms. A loud *crack* he told himself wasn't the breaking of bone sounded just before the camera fell to the ground. The lens was pointed into a clump of ferns, and something dark and thick Cody told himself definitely was *not* blood dripped onto the leaves.

"Fuck me," Tonya said.

Ollie reached for the camera to stop the playback, but then footsteps came through the speakers.

"Here," a woman whispered. "Look. His camera. But where's Don?"

Someone lifted the camera, its lens pointed at the ground.

"Is that blood?" a man asked, his voice low.

"Jesus," the woman said. "I think it is. How do you turn this thing off?"

"What is that?" the man asked.

"Where?"

"Up in the tree above us. Right up there."

The woman aimed the camera up along the thick trunk of a tree. The auto focus blurred the glowing green images as it worked to find a focal point. After several tense seconds, the image sharpened. Two glowing eyes stared down into the camera from a shelter of leaves.

"What is that?"

"Run!" the man shouted.

Another minute of footage of trees passing by while the woman panted for breath and shouted for help until the picture went black.

They all looked at each other in silence for a long moment.

"We have to give this camera to the police," Ollie said.

"Enjoy jail," Tonya said, tipping her head toward Madison. "We're going to Mariner's Ridge."

"What?" Demmy asked, his voice in that octave range that meant he was about to lose it.

"That thing is out there," Tonya said as she stomped across the office to a set of lockers in a corner. "We're sitting here wasting time when we could be collecting $250,000."

"We just saw that thing kill at least one person," Demmy said. "And you want to go out and find it?"

"Damn right I do."

"What about Meghan?"

Madison's voice was quiet but firm as she stared at the back of Tonya's head. Tonya had gone very still, facing the locker.

"Who's Meghan?" Demmy asked.

"No one," Tonya said, shooting Madison a withering look over her shoulder. "She's no one."

"She's Tonya's half sister." Madison stared at Tonya. "And she's a reserve police officer."

"Shut your damn mouth."

"You've heard the police scanner going off all night," Madison said. "You know they probably called in the reserves to help out. With her forensic training it makes sense she would be out in the woods at the crime scene. We could turn over the camera without any issue. Maybe get some information."

"No." Tonya's voice was hard.

"It's a good plan," Ollie said, looking hopefully at each of them. "I especially like handing off the evidence without any issue. Like no jail issues."

"I said no."

"What's the deal with them?" Cody asked Madison. "Tonya and Meghan?"

"There's a lot of history there. Tonya, it's the best possible course of action. You know I'm right."

Tonya sighed and lowered her head. "Damn you, Madison."

"I know," Madison said in a quiet voice. Her small smile signaled to Cody the storm between the two women might have passed. For now.

"Fine. I'll call Meghan. But I'm going out there locked and loaded." Tonya turned away from the locker, and Cody's eyebrows went up when he saw she held a pump action shot-gun. "And I intend to bring that motherfucker down and have it stuffed so I can put it in the corner of this office. Because we're the Critter Ridders, and that is one big fucking critter this city needs to be rid of."

CHAPTER SEVENTEEN

Demetrius was surprised at the difference between Tonya and Meghan. Where Tonya was broad-shouldered with a plain face and wide hips, Meghan was slender and beautiful, her light brunette hair pulled back into a ponytail that stuck out of the back of the bright orange hat she wore with RESERVE across the front. She frowned at Tonya as she grabbed the video camera.

"You were the ones who took this from the scene?" Meghan looked over Tonya's shoulder at Madison. "I would have expected better from two small business owners in town."

"Can the holier than thou stuff, Meg," Tonya said. "We brought it back, didn't we?"

"After you contaminated it with fingerprints and who knows what else."

"Oh hell, come on. We didn't film some porno with it or anything," Tonya said. "Jesus God."

Meghan took a step closer. "Toni, this could be a very serious charge."

"Just let us go out to Mariner's Ridge and look around,"

Tonya said. "Okay? After that, we'll come back in and clear all of this up at the station. All right?"

"What do you think is out there?"

"We won't know that until we get there and look around, will we?"

Demetrius had a feeling it was the wrong tactic, and Meghan proved him correct seconds later.

"I'm going with you."

Tonya blinked. "What?"

"Yes. If you're bound and determined to go out there, then I'm going along to ensure you go directly to the station once you're finished."

A police officer strode up and shined a flashlight in all of their faces. "What's going on over here?"

"Talking with my sister, lieutenant," Meghan replied.

The lieutenant directed his flashlight at the video camera in her gloved hand. "What's that you're holding, reserve officer?"

"A video camera, sir," Meghan said. "It was… It was found off the trail near the scene."

"Found?" He flipped the light up into Tonya's face. "By whom?"

Demetrius and apparently everyone else couldn't help looking at Oliver. When the lieutenant shone the flashlight in Oliver's face, his eyes were wide and his skin pale.

"Where did you find this camera?"

"Out… out in the woods there. Near a tree."

"Did you see any officers out there?"

"Not when I found it, no sir," Oliver said, and Demetrius had to give him that one. Technically, it wasn't a lie.

"Did you view the footage on this camera?"

"I looked through it, yes. I wanted to try and figure out who it belonged to."

"And did you figure it out?"

"I don't know any of the people in the footage."

"Fine." The lieutenant looked at Meghan. "Process the camera as part of the scene. Take all of these people back to the station to be printed so we can tell their fingerprints from any others on the camera." He moved the light from one to the other of their faces. "Would one of you be Cody Duran Bower?"

Demetrius tried to keep from gasping. Cody managed to look completely calm as he said, "Yeah, I am."

"Duran?" Tonya said with a thick chuckle. "What the hell?"

"You leave your truck out on the trail earlier?" The lieutenant had stepped close to Cody and directed the flashlight beam at his face.

"I did," Cody said as he squinted against the glare. "Could you lower that a bit, please? Thank you." Cody blinked a few times before he continued. "We were out driving around and had a bit of engine trouble."

"You sure about that?" the lieutenant asked.

"With that truck? Yeah, I'm sure."

"Started right up when we looked in the cab. You left your keys in the ignition."

Cody shrugged and gave the man his best "aw shucks" grin. "Guess I'm just a trusting country boy. Crazy that it started right up for you."

The lieutenant didn't look amused. "Yeah, crazy. And you're kind of far from home, according to the registration we found in your glove compartment. I'm assuming you have some ID?"

Cody pulled out his wallet and showed the lieutenant his driver license.

"All right. The truck's on the trail. You're lucky we haven't called for a tow truck yet or you'd be out five hundred dollars."

"I appreciate that, sir," Cody said in a respectful tone

Demetrius knew signaled a bit of a rant once they were alone. "Is it all right for me to go get my truck now?"

The lieutenant waved him off. "Fine. But don't go driving deeper into the woods. I want you to turn around and follow them to the station to be printed. Then you're to return to your residence for the rest of the night. Understood?"

"Yes, sir," Cody said.

The lieutenant blasted each of them with the flashlight once again. "That goes for every one of you. I don't want to find any of you back out in the woods tonight. Once you're done at the station, go home. Let the police look through the woods for those who are missing."

Demetrius exchanged a look with Cody. Was the video team simply missing, or worse? He wondered what the police would think when they saw the video on the camera. More than likely they would go out to Mariner's Ridge. But would they go right away or wait until daylight?

Either way, it was best they had handed over the camera, and the investigation was now in the hands of the police. Letting them handle the situation from here would be the right thing to do.

They all murmured some form of agreement for the lieutenant.

"Come on, Demmy," Cody said, turning toward the trail.

Demetrius set off after Cody, and Oliver followed along. Cody got into the driver's seat of the truck, and Demetrius slid in first on the passenger side, sitting between him and Oliver. Cody cursed then reached down for the seat adjustment as he glared at Oliver.

"Whatever asshole started my truck has shorter legs than Ollie."

"That's too bad," Oliver said with absolutely no sympathy in his voice.

Cody started the truck and took a few tries to get turned

around on the trail, grumbling the entire time. As he followed Tonya back into town, they were all silent. Demetrius kept replaying the video in his mind as they bounced along the dirt trail. Once Cody pulled off the trail onto the two lane blacktop, he figured they should talk about their next steps.

"We're not going back out in the woods tonight, right?" Demetrius looked between the two men, suddenly realizing he was seated in a truck between two men with whom he'd had sex. He had never been in that position before, and he wasn't sure what to think of it now.

Strange days.

"Do you remember the swamp?" Cody asked.

"Very clearly," Demetrius said. "Which is why I'm making sure no one has any ideas of trying to find Mariner's Ridge in the dark."

Oliver sighed. "I'm not planning on it. But I can't say what Tonya and Madison will do."

"That's their business," Cody said. He shot a dirty look Oliver's way. "Now my fingerprints are going to be on file with the police, thanks to you."

"Hey, we got to see the video footage, didn't we?" Oliver shot back.

"And what good does that do us besides give us nightmares?"

"Now we know there is definitely something out there," Oliver said. "Something big enough to lift a full grown man up into a tree and… And kill him."

Demetrius saw Oliver's Adam's apple work as he swallowed hard. He laid a hand on Oliver's arm and gave him a gentle squeeze.

"Still shouldn't have taken the camera," Cody said.

Demetrius saw Cody noticed him touching Oliver's arm, and he pulled his hand away. How did things get so damn complicated?

"Every other police station in the country has gone digital," Cody said over the sound of running water. "But not Pinesville, New Jersey. Nope. Still using ink pads and card stock for their fingerprints."

Demetrius lay on his bed in the loft with his hands behind his head. He stared at the slats of the barn roof as he half-listened to Cody's griping. The other half of his brain kept replaying the images on the video and the panic in Don's voice as he was carried up into the trees, followed by the sharp crack of bone. How awful. He couldn't imagine what that had been like for the man, though he and Cody both had come close a few times now.

Maybe this animal control business hadn't been the best idea.

"Hey."

Demetrius looked over to where Cody leaned out of the bathroom doorway. "Yeah?"

"I need some help in here." He disappeared once again.

Demetrius pushed up from the bed. "Is this some trick to get sex? I know I said we'd do it later, but after what we saw in that video—"

The words died in Demetrius's throat as he stepped into the doorway of the bathroom. His eyes widened. "What did you do?"

Water sprayed up into the air from the empty hole in the sink where the hot water faucet used to sit. Cody repeatedly tried to put his hands over the fountain of water, but pulled away with a yelp each time. Demetrius could feel the heat coming off the fountain of water from where he stood.

"What happened?" he shouted.

"The faucet just came off in my hand! Ow! Motherfucker!"

"What in all that's holy and good is going on up here?"

Eileen hurried up the steps to the loft, her small feet splashing in the shallow waterfall.

"The hot water faucet came off," Demetrius said.

"That damn thing." Eileen shoved past Demetrius and dropped to her knees in the pooling water. She reached under the sink and twisted the shut off valve until the water stopped.

Cody stood with his back pressed against the linoleum-covered wall, his hair plastered to his skull and his clothes soaked. His eyes were wide, and he held his hands palms up as he looked at Demetrius.

"All I did was try to shut it off," Cody said. "I swear."

Eileen grunted as she used the sink to pull herself to her feet. "It's been wonky since we added the bathroom. Going to have to shut off the water out here. You're welcome to come stay in the house for the night. We've got sleeping bags and foam pads you can use to bed down in the living room."

"That's probably a good idea," Demetrius said. "Once Cody dries off."

Eileen looked him up and down. "You're just as big soaking wet as you are when you're dry. Grab your things and follow me. I've got plenty of towels and a hair dryer that probably won't short out the whole house."

"All I did was turn the faucet off," Cody said as he plodded through the water that had pooled on the linoleum flooring.

"Should I mop up the water on the floor?" Demetrius asked.

Eileen waved a hand. "I had it designed with this possibility in mind. The water will drain down into the barn in no time. Come to the house when you're ready." She descended the steps out of sight.

Demetrius stepped back to allow Cody to move past, leaving wet footprints.

"Did you get burned from the water?" Demetrius asked.

"No, it's not bad. I'm just wet and now I feel cold."

"Let me check and see if there are dry towels."

Demetrius walked into the bathroom and looked in the open shelves of the linen cupboard. The water had sprayed everything, none of the towels had escaped. He leaned out of the bathroom doorway and started to explain the situation to Cody, but the words stopped in his throat as he watched Cody push his wet jeans down his legs. He wore his purple briefs that always made Demetrius smile, and the wet material clung to his cock and balls.

At moments like this, just the sight of Cody took Demetrius's breath away. Amazement and, if he were honest, a small slice of fear went through him at these times. It amazed him Cody had wanted to take their friendship to a physical relationship, but it frightened him a bit as well. He was in over his head with Cody, he knew it. He tried to keep his heart in check about the reality of the situation and the possibility that the relationship could end at any time, but if Cody was anything, he was intoxicating.

And how many women had been through this before Cody had turned to him? Other than the obvious physical differences, what made Demetrius think he could keep Cody's interest for a longer period of time?

"Any towels in there?"

Cody's question brought Demetrius out of his thoughts, and he shook his head and shrugged. "None of them escaped."

"Stupid cheap ass plumbing hack job." He hooked his fingers beneath the waistband of his briefs and slid them off.

Demetrius stared a moment, taking in the sight of Cody's soft cock, an unusual condition for it. Then he forced himself to look away to begin packing up his own things as Cody pulled the sheet off his bed and used it to dry himself.

"How do I look?"

Demetrius couldn't help grinning. Cody stood with the sheet wrapped around him toga style, hands on his hips and his head turned in profile as he looked stoically off into the distance.

"Very Roman."

"Yeah, well, let's hope the plumbing in the house is of a better quality." Cody dried himself a little more with the sheet before tossing it aside and pulling on a pair of sweats and a button down flannel shirt.

When they'd both packed up their duffel bags, they headed to the house. Oliver was laying out the foam pads on the floor by the fireplace, and Eileen tromped down the steps with a rolled up sleeping bag under each arm.

"Cody, you go get a warm shower in the bathroom off the kitchen," Eileen said. "The hair dryer is in there under the vanity. We'll set up the sleeping bags."

"Sorry I broke the faucet," Cody said with a sheepish shrug.

"My cousin Blake did the same thing two years ago," Oliver said. "It happens."

"I'm going to give that plumber scam artist Sol Jeffries a stern talking to," Eileen said as she unrolled a sleeping bag. "You just get yourself cleaned up and we'll all bunk down for the night."

Demetrius checked the time on his phone and was surprised to find it was almost ten-thirty. The whole evening had been a blur.

"We'll get up early tomorrow and head out to Mariner's Ridge," Eileen said.

"We?" Oliver asked. "What makes you think you're going with us?"

Eileen's eyebrows shot so far up her forehead, Demetrius thought she might topple over backward. "I don't think I'm going with you, I *know* I'm going with you. And if you know what's good for you, you won't give me any guff about it."

"It might be—"

"Dangerous?" Eileen huffed. "Who in this room has seen the Devil in person?" She raised her hand and shifted a challenging look back and forth between Demetrius and Oliver. "You got anything else to say about it?"

Oliver sighed. "No."

"That's right, you don't. And don't try to set out early in the morning and leave me behind. I can change a lock faster than those clowns at McMurtry Safe and Secure." She stared at Oliver until he held up his hands in surrender.

"Fine, you're going," Oliver said.

Eileen gave a single nod before turning away and stomping up the steps and out of sight.

Demetrius stared at Oliver. "Wow. She's a powerhouse."

"You have no idea."

Cody emerged from the bathroom in a cloud of steam. He wore his sweats and flannel shirt and had a towel around his neck, the end of which he used to rub his wet hair.

"What time should we plan to leave tomorrow morning?" Oliver asked.

"I'd like to set out as early as possible." Demetrius looked at Cody. "Can you be up and ready to leave by six?"

"In the morning?"

Demetrius sighed and looked at Oliver. "Let's try for six."

"But anticipate seven?" Oliver grinned and nodded. "See you in the morning."

As they got ready to go to sleep, Cody grumbled about getting up early and faulty plumbing and New Jersey in general. Demetrius ignored him for the most part, and was already zipped into his sleeping bag and yawning when Cody sat down and pushed his feet into his own sleeping bag. He stopped and made a face, then leaned down to sniff at the sleeping bag.

"Think they washed these after the last forty people used them?" Cody asked.

Demetrius sniffed at his own sleeping bag. "Mine smells fine. You're pretty cantankerous today."

"Must be my blue balls."

Demetrius smirked and felt comforted a bit by the statement. "Well save some of that feistiness for tomorrow and the Devil."

"I doubt even the Devil will be up at six in the morning."

"All the better to surprise it, don't you think?"

Cody slid into the sleeping bag and laid down. He changed position several times as the fire crackled and popped. The last thing Demetrius heard before he nodded off was Cody muttering, "I know we're going to get bed bugs from these sleeping bags."

CHAPTER EIGHTEEN

Cody parked his truck on the side of the two lane dirt road and hid the keys under the driver's seat. "Just in case I'm not part of the return group, the keys are right here."

"That's an optimistic outlook," Eileen said.

"My optimism tank is usually pretty dry this early in the morning."

"Does it ever get above an eighth of a tank?" Ollie asked.

Cody glared. "It used to."

"Okay boys," Demmy said. "Let's save the testosterone for the Devil."

"I thought I had," Cody said, giving Ollie a cool smile.

"Wasn't really funny the first time," Ollie said. "And now it just sounds like a desperate attempt to recycle old jokes."

"And we're off!" Demmy headed toward the foot trail at a quick pace, and Eileen fell in behind him.

"If I didn't know better," Ollie said as he adjusted the camera bag strap over his shoulder, "I'd say you were acting even more possessive of Demetrius than usual."

"Yeah? Well, maybe you really don't know better."

Ollie frowned as he thought about it. "What?"

Cody gave him a gentle push toward the trail. "Just get hiking."

"Don't look at my ass," Ollie said over his shoulder as he hurried off into the trees.

"Don't worry," Cody called after him.

He thought about what Ollie had said as he hiked after the rest of the group. He'd had that realization back in Polly's Place about being in love with Demmy, but what did that mean for them in the world at large? How was he supposed to express what he felt when no one knew they'd even been dating? And he did have to admit he was a bit jealous. But he wasn't overly possessive. He didn't love seeing how comfortable Demmy felt around Ollie, and he sure as hell didn't want to think about the two of them having sex. But was he going too far? Would his jealousy turn Demmy off and push him away?

He was so absorbed by his thoughts, he hadn't realized the others had halted until he almost walked right into Ollie.

They had come to the trailer. It was much creepier in person than on video. They all stood on the trail and stared at the metal hulk, crouching under low hanging branches on flattened tires that were faded and cracked. The once white sides were stained from years of exposure, and moss and vines grew on and around it. The windows were caked with dirt, making it impossible to see inside.

"That's not creepy at all," Cody whispered.

"It's like the setting of every Stephen King novel rolled into one," Ollie said.

"You boys are a bunch of scaredy-cats," Eileen said. "It's just an old camping trailer."

She stepped off the trail and marched through the ferns and heavy layer of fallen leaves.

"Grandma, wait!" Ollie hurried after her.

"She's got guts," Demmy said in a low voice.

"Yeah, and I'm afraid they're about to end up on the ground," Cody said.

"Come on."

Demmy struck out after Eileen and Ollie. Cody took a breath and let it out before he followed. They cautiously stepped through the long grass along the side of the trail and approached the trailer. Eileen led the way, and Cody walked around Demmy and Ollie to the front.

"Everyone stand back," he said and reached out to slip his fingers beneath the flip latch of the trailer's door. After a moment of hesitation, he popped the latch and the door swung open with a squeal of rusted hinges that sent a chill through him.

"Well, now that the gratuitous creaky door effect is out of the way," Ollie said with a dry, humorless laugh.

Cody stuck his head inside and looked around. The interior was heavily shadowed and details were hard to make out, but it looked like a standard camping trailer. Just super creepy and possibly haunted.

"Looks okay," he said. "I'll go in." He looked over his shoulder. "Demmy, you come, too. Ollie and Eileen wait out here for our signal."

Ollie looked irritated. "Why do you get to go inside?"

Cody took a step back and waved toward the open door. "If you'd like to go inside, be my guest."

Ollie straightened his spine, grabbed a small video camera from his bag, switched on a small light set just above the lens, and stepped past Cody into the trailer.

"Stand back," Eileen said, following after Ollie.

"Oh for fuck's sake," Demmy said as he climbed inside after her.

"Well, I guess we all rush inside and die together," Cody muttered to himself, following Demmy.

Ollie and Eileen moved deeper into the gloomy interior. A

table surrounded by bench seating sat in shadows to their right, just in front of a short counter with cabinets underneath. Ollie shone his light over a gas powered cooktop and a small refrigerator. Beyond Ollie, right near the back wall, a hole in the roof allowed in a bright shaft of light. But the glow didn't spread very far as branches and vines had grown through the opening and took up much of the space.

"Something busted through the roof up there," Ollie said, his voice low.

Cody inspected the hole and saw that the edges were ragged and pushed in as though something had pounded its way inside.

"What is this?"

Demmy had opened one of the cupboard doors. Plastic wrapped bricks of a dark-colored material were stacked inside. Ollie moved up beside Demmy and shone his camera light inside.

"Don't touch it," Cody said. "Step back from it."

Demmy jerked a hand back and looked at him. "What is it?"

"Heroin."

"What?" Ollie, Eileen, and Demmy all said together.

Ollie moved his camera in closer and slowly panned the bricks.

"Heroin?" Demmy moved back to stand beside him, and Cody resisted the urge to put a protective arm around his shoulders.

"This is where they've been selling it," Eileen said. "This is how they've avoided the police."

"How'd they get a damn trailer out this far?" Ollie asked.

"It's been here for a while from the looks of it," Cody said. "They could have towed it along the footpath some night. It looked wide enough as we hiked up here."

"But—" Demmy started, then cut himself off as he looked toward the back of the trailer. "Is that blood?"

"Where?" Ollie shined his camera light in that direction. "I don't see it."

"Past the hole in the ceiling," Demmy said. "Against the back wall, beneath the busted window."

They moved as a group past the branches and leaves that dangled through the hole in the roof. To the right the sliding door of a tiny bathroom stood open. Seated on the lid of a chemical toilet was the body of a man. He was thin and pale, and the body had been there at least a few days, Cody guessed. Flies buzzed around him, the sound making Cody feel frantic and closed in.

"Shit twice and cry Jesus!" Eileen exclaimed as Ollie's light revealed the corpse's gaping mouth and wide eyes.

"I wonder if that's Carl," Demmy said.

Cody couldn't pull his eyes from the body, and he had no idea who Demmy was talking about. "Carl?"

"Wasn't that the name being repeated by that guy Ollie almost ran over the other night?" Demmy asked.

"I did not almost run over him!"

"I'm not checking him for a wallet," Cody said. "He's still got both arms, so he wasn't in the tent."

"I need some air."

Eileen moved past them and stepped down out of the trailer.

"I think she's got the right idea," Cody said. "Come on."

He was surprised when Demmy and Ollie both followed him outside. Cody took several deep breaths of fresh air before he looked over at Demmy.

"Now what?"

"I want to look around this area," Ollie said. "I want to try and find out what busted through that roof and what it wanted."

"Might I suggest the life of that guy inside the bathroom?" Cody said.

Ollie ignored him, picked up his camera bag, and headed for the rear of the trailer. Eileen and Demmy followed.

"Just another walk in the woods," Cody said to himself, bringing up the rear.

As he rounded the back of the trailer, Cody stopped to stare. The large window in the rear of the vehicle had been broken, and bits of glass littered the ground. A dark trail of dried blood led off into the woods, protected from rain by the heavy canopy of colored leaves overhead.

"Someone busted out of there in a hurry," Eileen said.

"Or something," Cody said.

"This way." Ollie set off along the diminishing trail of blood that disappeared into the trees, recording every step with his camera.

As Cody followed the others, he noted blood splashes on ferns and leaves, along with claw marks across a few of trees. He was about to suggest they turn back when the path opened from the claustrophobic trees into a small clearing at the base of a rocky slope. A number of tall pine trees grew up along the slope, the air spiked with their juniper scent.

"A small opening there in the rocks," Ollie said, as he hurried out into the clearing.

"Oliver!" Demmy called after him. "Wait a minute!"

Everything happened fast after that.

A loud, shrieking roar stopped them all in their tracks.

The branches of one of the larger pines shook and rattled as they were pushed aside, and the Devil moved out from beneath the umbrella of pine needles into view.

Cody forgot to breathe as he stared. It was perfectly

camouflaged to hide in the woods, its leathery skin a mottled brownish green. Standing at least eight feet tall, it had folded its large wings against its strong back. Heavily muscled arms and legs ended in claw-tipped fingers. The head was shaped like a goat's, with a heavy brow and a jutting jaw filled with sharp teeth. A long tail curled around its feet, the tip twitching and skimming across dead leaves as the Devil fixed its black eyes on Ollie.

"Ollie," Demmy whispered, and started to go forward.

Cody reached out to grab his arm. "No! Stay still."

"Oliver," Eileen said. "Don't move."

Ollie held his video camera up, recording the Devil as it stared at him. "I can't believe it. Look at it. I can't believe it. Holy shit."

The Devil pushed off the ground and unfurled its wings. Shaped like a bat's, they were ten feet across and easily lifted the monster into a hovering pattern several feet off the ground. Leaves, pine needles, and dust fluttered out from its down draft. It glared down at Ollie and Eileen, parting its black lips and letting out an angry shriek-roar.

Cody was frozen in place, unable to move. The rest of the group stood similarly transfixed, staring at the monster hovering above them. Cody's brain kept trying to make sense of the thing he was looking at. How had it come into being? How old was it? He had felt much the same way about the swamp monster when he'd first seen it down in Florida, and he still didn't seem to have the capacity to process the sight before him.

The Devil leaned forward and angled its wings to swoop in toward them.

"Down!" Cody shouted, pulling Demmy to the ground beside him. He ducked his head and shielded Demmy as best he could.

Ollie screamed, and the piercing terror of it made Cody

look up.

The Devil had Ollie by one arm and was lifting him up into the air. He kicked his feet and swatted at the Devil's claw with his free hand, but the monster lifted him even higher into the air, heading up over the slope.

"Oliver!" Eileen ran after the Devil, reaching up in a vain attempt to grab one of Ollie's feet kicking several feet above her head.

"No!" Demmy was up and out of Cody's grasp before he knew it, running after Ollie.

"Fuckin' monsters," Cody muttered, and he took off after Demmy.

"Grab him, Cody!" Demmy shouted at him over his shoulder. "You're taller."

"I'll tr—" Cody started to shout back but never finished as the ground went out from under him.

He closed his eyes as he fell. Dirt and rock scraped his palms and a sharp outcropping tore a gash in the seat of his jeans as he skidded down a long slope into darkness. He came to rest on a shallow ledge, one leg canted at an angle. His back pressed against something heavy with a bit of give to it. A bout of coughing hit him as dust slowly settled, and he blinked to clear his eyes.

He'd fallen right into the mouth of the cave they'd seen in the rocky hill. Well, wasn't that just fucking perfect? At least he wasn't seriously injured, but how in the almighty hell was he going to get out of this place?

"Cody!"

Demmy's voice echoed down from above.

"Here," Cody said, then coughed some of the dust and dirt from his throat before shouting louder, "Down here!"

He listened to some shouted back and forth that drifted down into the cave, which made it sound as if the Devil had released Ollie, and he had landed safely on the ground. Cody braced himself better, planting his feet flat on the rocky slope and pressing his back against the rock behind him. The ground beneath him sloped off into darkness and who knew how deep of a hole. He really didn't want to find that out.

The rock he leaned against shifted a bit, and just as he was turning to try and see behind him, a shadow passed through the shaft of sunlight that came in from the mouth of the cave. Small rocks rattled down the slope past him, and a thin line of dirt slithered around his foot.

"Cody?" Demmy's voice echoed around the rock walls.

"Yeah, I'm here. Stepped right into the cave and slid down inside."

"Oh, shit. Are you hurt?"

"Scraped up a bit, but otherwise okay." He altered his position, and the rock behind him shifted again. "I'm about twenty feet down from the mouth of the cave. Not really secure, but not going any deeper. Yet."

"Hold still, we'll get some rope from the truck."

"We have rope in the truck?"

"I put rope in both of our trucks. Just stay still, and we'll be right back."

"Where's the Devil? And how's Ollie?" Cody shouted.

"The Devil dropped him and took off into the trees."

"Is he okay?"

"Careful, Cody," Ollie said. "Almost sounds like you care about me."

"Yeah, yeah," Cody said.

"I can't believe I dropped my camera! It's busted to shit now. Fuck!"

"Oliver and I will go back to the truck. Eileen's going to stay here and talk to you."

"I am?"

"Just keep a lookout," Ollie whispered, his voice carrying perfectly down into the cave.

"What do I talk to him about? He's pretty to look at, but we don't have a lot in common."

"I don't know," Ollie replied. "Just talk about the weather."

"Why's it take two of you to go to the truck?" Eileen asked.

"I know where the rope is," Demmy said.

"And I'm going in case the Devil follows him," Ollie said.

"What about me?"

"You've got Cody," Ollie said.

"He's stuck in a goddamn cave!"

Cody blew out a frustrated breath. "Jesus Christ, all three of you just go get the fucking rope."

"Now look, you made him mad," Ollie whispered.

"It wasn't me who did it," Eileen said.

"Just come on, both of you. We'll be right back, Cody. Don't move."

"Hurry it up."

"Fast as I can."

Shadows shifted, a few pebbles rolled down the slope past him, and they were gone.

It was quiet for a while, then a sudden wind blew dirt and stones down into the cave. Cody turned away and pressed his lips tight as he squeezed his eyes shut. When he opened his eyes again, the cave was darker, and he looked up as a low-grade alarm simmered in his chest. Had something fallen over the opening to the cave and trapped him inside?

A large shadow moved in and out of the sunlight, and Cody let out a breath of relief only to suck it back in when the Devil's frightening shriek-roar boomed down into the cave.

Cody turned his face away from a barrage of rocks and dirt that streamed down on and around him. He heard the crack of stone and the splinter of tree roots torn out of the ground, and full-fledged panic burned to life inside him.

The Devil was digging out the mouth of the cave, right down to him.

CHAPTER NINETEEN

Demetrius jogged through the woods, Oliver and Eileen a ways behind him. He checked the tops of the trees every few steps, afraid he would see the Devil swooping down on him with its giant batwings stretched wide and claws curled and ready to grab. The trail opened to the clearing where the trailer sat in rusty decline, and he started to go around it.

"Hey!"

The shout startled a scream out of him, and he careened off his intended path into the trees. He stopped with his back against a tall hardwood tree and gripped the rough bark tight as he looked over at the trailer.

Tonya stood in the doorway. She grinned as she held a shotgun in both hands across her chest. Demetrius could see the straps of a back pack hung over her shoulders.

"Did I scare you?" Tonya asked.

"No!" Demetrius said, but heard the lie in his voice. Damn her.

"Who is that?" Madison appeared behind Tonya, peering

over her shoulder. "Oh, it's Demetrius." She looked around. "Is Cody with you?"

"Seriously?" Tonya asked with a snarl.

"What?"

Oliver and Eileen hurried out of the trees, both coming to a sudden stop at the sight of the Critter Ridders.

"What are you two doing here?" Oliver asked.

"Nice to see you, too," Tonya said, then added with a mean little smile, "Ollie."

Demetrius hesitated. Tonya and Madison must not have seen the heroin or body yet because they seemed far too relaxed. Unless they had been the ones who had killed the man. But from the quick look he'd had, Demetrius had thought the man had overdosed.

So Demetrius assumed they hadn't seen the corpse. And, therefore, they had no idea the Devil was so near at hand. And while having a shotgun among them would provide a nice level of protection, Demetrius didn't want the Devil killed unnecessarily.

His first thought, though, was, of course, for Cody's safety. "Cody fell into a small cave at the end of that trail and is stuck. Do you have any rope we can use to get him out?"

Tonya and Madison stared a moment, then Tonya threw back her head and let out a long, loud laugh. Madison frowned at Tonya from behind her back before pushing her way past to step out of the trailer and onto the ground.

"I've got some rope in my backpack." Madison slid it from her shoulders and set it on the ground, dropping to one knee to unzip it.

"Stretch slid into a tight hole, and now he's in trouble, huh?" Tonya said, shaking her head. "What a shock. And you're running to rescue him just like usual, aren't you? The dutiful best friend who's been harboring a secret crush on him your entire friendship."

Demetrius glared and hated that he could feel his cheeks burning. "That's not how it is."

Or was it? Dammit, this wasn't the time for him to be thinking about this. Fucking Critter Ridders. Fucking Tonya.

"Here it is." Madison produced a rolled up length of rope, then stood and pulled on the pack once again. "Let's go."

"Oh, um…" Demetrius looked at Oliver and Eileen before he turned back to Madison. "You know, we can manage getting him out." He stepped forward and reached for the rope. "I really appreciate this. And we'll get the rope back to you at your office later today."

Tonya stomped down out of the trailer and grabbed the rope from Madison's hand. She stared at Demetrius and said with a wicked little grin. "We insist on helping. Gotta make sure good ol' Cody is safe and sound and all in one piece."

"I don't want to trouble you."

"No trouble at all." Tonya gestured toward the trail. "Lead the way."

DIRT SHOWERED Cody as rocks tumbled past. One bounced off his shoulder and another just missed striking him in the temple. He lurched backward and shouted as loud as he could, hoping to scare the Devil away.

But the Devil roared at him. The sound echoed throughout the cave and set the hairs up and down Cody's arms on end.

The sound of a loud gunshot ricocheted around the stone walls, and sunlight returned as the Devil fled. Dust clouded the light, and Cody squinted toward the mouth of the cave, now a bit larger thanks to the Devil.

What the ever-loving fuck had that been about, anyway? First it had gone after Oliver—and, really, Cody couldn't blame the monster for that—and then it had tried to dig into the cave and right down to Cody. Why was it so hell bent on attacking people all of a sudden?

"Cody?"

Demmy's anxiety-ridden voice soothed his frazzled nerves.

"Yeah, I'm here."

"Are you okay?"

"I'm fine. Just scraped and bumped, that's all."

"What the hell was that thing doing?"

Demmy sounded like he was on the edge of a panic attack, and Cody didn't want him freaking out, so he said as calmly as possible, "Maybe it was trying to help me get out of here?"

"Really?" Demmy sounded hopeful now, like he wanted the Devil to have a good side or something.

Cody's patience ran out. "I don't know, goddammit! I didn't ask it why it was trying to dig the cave out and get to me. I was trying to avoid boulders and dirt and shit like that. Did you get the rope?"

Shadows shifted in the sunlight, and a length of nylon rope dropped into his lap.

"Big strong man need a woman to help him climb out of a hole?"

Cody bristled and paused in the act of wrapping the rope around his waist. He looked up to find Tonya's big head in the opening of the cave, her smile beaming in the diffused sunlight.

"What are you doing here?"

"Saving your ass. Ready to come up top?"

Before Cody could respond, his foot slipped on some loose dirt and stones. He held onto the rope, but his torso pitched backwards against the rock behind him, and he let out a grunt. Something landed on his shoulder, and from the corner of his eye, Cody saw a branch or something tremble in the dusty sunlight. He turned his head and found a claw with sharp talons at the end of each finger dangling next to his face.

His scream echoed around the cave as he tried to scramble out of the monster's reach, but his feet went out from under him, and he slipped deeper into the cave.

The rope burned his palms as it slid through his hands. He finally managed to tighten his grip and stopped his descent a dozen feet deeper inside the cave. Cool, damp air made him shiver as the opening to the cave seemed so much smaller and farther away now. A shape leaned out of the shadows on the narrow ledge where he'd been sitting before, a head and upper torso along with an extended arm and claw. The sunlight coming down from above cast it as a silhouette, but he could tell from the outline it was the Devil.

Or *a* Devil.

Now that he had a chance to look at the thing, it was smaller than the one that had grabbed Oliver and been digging at the cave. And it was motionless, much too still for Cody's liking. He didn't trust it. In his book, nothing with a goat's head that didn't also come with a goat's body should be trusted.

"You okay?"

Tonya almost sounded concerned when she called down to him.

"I'm okay. Just slipped and ended up a little lower." He felt a couple tugs on the rope.

"You're still holding on to the rope, right?" she asked.

"Yeah, I've got it. There's, um… There's something else down here with me."

"Something else?" Tonya moved back from the opening, and Cody heard her exchanging some words with someone.

Demmy's voice soon echoed down to him. "What's down there? Are you hurt?"

"I'm not hurt, and I don't think this thing is a threat, actually," Cody said. "Can you guys pull me up about a dozen feet?"

More back and forth followed before they slowly dragged Cody up the sloping floor of the cave. His heart thumped harder the closer he got to the thing, and he forced himself not to think that he had been leaning against it. If it hadn't attacked him by now, it should be safe to approach.

Half of the Devil's face was illuminated, the iris of the visible eye cloudy and unmoving. A shiver ran through him as he came even with it. His mouth was dry and his throat constricted, but he managed to call out, "Okay! Hold up!"

The pull on the rope stopped, and he lay flat against the rocky slope. He stared at the Devil looking back at him with dead eyes. The shiver turned into a full on shudder that shook him head to toe. He didn't know what was worse: being stuck in this cave with a living Devil of Pinesville or a dead one.

"What's going on?" Demmy called down. "You okay?"

"Well, I'm not hurt," Cody replied. "But I'm officially creeped right the fuck out."

"By what?"

"There's a dead Devil down here with me."

"What?" The pitch of Demmy's voice went up three-fold and made Cody flinch. "Are you kidding me?"

"Nope, not kidding."

"What did it die from?"

"I don't know, I'm not goddamn Agent Scully doing a fucking autopsy down here, okay?"

"Okay, okay, I'm sorry."

There was some whispers above ground while Cody literally stared into the face of the Devil.

"So, what do you want to do about your, um, discovery?" Demmy asked.

Cody was having trouble focusing, but one thought stuck out in all the noise inside his brain. If they could get this body to the cable channel team for an autopsy, they'd be a quarter million dollars richer.

And Cody was going to make damn sure he got a bigger slice of that money than any of the others up there.

"Fuck." Cody heaved a sigh. "I've got an idea. Give me some slack in the rope and a few minutes while I see if I can do what I'm thinking."

"Okay," Demmy said. "Go ahead."

Cody shifted around until he found good footing. He braced himself against the sloped floor of the cave and a couple of larger stones as he gathered up the rope. There was no good or easy way to do what he had planned, so he just leaned in close to the Devil and turned his face away as he wrapped the rope around its torso. Even though he tried to avoid touching it, he couldn't keep from cringing each time his hand brushed the cold, scaly skin.

Once he'd knotted the rope, he checked to make sure the Devil wasn't wedged in place too tightly. Touching it made him shudder all over again, and he nearly lost his footing and slid down into the depths of the cave. Probably a whole fucking nest of Devils down there, only alive and hungry.

Well, that thought completely freaked him right the fuck out.

"I've tied the rope to the Devil," Cody called. "Slow and steady now to pull it up."

The rope tightened, and the Devil shifted slightly, dislodging small rocks and dirt that disappeared into the darkness. As the group aboveground pulled, the Devil slid out of where it had been wedged for who knew how long and swung directly at Cody. He barely held a scream in check and put up his hands to avoid having the thing land right on top of him. Instead, one of the tattered wings dragged over his face as it slid up toward the surface, and he gagged then turned away to spit.

Cody wiped his mouth and tipped his head back to watch the Devil rise toward the light, its tail slithering up after it like the most awful snake in the world. He wondered if the pressure of the rope around its midsection would create pressure on its bowels or bladder, then quickly and carefully moved so he was not directly beneath it.

He comforted himself with the thought of the money they were going to get from the body as Demmy and the others pulled the Devil higher. That money would sure as hell pay off a lot of bills.

DEMETRIUS STOOD BACK and stared at the corpse stretched out on the ground before them. It was smaller than the one they'd seen earlier, and he wondered if it was an offspring. If so, it made him sad to look at it. From the condition of the body, something had happened to this one. It looked much too thin, its ribs pronounced beneath the pale flesh. And a long trail of black bile had dried from the corner of its misshapen mouth down along its torso. The wings were torn in several places, so even if the thing had been alive, it most likely would have been unable to fly.

"What the hell happened to it?" Oliver asked in a low voice.

"Who cares?" Tonya said and smiled as she looked at each of them in turn. "We're going to be fucking rich."

"Hello?" Cody's voice echoed out of the cave.

"Shit, we need to get Cody out," Demetrius said.

He took a step toward the cave then stopped. The rope was still tied around the middle of the Devil.

"Well, go on," Tonya said, dark humor lacing her tone. "Untie the rope so we can get your boyfriend out."

"I'm going," Demetrius said, pointedly ignoring her comment about Cody being his boyfriend. "Let's pull the Devil over to the shade of the tree and out of the sun."

"To keep it nice and cool?" Madison asked.

"So it won't disintegrate or something. I mean, it's already started to decompose down in that damp cave."

"Hell-Oh!" Cody's voice was louder.

"Just a minute!" Eileen shouted toward the cave, smoke drifting out of her mouth from the cigarette she clutched in a shaking hand. "We're making sure the dead Devil is comfortable."

As he, Oliver, Tonya, and Madison pulled the Devil across the grass and into the shade of a towering pine tree, Demetrius looked into the sky. He wondered where the other Devil had gotten to and whether it might show up again. Tonya had missed it with her shot, and it had flown off out of sight behind the pine trees. It had to be related to this one somehow, either a parent, sibling, or mate. But what had happened to this smaller one that had led to its death. And how had it ended up down inside that cave?

"Any day now!"

"He's kind of short-tempered, isn't he?" Madison asked.

"You have no idea," Oliver said.

"He's stuck in a cave, where he was trapped with this dead monster," Demetrius snapped at them. "What the fuck do you expect?"

Tonya raised her eyebrows. "Protective of your boyfriend. That's commendable."

"They're not boyfriends, okay?" Oliver was fed up with Tonya, Demetrius could tell by his tone and angry expression. "Just let it the fuck go, Tonya. Just because you and Madison are bisexual doesn't mean everyone else is."

"World would be a lot happier if they were," Tonya said.

Demetrius tried to ignore them as he squatted beside the Devil. He reached for the knot in the rope, then stopped as something in the corner of the Devil's mouth caught his eye. Shifting position, he leaned in for a closer look.

"What the hell are you doing?" Eileen asked. "Giving it a goodnight kiss?"

"There's something in its mouth."

"A shit load of teeth?" Tonya offered.

"No, something dark and—" Realization struck like a lightning bolt and Demetrius stood up quickly, the rope and its knot forgotten as he stared at the Devil's corpse. Everything that had happened became clear, and he felt a little unsteady at the rush that went through him.

He now understood why the Devil had been attacking people, and how this one had died.

"What is it?" Oliver stood beside him, squinting as he looked down at its mouth. "What did you see?"

"Oh, um, just some dirt or stones or something," Demetrius said. He didn't want to waste time talking to the others about his insight; they needed to get Cody out of the cave. He dropped to one knee and made quick work of the knot before pulling the rope from around the Devil. Getting to his feet, he gathered the rope into loops as he walked toward the cave. "Let's get Cody out of there, then we can make a plan about the corpse."

It didn't take long for them to pull Cody back above ground. As Cody freed himself from the rope, Demetrius looked over his scrapes and decided they weren't too severe. He wouldn't need to go to the hospital.

A strong breeze ruffled Demetrius's hair and sent leaves skittering across the clearing. Eileen gasped, and Demetrius looked around, barely holding back a shout himself. The larger Devil they'd been following must have been waiting in one of the pine trees and flown down to crouch over the body of the smaller one. It bared sharp teeth at them as it drew the corpse closer and folded a wing over its head.

"Fuck," Tonya whispered. "I left my shotgun over there to help get Sasquatch out of the hole."

"You're not that good of a shot anyway," Demetrius said.

"What did you say?"

"Knock it off," Madison snapped, then her expression and voice softened as she watched. "It's shielding the smaller one. Like it's a child or something."

"Maybe it is," Cody said.

"You think this thing has *feelings*?" Tonya sounded amazed.

"Animals can be very emotional," Eileen said. "Two of my goats were very attached to one of my sheep, and when she died they didn't eat for weeks. They just stood at the fence and looked for her out in the sheep pasture."

"That sounds more like a scene from *Babe* than something that actually happened," Tonya said. "Does no one else have a gun? Seriously?"

The Devil growled, rumbling like a diesel engine. They all took a step back, and Cody moved up close beside Demetrius. It shifted its black-eyed gaze between each of them in turn as it slowly bent over the body. With gentle movements, the Devil gathered the corpse in its strong, clawed hands and held it close.

"Oh, dammit," Cody said. "Come on. Don't take it away."

"No," Tonya said, then followed that with a louder, "You prehistoric bastard!"

A flap of its giant bat wings sent the Devil soaring up into the air, and it was gone from sight seconds later.

"Son of a..." Tonya rushed forward to grab the shotgun she'd leaned against a tree, and then she stomped out into the clearing and looked all around the treetops for any sight of the Devil.

"Well," Demetrius said to Cody, "another paranormal case done, and once more we have no proof anything weird happened."

"We'll always have our memories," Cody said with a grin.

"What is it with you two?" Madison asked as she came up beside them. "You fucking each other or what?"

"What?" Cody looked shocked and took a step back from Demetrius.

Cold stitches of grief ratcheted through Demetrius's gut, and he turned away, blinking against the sting of tears. The back of his throat burned as he walked back toward the cave and began to coil the rope. He needed to keep his hands busy, do something, anything other than stand there while Cody blatantly dismissed their relationship. Again.

Oliver approached. "Hey, you okay?"

Demetrius nodded, not trusting his voice.

Oliver looked over to where Cody and Madison were still talking, then back at Demetrius. "I left a few things back in Parson's Hollow when I moved up here. If you need a ride back home, I can drive you."

Relief surged through Demetrius, and he smiled as casually as possible when he looked Oliver in the eye and said, "You know what? That sounds great. I'd appreciate it."

"Of course, no problem. Just tell me when you want to leave."

"The minute we get back to your grandmother's house?"

Oliver blinked in surprise. "Yeah, sure. We can do that."

"I mean, I know we have to talk to the police about the body in the trailer—"

"Demmy..." Cody was beside him, leaning in close. "We have to talk."

Madison appeared at his side, her voice amping up in

volume and pitch, "Body? Where? In that trailer back there on the path? There was a fucking *body* inside there?"

"Where was there a body?" Tonya demanded as she stomped up to them.

"Demmy, talk to me." Cody was practically pleading.

"I've called the police," Eileen stated in her loud, raspy voice. Everyone fell quiet. "Most of 'em were up at Mariner's Ridge anyway, so they'll be at the trailer in no time. They want all of us to meet them there."

"What about the Devil?" Tonya looked at the treetops all around them, shotgun at the ready. "We had the proof right in our hands."

"But it was dead," Madison said. "Like that body in the trailer where we were just poking around." She did a jerky dance of revulsion that set Tonya off into a fit of laughter. Madison's spasms diminished to shivers, and soon she was laughing along with Tonya.

"Weirdos, the whole lot of you," Eileen announced. "Come on. Let's go."

Cody grabbed Demetrius's hand and held him back as the others filed off along the path. Demetrius could not bring himself to meet Cody's gaze and remained facing away from him.

"Demmy, I fucked up, I know it. Please, look at me."

Demetrius turned and knew the full extent of his hurt showed on his face because Cody flinched and dropped his hand as he took a step back. His cheeks turned pink and he looked at anything and everything but Demetrius's face.

"I know I fucked up. I'm sorry. She caught me off guard and I just..." He shrugged helplessly and finally managed to look Demetrius in the eye again. "I panicked."

"You panicked about us, Cody, about being with me. Again. I knew you weren't entirely comfortable, but I didn't know how deep it went. I can't go back in the closet about something and someone that's so important to me. It's not fair of you to ask me to do that. And I won't let myself do it. I'm sorry, too."

Demetrius left him standing in the small clearing. He managed to hold back the tears until he reached the first bend in the footpath, and then he allowed himself to cry for just a minute before he pulled himself together. A lot still needed to be done before he and Oliver could leave for Parson's Hollow. And even more to do once he got home.

His chest ached, and everything around him seemed strangely disconnected. It was as if he moved through a dream as he continued along the path to the trailer.

He only needed to answer the questions from the police, and then he could go. Just a little bit longer.

CHAPTER TWENTY

Cody tossed his duffel bag into the space behind the driver's seat of his truck. Demmy had left over an hour ago with that bastard Ollie. Granted, Ollie might actually have some things left in Parson's Hollow he wanted to pick up, but did he need to go and offer Demmy a fucking ride? Especially after seeing how strained things were between them?

He felt bruised and achy, like he used to after an especially brutal game back in high school. He'd argued with Demmy plenty of times before, and they'd always found their way back to each other. If he remembered correctly, the longest they'd ever gone without speaking had been four weeks. But that was a long time ago in middle school. At that time, they'd been best friends, and through that whole month they hadn't spoken, Cody never doubted they'd get back on track and be friends again at some point.

But this felt different. This fight had more weight and more bad decisions on Cody's part. The romantic element of their relationship added an extra layer of complexity to everything. Cody had been so worried he would fuck things up, he'd finally gone and fulfilled his own fear. And not just with another lover, but with his best friend as well. When he had broken up with a lover in the past, he had always had Demmy to turn to. Now that Demmy played double duty, the ache was especially severe. He really had no experience with this kind of fuck up. All he knew was he'd done something stupid, and he wanted—no, he *needed*—to fix things with Demmy.

But how?

"Sure you don't want to stay until tomorrow?" Eileen sat in a rocker on her porch, smoke spiraling up from a cigarette between her fingers.

"I think I've seen enough of Pinesville, New Jersey," Cody said.

"How about one drink for the road?"

Cody looked at her across the hood of the truck. "If you're trying to get me drunk and take advantage of me, you're going to need a hell of a lot of booze."

Eileen tossed back her head and laughed long and loud. "You should be so lucky. Get your ass up here, and I'll go get the whiskey."

Cody walked up the porch steps and sat in one of the rockers. He stared out at the woods and thought about Demmy. Even for him, this was pretty high on the fuck up scale. Demmy was his best friend and half of his heart. Hell, Cody was in love with him, for God's sake. So why was he so reluctant to admit they were in a relationship?

"You're awfully deep in thought for someone so handsome."

Eileen sat in her rocker and plunked a bottle of Crown Royal on the aluminum table between the chairs. She set a couple of jelly jars with the Flintstones painted on the sides beside the bottle and Cody grinned.

"Breaking out the fancy glassware for me?"

"Hey, these things are collectibles." Eileen had a cigarette in the corner of her mouth, and it dribbled ash as she spoke. "Don't go breaking them, or you're going to owe me big."

"Okay, I'll be careful."

Eileen poured them each a generous serving and handed him a glass. Lifting hers, she said, "To the Devil of Pinesville."

Cody grinned. "To the Devil of Pinesville."

They each took a long drink, then sat and rocked for a time in silence.

"I feel bad for it, you know?" Eileen finally said.

"For what? The Devil?"

"Yeah. It lost its child. Or its mate. Or at least another one that was just like it. One that understood what it was like to be whatever it is. It's probably out there right now, mourning the only other one it might have known. It's feeling lost and alone and angry, and it doesn't understand anything that happened."

Cody stared at her profile with tears in his eyes. "Jesus, Eileen, you're killing me here."

Eileen pressed her lips tight and nodded, then she looked at him. "How long have you ever stayed with someone?"

He sat forward with his elbows on his knees, the Flintstones glass in both hands as he stared at the boards beneath his feet.

"I've been in a lot of relationships, but nothing long term." A quiet and sad huff escaped before he could stop it. "Demmy's been my longest relationship."

"You screwed up, didn't you?"

He turned his head and scowled. "Is this you trying to help?"

"Just stay with me here a minute, okay?"

He sighed but nodded.

She smiled, then her expression turned serious. "How long you two been sleeping together?"

Cody groaned. "Come on, seriously?"

"Are you ashamed of him?"

"What? No!"

"Then tell me how long it's been."

"Fine. A little more than a month."

"And how long have you been friends before that?"

"Hell, I don't know. Demmy's the one who knows that stuff about us."

"Give it a shot. How long?"

Cody's vision blurred with tears. "Twenty-three years. No, twenty-four now."

"That's a long time."

"Yeah, it is."

"How long have you known he's gay?"

Cody chuckled. "A long time. Years before he came out to me in high school."

"Did you have a problem with it then?"

He sat straight up and tightened his grip on the glass. "No. I never have."

"Did you ever stand up for him? Protect him from getting picked on?"

"Yeah. Of course."

"Are you ashamed you're with him?"

"What? No!"

"Then what is it? Answer me right now."

Cody opened his mouth, but there were no words.

"Right now, dammit. Say it."

"He's the best relationship I've had, and I'm afraid I'll fuck it up."

Eileen sat back and slapped another cigarette out of her pack. She smiled in a satisfied way as she lit up and blew smoke out of the side of her mouth. "Feel better?"

Cody sat and stared at his truck as connections in his

brain fired and realigned themselves. He slowly turned his head to stare at her. "Holy shit."

"I thought as much." She leaned in closer and pointed her cigarette at him. "You're not ashamed of what you have with Demetrius. You're afraid you're going to ruin it."

"I've never been able to make a relationship last," Cody said.

"Have you ever tried to make one last with him?"

He shook his head as he stared at her.

"There's the problem. You don't have a problem being in a relationship, you just needed to find the right person to be in one with."

"For the love of oak trees, I've been making this a lot harder than it needs to be."

"Oak trees?" Eileen let loose one of her raspy cackles. "Where'd you pick that up from?"

Cody grinned. "Demmy's Aunt Amelia uses tree names instead of swear words." He gulped the rest of his whiskey and carefully set the glass on the table before standing up. "Thanks for the drink, Eileen, but I've got to hit the road."

Eileen pushed to her feet. "You okay to drive?"

"I'm better than okay." He grabbed her in a hug and lifted her off the porch.

Eileen laughed and slapped him on the arm until he set her down again. "Go on, get out of here." He turned for the steps, but she grabbed his arm tight. "Don't you even think about hurting my grandson, either. When he comes back, he'd better not have any injuries, or I'll make you suffer twice as much. You hear me?"

Cody sighed but nodded. "Fine. I hear you. I won't mess Ollie up." He bounded down the steps and raced around the front of the truck. "You be careful walking out in the woods. There's at least one Devil still left out there."

"I'm not afraid of that Devil any more. Bring him on so I can get a picture of him and get that quarter million dollars."

Cody waved to her, and then he climbed in the truck and started the engine. He pulled out of the gravel drive and onto the road, turning toward Parson's Hollow.

He thought about calling Demmy but figured he wouldn't pick up anyway. No, for this he was going to have to do something bigger and more meaningful. He had the bare beginnings of an idea and hours of driving time to figure out the details.

It was time for him to take the next big step. And he was more than ready for it.

CHAPTER TWENTY-ONE

"You're sleeping with Cody, aren't you?"

Oliver didn't waste any time getting right to the point as they left Pinesville city limits.

Demetrius sighed. "Why is everyone so interested in what's going on between us?"

"Are you serious? You do realize that the entire town of Parson's Hollow has been waiting for the two of you to get together, don't you?"

"What?" Demetrius blinked as he stared. "Shut up."

"I'm not kidding. It's all anyone talks about at Margie's Diner, or Antonio's Italian, or the freaking Herald newspaper office where I used to work. They've watched you two grow up all these years, and they've seen how you are together. Most of the town thinks you've been sleeping with Cody since high school."

Demetrius looked out the window as he tried to put it all right in his head. "Everyone assumes we're a couple?"

"Yep. Pretty much everyone."

"But, all those women Cody dated…"

"And then broke up with a few weeks later? Yeah, that

doesn't matter. They most likely saw him as a challenge and wanted to be the one to land him for good."

"Do you think all of his ex-girlfriends hate me or something?"

Oliver shrugged. "Not that I'm aware of. And not because you might be sleeping with Cody. They all like you, I mean, come on, who doesn't like you? If anything, they might be jealous of you."

"Really?" Demetrius wasn't sure how to feel about that.

"Wait, I don't think jealous is the right word. They're more envious."

"Well, yeah, because Cody's a really hot guy."

"Not just that, though. They see the depth of emotion between the two of you and wish they could have that with him, too. And, by the way, you're just as handsome as he is, and way more caring and compassionate."

Demetrius said in a quiet voice, "Cody's like that, too. And more."

"He just can't admit you're together?"

"Yeah. He has trouble with that. I mean, I get it, in a way. I'm his first gay relationship."

"You sure about that?"

Demetrius shrugged. "Pretty sure. We talked about this on the drive back from Florida."

"It happened down in Florida?" Oliver grinned. "That state brings out the horn dog in people."

"What does that even mean? And, no, we weren't in Florida. Well, we were when we kissed for the first time. Cody stopped in the parking lot of a McDonald's near Jacksonville so we could talk."

"Romantic."

Demetrius smiled. "Actually, it *was* pretty romantic."

"So that was, what, a month ago?"

"A little longer, yeah."

"And since then you've been having sex?"

Demetrius blushed. "Yeah."

Oliver smirked and kept his eyes on the road as he asked, "How was it?"

"What? I am not going to answer that."

"That bad, huh?"

"No! He's… Cody's…" Demetrius sighed in frustration. "Dammit, Cody's amazing, okay? There, I said it. He's hot as fuck and he knows what he's doing. He's playful and fun and sexy and…" Demetrius looked out his window as tears blurred his vision. "And I don't know if he wants to be with me any longer."

"Oh, Demmy," Oliver said, and his use of Cody's nickname pushed Demetrius into a heavy sob.

DEMETRIUS WAVED to Oliver from the door of his apartment building and watched him pull out of the parking lot and drive out of sight. He rode the elevator up to his floor, walked down the hall, and let himself into his apartment.

Oliver had let him talk pretty much the whole way home, and he felt hollowed out. The air inside his apartment was still and lifeless, very much in sync with how he felt himself.

What was going to happen now? If Cody couldn't openly be in a relationship with him, what was left between them? It was just as Demetrius had feared. Sex had changed everything, and now he had nothing but an aching emptiness he didn't think would ever be filled.

He unpacked his duffel bag and avoided using the drawers he'd let Cody put his stuff in. He'd figure out how to return Cody's things later.

And then they would have to decide what to do about the business. Demetrius didn't think he'd be able to handle sitting across from Cody every day and no longer be involved with him.

He'd been an idiot to start this relationship in the first place. What had he been thinking? Obviously he hadn't been thinking. Or, rather, he'd been thinking with his little head.

God, the sex had been so good though.

And it had been comforting to have someone sleep beside him. Someone to eat breakfast with and watch TV with and argue with, then make up later.

Ugh, this wasn't getting him anywhere. Maybe he'd go to Amelia's and see what she was doing.

Demetrius grabbed his keys, wallet, and phone. Checking to see if he had any calls or texts from Cody, he hated himself for being disappointed there were none, and headed for his truck.

Amelia was out of breath when she answered the door, her cheeks pink and forehead beaded with perspiration. She had tied a bandana around her hair, and she wore her grubbiest clothes. When she saw him standing on the porch, she brightened immediately and pulled him into a strong hug.

"Demetrius! Oh, how are you? How was the trip? What did you find?" She pushed him away and lowered her voice. "Did you see the monster? Did you catch it?"

Demetrius managed a shaky smile before he dissolved into tears.

Some time later, Demetrius sat at Amelia's kitchen table, in a spot she had cleared by carting away several moving boxes. She had brewed a pot of tea and sat in the chair beside him.

"Tell me all about it," Amelia said.

"It's a long story, and you're in the middle of packing." He gave her a sheepish look. "I completely forgot you were planning to move in with Otis. I'm so sorry. I should be helping you pack."

She waved dismissively. "Oh, spruce trees. The packing can wait. I've been at it for days, and I could use a break." She lifted her cup of tea and took a dainty sip. "Now, tell me everything."

Demetrius told her everything, including what the Devil's body told him. "And I figured it all out then," Demetrius said with a sad and shuddery sigh. "I knew what had happened."

"What?"

"The younger Devil had gotten into a backpack or maybe, I don't know, found a syringe left by a hiker who had shot up with heroin. I think it got addicted and started grabbing hikers it could tell were heroin users. Maybe it had a good sense of smell or something and could smell on them. At some point, it found the trailer where the heroin was stored and busted in to get to it. Maybe the guy in the trailer was shooting up when it happened, and it caused him to over-dose, I don't know. Anyway, I found pieces in the corner of the smaller Devil's mouth that looked like they came from the bricks we'd seen back in the trailer. I think it was really high and stumbling and trying to fly when it fell down that cave and died of an overdose down there.

"Then the larger, or what I think of as the parent Devil, was trying to find it and that's when we came along. Cody found the body of the offspring, we pulled it up, and the parent came and took the body away."

Amelia looked stricken. "That's the saddest monster story I think I've ever heard."

"I know. And even if the parent hadn't come and taken the body, I don't think I could have handed the body over to that cable channel. What would that have meant for the parent Devil? And the forest? And even Pinesville itself? Everything would have changed, and for what? Sure we would have gotten a reward, but some living creature would have been hunted out of existence." He shrugged. "I'm glad Oliver's camera got smashed, actually. All the evidence is gone and maybe the Devil will go back into hiding."

She gave his hand a squeeze and smiled sadly. "And what's become of you and Cody?"

Demetrius sighed. "I don't know, Aunt Amelia. He might as well have bolted and run when Madison asked if we were sleeping together. I can't live a lie like that, I just can't. But it hurts, you know? He's my best friend." Tears stung his eyes, and his lower lip quivered as he continued. "He's my very best friend. And now I don't know what to expect. I mean, we have a business together. And we, you know, are always together. And now…"

"And now you just don't know." Amelia took a breath and dabbed tears from her own eyes. "I understand, my wonderful, loving, and kind Demetrius. And I know just the thing to help you put all of this out of your mind."

Demetrius smiled. "Oh? And what would that be?"

"Packing boxes!" Her smile was bright and infectious, and despite how he felt, Demetrius couldn't help smiling himself.

"I had a feeling you'd say that."

"Oh, apple trees. Come on, a little busy work will help put you right as rain. Or at least right as a light mist."

A few hours later, Demetrius had to admit Amelia might have been right. He had emptied the cupboards in her kitchen, wrapping glassware in newspaper and using Amelia's complex color and abbreviation system to label the boxes. He was sweaty and tired and thought he might actually be able to sleep that night.

And still no call or text from Cody.

Well, he supposed he knew where that left him.

"Hey, how about you spend the night here?" Amelia asked as she carried several flattened boxes up from the basement.

"We'll order a pizza from Antonio's, and I've still got some Ben & Jerry's in the freezer."

Demetrius smiled as he wiped sweat from his brow. "That sounds really nice. Thank you."

"Oh, don't thank me," Amelia said with a wicked laugh. "It's my plot to keep you here all night helping me pack."

He couldn't help a laugh of his own before he went back to clearing out the cupboard.

HOURS LATER, Demetrius stared up at the moonlit ceiling as he laid on his back in Amelia's guest bed. Tomorrow was Friday, and he would go to the office early and see what kind of calls Jugs had received while they'd been gone. He hadn't gotten any calls or texts from Cody, for which Demetrius was somewhat grateful but also more than a little hurt.

Talking with Oliver and Amelia had been helpful, of course, but he missed being able to talk about something like this with Cody. Sure he would say something stupid and crack a bunch of jokes and probably bring up farting for no apparent reason, but at the end of it all, once Demetrius was good and frustrated with him, Cody would turn serious and spout some wisdom that would rock Demetrius back on his heels and leave him out of breath.

What a bastard.

What a handsome, sexy, caring, loving, all around amazing fuck of a bastard.

Demetrius rolled over and pulled his pillow against his chest. He squeezed his eyes shut and focused on clearing his mind. He would not think about Cody, not even a little bit. He would put from his mind all thoughts of Cody's brown eyes, the way he liked to wear his slightly wavy brown hair a little long, and the smell of him, like clean work-sweat and fresh air and spices.

When he finally fell asleep, Demetrius dreamed he sat in front of Cody, both of them straddling the back of the larger Devil as it flew over the Wharton State Forest toward the setting sun. They were so low the Devil's clawed toes rustled the top leaves of the trees and sent birds fluttering into the darkening sky. And even though he was scared, Demetrius also felt thrilled and alive, and Cody wrapped his strong arms around him and leaned down to whisper in his ear, "Hold on tight. We're going to go really fast."

CHAPTER TWENTY-TWO

After a big breakfast with Amelia and a promise he would return soon and help her finish packing, Demetrius stepped out of her front door and crossed the lawn to his truck in her driveway. He made sure the absence of a note from Cody under his wiper did not slow him down one bit. He had a lot of things to check on, so he would be plenty busy today. Much too busy to worry about hearing from Cody Duran Bower, that was for sure.

He was concerned he would run into Cody at their office, and wanted to take his time getting there, but of course the one traffic signal in town was green. If he had been running late for a meeting at the office with a client, he knew that signal would have been red. He pulled into the long, narrow parking lot of the strip mall and was relieved—disappointed? —to not see Cody's truck. Jugs's copper colored 2003 Ford Escort was in a spot just outside of the office door, however, and Demetrius took a moment to summon his courage to go inside. Jugs was going to ask what happened and want to hear all about it. He'd then ask where Cody was, and Demetrius needed to stay calm and not talk Cody down.

And not burst into tears.

A last deep inhalation and exhalation, and he was ready.

"Demetrius!" Jugs's big smile helped Demetrius feel a little bit better, and he smiled back.

Enid Helen pawed at Demetrius's legs and barked to be picked up. She was so excited the little pink bow in the fur on the top of her head was askew. Demetrius swooped her up into the crook of his arm and let her lick his face before giving her some scratches and handing her off to Jugs.

"So, tell me all about it," Jugs said as he leaned back in the chair at Cody's desk. Enid Helen settled into a tiny furry ball on his lap and closed her eyes. Demetrius envied the dog her ability to just turn everything off and go to sleep. What he wouldn't give to be able to do that.

"Well, it was a lot like what we do here. And Pinesville is almost a direct copy of Parson's Hollow, if you can believe it. So what went on here. Any calls?"

"A few, but I handled them on my own. A couple of possums." He made a face and shook his head. "I do not like those things. Just great big rats, that's all they are."

"Yeah, they are pretty gross. I had a whole nest of them land on me one time. Cody nearly wet himself laughing about it."

A hot, sticky ball of emotion wedged in his throat, temporarily blocking his ability to speak.

"I can just imagine." Jugs shook his head, then looked around as if Cody might have snuck in behind Demetrius. "Where is the big ape? Sleeping off a drunk?"

"Could be. He had some stuff to take care of when we got back last night. I ended up helping my Aunt Amelia pack up her house."

They talked a little longer, then, with no clients to see to, Demetrius asked if Jugs would mind manning the office phones. He agreed and Demetrius picked up his keys and turned for the door.

"You headed out Main Street to the other side of town at all?" Jugs asked.

Demetrius shrugged. "I could. What can I get you?"

"Enid Helen loves this brand of dog food I can only find at that little market out past the Hollow Leg. You know the place I'm talking about?"

"Yeah, it's called Ike's Market, right?"

"That's the one." He wrote something on a sticky note and handed it over. "Here's the brand and flavor she likes. I mean, it's like crack to this girl."

Demetrius chuckled as he walked out the door. He felt better after talking with Jugs, but he still had an ache high up in his chest that felt like he'd tried to swallow an ice cube whole and it stuck there.

After a stop at the bank to deposit some checks, Demetrius turned toward Ike's Market. He drove slowly through the downtown area, searching for Cody whether or not he admitted it. There was no sign of him or his truck, and Demetrius told himself that was for the best.

When he was just about at the Hollow Leg bar, the quick blip of a police siren made him jump. He looked into the mirror and frowned at the flashing blue and red lights, then checked the speedometer. He wasn't speeding, and he hadn't had his phone in his hand, so no distracted driving infraction. What the heck was he being pulled over for?

He pulled in at the driveway to the Hollow Leg parking lot and stopped in a spot close to the street. Quite a few cars in the lot for eleven thirty on a Friday morning, but he didn't give it much thought. He powered down his window and looked out at Lucia Durant's smirking face.

"Well, well, well," Lucia said. "Look who it is."

Demetrius frowned. "Don't act so surprised. You know my

truck on sight, and you probably have my plate memorized. What's this about?"

Lucia's eyebrows went up. "Are you sassing an officer of the law?"

"When I get pulled over for no reason, I guess I tend to be sassy."

"I could write you up for that," Lucia said.

"And I could fight it in court and win," Demetrius said. "So why are we here talking about this?"

She stayed quiet and gave him a long, cool look. Finally, she took a deep breath and let it out, then said, "You're right. I pulled you over for a simple reason that goes beyond my responsibilities. But since you seem to be in a rush to get somewhere, I'll just let you be on your way."

Demetrius frowned as she turned away to walk back to her police cruiser. He watched in his side mirror as she went, fidgeting a bit as he thought over what she'd said. What simple reason had she had to pull him over? His curiosity got the better of him, and he leaned out the window.

"Lucia!"

She had been reaching for the door handle, but stopped. "Do you mean Deputy Durant?"

Demetrius sighed. "Yes, sorry. Deputy Durant. Would you please explain the reason you pulled me over?"

Lucia looked up to the sky, then pulled her phone from a pocket and looked at it. Her fingers sped over the screen of her phone as she slowly approached his window once again.

"Tell you what," Lucia said when she once more stood beside his door. "It's my lunch hour. How about we grab a burger and a beer inside and talk it over."

"Burger and a beer? You can't have a beer, you're on duty."

"You have the beer, and I'll have an iced tea. What do you say?"

Demetrius hesitated. He'd never spent time with Lucia

just one on one. But her cryptic statement did have him intrigued.

And, seriously, where the hell did he need to get to anyway?

"Yeah, okay. Why not?"

Lucia gave him a droll look. "Why not, indeed. I'm going to park closer. You're free to move your vehicle if you'd like."

After moving his truck to a closer spot, Demetrius followed Lucia through the heavy wooden door and into the Hollow Leg. He was nervous about having lunch with her, wondering what topics they'd discuss, and how he should react when the conversation turned to Cody, as it inevitably would.

The Hollow Leg was always dimly lit, and it took some time for Demetrius's eyes to adjust. In the meantime, he followed Lucia as she wound her way through the smaller tables scattered about the old carpeted area to one of the large, round tables situated along the wall.

Demetrius stopped and stared. His eyes had adjusted, but he thought they might be playing tricks on him.

"Is he all right?"

Lucia looked back at him. "He's fine. I think I just caught him off guard." She pulled out a chair at the large table and gestured for him to sit.

Demetrius sat down and looked at the women seated all around the table. He knew all eight of them by first and last name. They were all Cody's ex-girlfriends who still lived in town.

Lucia sat in the chair next to his and folded her arms on the table as she grinned at Demetrius. "I assume you know everyone at the table, but in case you don't, we'll go through a quick round of introductions."

The beautiful woman with long dark hair who sat beside Lucia smiled. "Zenona Baldwin."

Demetrius returned her smile, though he felt a little numb. Zenona was a doctor at the hospital, and had treated both him and Cody now and then. She'd given Cody a second chance last year, but they'd broken up after two weeks.

"Tracey Mumm." She was a librarian and helped Demetrius with his paranormal research now and then.

"Darcy Saunders." She worked at the Homeless Pets animal shelter where they'd dropped off the kittens they'd caught in the Widow Monroe's garage.

"Bridgett Webster." She was a waitress at Antonio's.

"Jocelyn Batting." She was a realtor.

"Melanie Pointer." She was married and stayed at home with her two kids.

"Diane Conner." She was an auto mechanic at Bill's Garage.

"Hilary Lubbock." She was a manager at Winston's Groceries.

Demetrius lifted a hand and said, "Hi."

The women laughed, and then another of Cody's exes, Gwen Young, came up to the table. She was a waitress at the Hollow Leg, and she took their orders.

"I bet you're wondering what this is all about," Zenona said.

"I'm afraid to ask," Demetrius said.

Another laugh from all of them. But Demetrius wasn't laughing. He was nervous. Sweat had collected in the small of his back and ran down his sides. Why had Lucia brought him in here to this table filled with Cody's ex-girlfriends? Did they want to get revenge on him? Were they going to yell at him for enabling Cody's behavior all these years? Were they going to ask him what was wrong with Cody that he couldn't stay with a woman for longer than a few weeks?

And what the fuck was he going to say in response?

He feared he might throw up, but then Zenona started to

talk and he tuned into her voice. She was always kind and polite to him. He genuinely liked Zenona, and had always felt she liked him, too.

"Demetrius, you don't have to be scared. We're not here to yell at you or try to get you to explain away Cody's behavior with each of us."

He lowered his shoulders a bit, and managed a quick smile as he looked around the table. "Okay. Well, that's good."

"We're here to tell you something we don't think you understand."

He became nervous all over again. "Oh?"

"It is about Cody," Tracey Mumm, the librarian, said. She pushed her dark framed glasses up her nose as she leaned in over the table. "But it's not an angry tirade. We do that enough on our own."

Demetrius frowned and looked at Lucia. "On your own?"

Lucia shot Tracey a quick dirty look before she faced Demetrius again. "We meet up every now and then for a drink."

"Twice a month," Darcy Saunders said as she picked animal hairs off her shirt.

"Sometimes twice a month," Lucia said. "We just have drinks and some food and hang out."

"That's it?"

"Well, it used to be a kind of support group for those of us who had dated Cody," Tracey said, then she shrugged. "But we all got to like each other, and now we just hang out."

"A support group?" Demetrius looked at Zenona. "Because of how he treated all of you?"

"Demetrius, that's not what's important here," Zenona said. "What's important is the reason we all came here today. And that reason is all about you."

"Me? What did I do?"

The women all laughed, but Demetrius didn't. He was still too nervous.

"You didn't do anything," Lucia said. "We all actually really like you."

"Now," Tracey muttered.

"Tracey, you agreed," Zenona said.

She shrugged and looked away.

"Once we started talking about Cody, we couldn't help talking about you, too," Zenona said. "You and Cody always came as a set. And even though he traded us out for each other, you were the one constant in his life. You always have been."

"When you two came into the shelter this week, I couldn't help saying that to you," Darcy said. "We were his fun, but you were always his heart."

"His heart?" Demetrius whispered as his head spun and his mouth felt dry.

Zenona reached past Lucia to put her hand over his, and her touch helped him focus on her words.

"He loves you in a different way than he loved any of us. In you he has a perfect match, and he's just starting to figure that out. It's taken him twenty-plus years to do it, but I think he's finally getting there."

"Wait. What? What are you—?"

His question was cut off by a song starting on the jukebox at the other end of the bar. It was a fast, electronic beat straight from the heart of the eighties. A chorus of singers came in over the roll of electric drums, singing, "Doo doo doo," and a few beats later, Bonnie Tyler's deliciously raspy voice asked for the whereabouts of all the good men and gods.

Demetrius slowly turned his head. It seemed to take forever to peer across the sparsely populated tables and the empty expanse of dance floor to where Cody leaned back against the jukebox. He wore faded jeans and a blue button-down shirt with the top two buttons open. His elbows rested on the curved glass and one foot was crossed over the other as Cody stared right at him.

Demetrius couldn't breathe. Every thought he tried to form plowed into a brick wall of nothingness as his brain emptied of everything except the sight of Cody.

Bonnie Tyler continued singing "Holding Out for a Hero" as they stared at each other.

It was Demetrius's favorite song, the song of his life, and Cody knew it.

When he'd been in the Hollow Leg last year with Cody, drunk off his gourd, Demetrius had played this song and told Cody that all the artists in the world had it wrong. It wasn't the first kiss that was so important to a relationship, it was the first look. Everything could be found in that first instant when two people see each other, really *see* each other, for the first time.

And now Cody was here, looking at him like he had never seen him before. And he had somehow arranged all of this, just for him. He'd gone to each of his ex-girlfriends—or had Zenona go to them to avoid facing injury—and asked them to be here to witness this.

Cody pushed himself up from the jukebox. He walked slowly across the dance floor, stopping halfway to do a little shimmy in time to the music.

Demetrius couldn't help laughing, and he couldn't take his eyes off him.

Cody grinned, and the sight made Demetrius's heart pound until he thought it might burst right through his chest.

The next moment, Cody stood in front of him, his grin widening to a smile as he looked him in the eye. He held out a hand and Demetrius didn't hesitate to lift his own and take hold. Cody pulled him to his feet and into an embrace. He wrapped his strong arms around him and kissed him hard and deep, right there in front of everyone in the Hollow Leg as Bonnie Tyler's scratchy voice climbed higher and higher.

It wasn't until the kiss ended that Demetrius heard all of Cody's ex-girlfriends cheering behind him. He blushed and pressed his face into Cody's chest as he caught his breath.

What just happened?

"Hey," Cody said, his voice so rough and sexy it made Demetrius's stomach tighten.

"Hey."

"Just so you know, this song isn't about me. I'm not the hero."

"Okay."

"You are."

Cody leaned down for another kiss, and Demetrius lost himself in it. When Cody pulled back, Demetrius looked around and was stunned to see not only Cody's ex-girlfriends watching and smiling at them, but Aunt Amelia and Jugs with Enid Helen as well. Oliver sat at the bar, and when he caught Demetrius's eye, he grinned and raised his glass in a toast.

"How long have you been planning this?" Demetrius asked.

Cody smiled. "All my life."

CHAPTER TWENTY-THREE

"It won't go in that way! You have to pivot!"

Cody's back was sore, and his arms were about to give out, but he couldn't help busting out into laughter. The sofa slipped from his grip and thumped to the floor, jammed halfway in Amelia's front door.

Correction: his and Demmy's front door.

Demmy set his end of the sofa down and leaned on it as he glared at Cody.

"Come on, how could you not laugh at what you just said?" Cody asked through his laughter as he wiped away tears.

"Maybe because I'm an adult."

"Or you're just tired and cranky and you didn't eat when I told you to three hours ago, so now you're hitting rock bottom and taking all your hangry issues out on me." Cody arched an eyebrow and stared back until Demmy put his hands on his hips, his actions making Cody fall in love with him all over again.

"Fine. I should have eaten the rest of my sandwich. Are

you happy? Can we get this last piece of furniture inside please?"

Cody twisted up his face in mock concentration. "You know, it's like all those words really, truly wanted to be an apology, but they just couldn't get it together."

"You're an ass."

Cody leaned in over the sofa and lowered his voice. "I'd like to be inside your ass right now."

Demmy blinked a few times as he blushed. "That's not fair."

"Ready to try again?" Cody smirked as he crouched down and got a grip on the sofa.

"You play dirty."

"That's what you love about me."

Demmy squatted down as well and they looked across the length of the sofa at each other. "Ready, set, lift."

Several minutes later, they finally set the couch down in the living room. Both of them groaned and stretched out on the carpeting in front of it, feet pointing in opposite directions and heads turned to look at each other.

"I don't ever want to move from this house," Demmy said.

"You're in luck, because we'll never be able to move with the little money we make catching critters."

"Thanks for the pep talk."

"Any time." Cody rolled right and then left, moaning as he stretched his back muscles. "Was that the last of it?"

"Just the cushions left."

"As my treat to you, I'll handle the cushions. You get something to eat so you don't yank my heart out of my chest."

"I only did that once," Demmy said with dramatic frustration. "God! Get over it!"

Cody chuckled. After delivering a soft, lingering kiss, he pushed to his feet and walked out the front door. He grabbed the cushions from the bed of his truck and turned back toward the house. Through the living room window he could see Demmy placing lamps and pillows and end tables, and he watched with a stupid grin on his face as he clutched the cushions to his chest.

This was their house. No, this was their *home*. They were going to live here, sleep here, and love here. After all the years of trying so hard, Cody had finally come to his senses and realized the person he needed had been with him the entire time.

Demmy stuck his head out the front door. "You going to stand there hugging those cushions all night, or are you going to bring them inside? I'd like to be able to sit on our couch at some point."

Cody threw back his head and laughed, then he climbed the porch steps and angled himself to be able to get through the front door.

IT WAS a little weird taking a shower in what had been Amelia's bathroom, and Cody wondered if he'd ever get used to the 1950s style pink tiled walls, pink toilet, and pink bathtub.

A bathroom remodel was high on the list of projects.

He dried off, brushed his teeth, combed his hair, and then gargled with mouthwash. With the towel around his waist, he left the bathroom and walked down the short hallway to the master bedroom. Demmy stood on the opposite side of the bed, slipping a pillow into its case. His thinning brown hair was still damp from his own shower, and he wore just a pair of boxer briefs. Cody leaned against the doorframe as he admired his toned and furry body.

"Ready for bed?" Demmy asked.

Cody nodded and stepped into the room, loosening the

towel and letting it drop to the floor to reveal his semi-erection.

Demmy raised his eyebrows. "I guess that answers my question. I'm glad I hung blankets in front of the windows."

"Me too." Cody got on the bed and walked on his knees to the middle of the mattress, his cock swaying side to side.

Demmy closed the distance between them, also walking on his knees, and still wearing his boxer briefs. He took hold of Cody's dick and slowly stroked as he leaned in for a kiss.

"You know just where to touch me," Cody whispered.

"Anywhere on your cock? Yeah, I know what you like."

They kissed again, and Cody slipped his tongue between Demmy's lips. As the kiss intensified, Cody slid a hand under the waistband of Demmy's boxer briefs and wrapped his fingers around him.

"Think you'll ever get used to Amelia's pink bathroom?" Demmy asked.

Cody snorted a laugh and rested his forehead against Demmy's shoulder. "Are you trying to kill the mood?"

Demmy laughed as he gave his dick a squeeze. "You didn't lose your hard-on."

"That's it." Cody pushed him down onto his back. "You're getting naked."

He pulled Demmy's boxer briefs off and tossed them over his shoulder, then braced himself above him.

"I love you, Demetrius Barnaby Singleton."

Demmy's smile softened, and he stared back with such love and trust in his eyes, Cody's heart ached. "I love you, too, Cody Duran Bower. Now fuck me."

Cody lifted Demmy's legs and draped them over his shoulders, never breaking eye contact. "You ready to get fucked hard and deep?"

Demmy's eyes were bright and he panted slightly. "So ready."

One more kiss on the lips, and then Cody kissed his way down Demmy's torso. He ran his tongue slowly up the length of Demmy's cock before taking him into his mouth. Slow movements soon gave way to more speed, and Demmy writhed and gasped beneath him. Cody stroked as he sucked, and just when he thought Demmy might be close, he pulled back and grinned at him.

"You had me really close," Demmy said through a gasp.

"I want you to save it for when my dick is buried balls deep inside your ass."

Demmy moaned. "Holy shit, you're killing me."

"I haven't even started yet."

He slowly ran his tongue down Demmy's length from top to bottom, then licked and sucked at his balls. As he worked on his balls, Cody eased Demmy's legs off the mattress, pushing them up high enough to expose his anus. He ran his tongue around the tight, wrinkled rim, then pushed the tip into the center. Demmy gasped and grabbed up fistfuls of the sheet as Cody rimmed him.

"Goddammit, Cody, put your dick inside me already."

Cody gave Demmy's anus a final soft kiss, then leaned over to grab the lube from the nightstand drawer. As he slicked himself up, Cody gave him a sloppy, tongue-heavy kiss before moving back into position between Demmy's legs. He rested Demmy's calves on his shoulders and slowly pressed into him, moaning at the hot, wet embrace.

"God, you're so fucking tight," Cody said.

"No thanks to you. Back it up a bit, big guy."

Cody withdrew and waited for Demmy to nod, then eased back in. This time he was able to fully seat himself inside Demmy and he leaned down for a quick kiss before pulling back and pushing in. His thrusts built slowly until at last he pounded into Demmy, both of them grunting and panting, sweaty skin slapping and sticking. Cody was close, and by the way Demmy stroked himself, Cody could tell he was as well.

"Oh yeah, right there," Demmy said with a gasp. "Oh, I'm almost there. Keep it up. Fuck my ass. Go deep, oh yeah, just like that."

Muscles clutched Cody in a steady pulse as Demmy came, each shot coating his sweat-slicked skin. Cody grabbed Demmy's ankles and held his legs straight up as he plowed into him. He closed his eyes and thought about Demmy over the years. He thought about how well they knew each other, and how he wanted to know even more about Demmy. This was it for him, the answer to everything, and Cody wasn't going to fuck this relationship up like all his others.

A final stroke toppled him over the edge, and he cried out as he came inside Demmy. When he'd finished, he lowered himself over Demmy and, still inside him, kissed his lips.

"That was amazing," Cody said.

Demmy pressed a hand against the side of his face. "Always."

Cody slipped out of him and got up to get a warm washcloth. He cleaned Demmy up, returned the washcloth to the bathroom, and climbed into bed. After turning out the light, Cody pulled him close, Demmy's back against his front. He kissed the top of Demmy's ear and whispered, "Sleep well, Demmy."

Demmy yawned in response, then brought Cody's hand to his mouth to kiss the back. "You too, Cody."

They were quiet a few moments, then Cody said, "You're going to make me breakfast in the morning, right?"

Demmy's whole body tightened, and Cody couldn't help laughing.

"Shut up and go to sleep," Demmy said.

"I can't sleep in a new place, you know that."

"You've been to Amelia's house before, it's not a new place."

"I've never slept here before."

"You did too."

"I did not."

"You did too! We've slept here a few times before. When that big snowstorm knocked out our power but not hers. When we both had too much wine at Easter dinner that one year and she made us stay over."

Cody nodded. "Okay, yeah. I remember."

"Good. Now go to sleep."

Cody let a few more minutes of silence pass. "But I've never slept in this *room* before."

Demmy twisted in his arms to face him, moving fast like a seal in the water. He slapped and tickled and pinched Cody until they were both laughing and shouting, and Cody didn't think he'd ever been happier in his life.

THE END

SCREAMS OF THE SEASON

CRITTER CATCHERS BOOK FIVE

Demetrius and Cody return for an all new adventure in SCREAMS OF THE SEASON: Critter Catchers Book Five, available now!

SCREAMS OF THE SEASON

A Christmas spent far from home. Cody's father gone missing. Clues that point to another monster case.

Demetrius accompanies Cody on a trip to visit his parents in Colorado for Christmas. The house is packed with Cody's four brothers and their extended families, which is something close to chaos and means Cody and Demmy are sleeping on the living room floor of Grant, his oldest brother. Soon after their arrival, they learn Cody's father's truck has been found in a ditch with no sign of his father and are out the door.

Everything going crazy around them makes Cody appreciate what he and Demmy have found together, and he opens up to his family about the true depth of their relationship. There are mixed reactions, but Cody's honesty with his family proves to Demetrius just how important he's become to Cody, and he realizes he couldn't ask for a better Christmas gift.

Between Greg Bower's disappearance, Grant's cannabis greenhouse, and a trip to the mall with Cody's nieces and nephews, the guys also manage to find themselves smack dab in the middle of another monster case when a sasquatch makes a terrifying appearance. As they high-step for their lives through the deep Colorado snow, they'll end up saving a movie stuntman with a terrible sense of direction and writing Cody's nephew an IOU for a brand new drone.

Screams of the Season is available in digital, print, and audio from these retailers: https://books2read.com/crittercatchers5

ABOUT THE AUTHOR

Hank Edwards (he/him) has been writing gay fiction for more than twenty years. He has published over forty novels and novellas and dozens of short stories. His writing crosses many sub-genres, including contemporary romance, rom-com, paranormal, suspense, mystery, wacky comedy, and erotica. He has written a number of series such as the funny and spooky Critter Catchers, Old West historical horror of Venom Valley, suspenseful FBI and civilian Up to Trouble, and the erotic and funny Fluffers, Inc. Under the pen name R. G. Thomas, he has written a young adult urban fantasy gay romance series called The Town of Superstition. He was born and still lives in a northwest suburb of the Motor City, Detroit, Michigan.

For more information:
www.hankedwardsbooks.com
hankedwardsbooks@gmail.com
www.facebook.com/groups/hankshangout

ALSO BY HANK EDWARDS

<u>Critter Catchers Series</u>

Terror by Moonlight

Chasing the Chupacabra

Swamped by Fear

The Devil of Pinesville

Screams of the Season

Horror at Hideaway Cove

Dread of Night

Critter Catchers Box Set 1

Critter Catchers Box Set 2

<u>Critter Catchers Universe Stories</u>

The Mystery of the Morelock Motel

<u>Critter Catchers: Level Up Series</u>

Grave Danger

Wet Screams

<u>Williamsville Inn Gay Romance:</u>

Snowflakes and Song Lyrics

The Cupid Crawl

Fake Date Flip-Flop

Star-Spangled Showdown

<u>Lacetown Murder Mysteries</u>

(co-written with Deanna Wadsworth)

Murder Most Lovely

Murder Most Deserving

Venom Valley Series

Cowboys & Vampires

Stakes & Spurs

Blood & Stone

Up to Trouble Series

Holed Up

Shacked Up

Roughed Up

Choked Up

Fluffers, Inc. Series

Fluffers, Inc.

A Carnal Cruise

Vancouver Nights

Standalone Gay Romance

Buried Secrets

Destiny's Bastard

Hired Muscle

Plus Ones

Repossession is 9/10ths of the Law

Wicked Reflection

Holiday Gay Romance:

A Gift for Greg (A Story Orgy Single)

Mistletoe at Midnight (A Story Orgy Single)

The Christmas Accomplice

<u>Story Orgy Singles Gay Romance</u>:

A Gift for Greg

By the Book

Cross Country Foreplay

Mistletoe at Midnight

The Cheapskate: Bad Boyfriends

With This Ring

The Story Orgy Singles Boxed Set

<u>The Town of Superstition (YA urban fantasy series)</u>

<u>Published under pen name R. G. Thomas</u>

The Midnight Gardener

The Well of Tears

The Battle of Iron Gulch

A Tangle of Secrets

<u>Gay Erotic Short Story Collections</u>:

A Very Dirty Dozen

Another Very Dirty Dozen

A Third Very Dirty Dozen

A Fourth Very Dirty Dozen

<u>Salacious Singles Gay Erotic Short Stories</u>:

Bear Market

Convoy

Double Down

Exchange Rate

Finding North

Hotel Dick

Kindred Spirits

Sacked

Stroking Midnight

Vanity Loves Company

Wet Lands

9 798223 742388